Café Shapiro Anthology

# Café Shapiro Anthology

*23rd Annual*

*2020*

*Cover Photo and Original Artwork provided by:*
*Erika Woo*
*University of Michigan*
*Junior, Major: Economics; Minor: Art & Design and Creative Writing*
*Image is titled: "growth despite – gouache on mulberry paper"*

*Published by Michigan Publishing*

# 23rd Annual
# Café Shapiro
# Anthology
# 2020

**February 10, 2020**
**February 11, 2020**
**February 17, 2020**
**February 18, 2020**
**February 20, 2020**

# Contents

# Anthology Introduction

LAURIE ALEXANDER

Welcome to the 23rd Annual Café Shapiro!

This anthology is a celebration of University of Michigan student authorship. The writings will inspire you and connect you with the undergraduate student learning experience.

Café Shapiro is an example of how past innovations become part of current campus traditions. When it launched over twenty years ago, Café Shapiro was a bold experiment, a student coffee break designed as part of the University's Year of the Humanities and Arts (YoHA). YoHA set out to explore the role of the arts and humanities in civic and community life through a variety of programs. Café Shapiro now continues the tradition of featuring undergraduate student writers nominated by their faculty to perform their works, and by during so, continues to demonstrate the value of the arts and humanities.

The act of reading one's work out loud is a new experience for many of our students. Throughout several evenings in February, students gathered in the Shapiro Library lobby to share their works. They were joined and supported by friends, faculty, coaches and family. Each reading demonstrated of the power of speaking and performing one's own work. The performed works are published in this anthology and discoverable through Deep Blue, the University's institutional repository. Through this process, students learned about copyright and related steps to publishing their scholarship.

Please join me in thanking the library community for making Café Shapiro possible. Events such this make visible our commitment to learning. We are enthusiastic partners with faculty and students, looking to enable the exploration of new ideas while capturing passions and self-expressions.

We hope you enjoy reading the works of these talented undergraduate writers.

Laurie Alexander
Associate University Librarian for Learning and Teaching
U-M Library

# MADDIE AGNE

**Freshman**
**Major:** Creative Writing and Literature
**Reading:** Poetry

Maddie Agne is a poet and writer from Chattanooga, Tennessee, and she is excited to be growing roots in arctic Michigan. She is also a musician with a passion for theater, television, and literature, but has been writing short stories and novels since second grade. She hopes to pursue all of these avenues while at Michigan, and aspires to maybe actually finish writing a book one day. Her poetry is usually either about love, blasphemy, or family, so let this serve as a warning for what you are about to hear.

*Nominated by: Laura Kasischke*

# My Women

These days
I am realizing more and more
How similar I am to my heroes
to my women

Éowyn
Ahsoka Tano
Yennefer
Hermione Granger
Morgana, Guinevere
Clara Oswald
Lucy Pevensie

They were the ones who dove
    headfirst
      into dark waters
And snarled in the face of death
    and fear
For me

Lonely
and intrinsically sad
all of them

I grew up with them
I played with them as children
They stayed with me as women

Confident, passionate
my mother calls me

Loyal
    to a fault
my father calls me

I try to tell myself
that those only mean
      brave
      courageous
      clever

But when my brother call me
      angry

I know
      When

Sitting in a movie theater
      Jo March announces she is lonely
My best friend and I
      point
at me

We laugh

I wish we hadn't
I wish we cried
I wish we cried because we are lonely

I wish I cried
      to thank my women
To tell them that it's
      all okay
That I am

Just afraid to love
Just afraid of commitment
Just afraid to be loved

So I wrote
      because I needed them
more than they needed me
And because woman
is such a fierce word on the tongue

and on the page
It will raze cities
and raise children

So I must look to my women
because they raised me
and dried my tears
and told me I could be strong
and beautiful and harsh
and gentle and irrational
and logical and caring
and reckless
like them
Without sacrificing
Me

So here I am
a byproduct of their love and their lessons
just
desperately and fiercely
Independent
and
desperately and fiercely
lonely

# Rumpelstiltskin

Rumpelstiltskin
works in deals
he always has
he always will

He spins lies
into life
opportunity
into wastelands

Always in exchange
always for a price
which we cannot conceive to pay
nor to kill

The creature
steals her necklace
her ring
her love and her firstborn

He has no interest in riches
or the sublime
or the fire
of nerve endings

He rather requests
and forces from her
a child
a baby

And one day
I have to wonder
why do villains
always want children?

Rumpelstiltskin
Mother Gothel
Hades
they make exchanges

Promises
for firstborns
because children, I suppose
are promises

But no villain
has ever raised a child
not properly
anyways

Don't they know?
children, they are
so easily
molded and formed

They are changed
with a word
a gesture
a command

They are gentle
inherently docile creatures
designed for
love

They are quick to cry
quick to forgive
and they don't know any better
because they are just children

They are so new
and so strangely perfect
that I wonder what planet they come from

certainly not earth
not these horrible hemispheres
where Hades and Hermes hover
over hovels and heretics
and hail hell on them for
harboring hatred

No, not earth
children don't know hate
they don't know pain and suffering
like Rumpelstiltskin did

Not earth
where they will be changed
with a word
an action

Not on earth
where they will be broken
and told
to put it back together

Not an earth
where they will cry
when they are lost
and you and I are not there

Not on earth
where villains will take them
for their own
and heroes are long gone

And there are no more revolutions
and no more gods
and no more saviors
and no more mothers

They don't know the anger

that so quietly intertwines
with their blood
it feels natural

They won't know hate
or anger
or pain
until it is taught

And one day
I think I know
why villains
always want children

# MAHMUDA AHMED

**Senior**
**Major:** English
**Reading:** Flash Fiction

Mahmuda is a senior at the University of Michigan, majoring in English with a Sub-Concentration in Creative Writing. She hopes to one day work in publishing. She has been writing fiction and poetry for as long as she can remember, and absolutely loves it! Aside from this, she also likes to spend her free time drawing as well as reading!

*Nominated by: Jeremiah Chamberlain*

# It's Called Love, Right?

"Fuck, can't you do anything right?"

The words hit me, a sharp and quick jab in the chest. The breath is knocked out of me, leaving me in a gasp. I've heard these words, all in this specific order, many times. And each time it hits like a battering ram, splintering the wood and bone. It's only a matter of time until the wall gives and leaves everything exposed.

I don't answer, I walk away. It would've been *no*, whispered softly, barely a breath that escapes through a thin chink in the armor. *Don't open your mouth*, I warn myself. I grind my teeth in my sleep. *Don't open.*

"Dumb bitch."

It's the sound of a match as it scratches and ignites a tiny flame, white hot at its core as it engulfs the thin piece of wood. It reaches my fingertips, and the *ow* that forms on my lips never escapes because I've stuck my burnt finger in my mouth to suck on the wound.

I drop the match and it meets the underside of my boot as I walk away, black and curled up, with hunched over shoulders and no amount of tears that will stop the burning.

"Just get the fuck away from me."

The words are detached, suspended in the air, ready to be plucked and tossed away. They're rotten. I've waited too long to harvest the fruit, and the one bad apple will spoil the bunch, I must get rid of it quick, quickly.

It gets easier to turn away, but I don't know if this is good or bad, like the fruit. If I stay will I only spoil and rot everything away, like the saying that misery loves company, is that all I am? Miserable?

"You're useless."

Short and sweet and to the point of a tranquilizer that digs into my flesh and renders me... useless. My arms and legs grow heavy, heavy fogs that settle at the base of my thoughts until everything is as clouded as my judgement.

I'm silent as I turn away, drag my feet, a loaded *yes* lodged in my throat, floating in the fog with no way out. The fog is thick and some part of me collapses.

"I'm sorry, I didn't mean to yell at you."

The words are like rain on a sloped roof, they roll right off. It rains quite a lot here in Michigan, and spring is coming but these showers won't sprout any flowers this year because the winter was especially cold.

I don't say anything, I walk away, but I know the words *it's okay* would've slipped out like rainwater through the waterspout. The gutters would've been washed clean until the next storm.

# Lovebug

Something has invaded my body and mind. A tingling has taken root at the base of my belly, slowly growing and spreading into my chest. It settles there with a light squeeze. Foreign thoughts, which have never existed before—or something that has existed long ago, squashed throughout the years—ring loudly and unclear in my head. It is almost like... a humming? Like a fridge, a fan, the wind, muffled voices from the TV in the next room? It's hard to pinpoint the sounds, the words formed on foreign lips from foreign faces that I have never laid eyes on. How does someone find something they've never seen before?

*What are you?* The question lingers, hanging gingerly like delicates on a clothesline. The streets of Paris are crowded like my mind. There is a light breeze that ruffles the laundry. But the humming in my head goes quiet and the silence is deafening. The narrow street clears. The whistle of the wind is frozen in the air, on my tongue. I hold my breath. The silence lasts for days.

In this moment, it is hard to remember why I left my comfortable life back home to move to this foreign country. Maybe it's just homesickness. Maybe it's just that things are much too crowded here, breaths shared by too many people, shoulders brushed at every turn. Derrick said it's just something to get used to, but we've been living here in his home for months now and I have still not adjusted. My mind drifts back home.

I can remember how good the water tasted, the field of daisies that grew behind my house in the summer, and my friend Cecilia who lived across that field. We would meet there every day at sunset and let our imaginations run wild along with our legs. And when the sky turned dark, we snuck around the daisies whispering each other's names until one of us was found. The stars were always bright when we were together. I haven't seen her since I ran into her at a friends party a few years later. She spotted the ring on my finger immediately, and it seemed that it created a barrier around her. I invited her to my wedding of course, but I wasn't sure that she heard me. And she didn't attend.

The tingling in my stomach has returned along with a pain in my chest, and I *must be homesick, that's all it is.*

I lean over the *petit balcon* and spot the woman again, seated at the café across the street.

Her hair is soft, her eyes are soft, her lips are soft.

The humming, the something, the foreign thoughts are back and *it's just her.* Today, she's wearing very short shorts and a wispy blouse, thin straps that keep finding their way off of her shoulder. Her long, bare legs stretch across the empty chair in front of her. She pulls her sunglasses down over her soft eyes, she ruffles her soft hair. A cappuccino is placed in front of her and I can see the word *merci* form on her soft lips, like soft, secret whispers in a field.

"Are you done with the laundry?" my husband asks as he takes my hand, releasing a clothes pin from my grip.

"Oh, yes, sorry," I say without looking at him. Across the street, the woman has just taken her first sip of cappuccino. Her tongue darts out from between her lips to capture the foam that has settled just above her cupid's bow. The action leaves another tight squeeze in my chest.

"What are you looking at?" he asks, following my gaze out the window.

"Nothing important," I reply, pulling his face back toward mine. He smiles and leans in close, captures my bottom lip between his, as his tongue searches for entry. I imagine instead the woman's tongue trying to capture cappuccino foam from *my* lips. She would laugh, her fingers grazing the back of my ear as she tucks strands back into place. Goosebumps rise as she slides her warm fingers down the back of my neck. Her lips tease mine, not quite kissing. *Je te veux,* I whisper in harsh French against her delicate mouth, but she swallows my words, and we're not at the café anymore because she's pushing me backwards onto my bed, straddling my hips. Her dark hair sticks to her face, her blouse sticks to her body in the summer heat. Everything is stripped off slowly until her body is flush against mine. Her tongue is searching for the cappuccino foam and she finds it.

Sunlight streams in through the window, warm, like our measured breaths.

"I love you," my husband tells me. I open my eyes and the woman is gone. He kisses me softly on the forehead, rolls off the bed, and pulls his shorts back on. He pushes through the thin curtain separating the bedroom and the kitchen, and I hear the clink of a glass, the faucet.

"I love you, too," I call quietly after him, drowned out by the rushing water. My gaze is frozen on the delicates that hang out the window. The grumbling in my stomach starts up again with the squeezing in my chest. Something has invaded my mind and it whispers in my ear, its warm breath trailing down my neck.

# HUSSEIN ALKADHIM

**Freshman**
**Major:** English and Classical Studies
**Reading:** Prose Fiction

I am a freshman and I plan on doing English and Classical Studies. I come from Dearborn, MI and I started writing short stories in my senior year of high school. I really enjoy reading literature in my free time, as well as philosophy. I like reading Albert Camus, John Steinbeck, Joseph Conrad.

*Nominated by: John Buckley*

# Goodnight

Sameen Bakery was a local hotspot during morning hours. Sweaty workers shouted the orders to the dough powdered baker in back, who tightly held the metal peel with a wooden handle to look like a disciplined war soldier. All the round cheese and meat manakeesh, zataar, and mini pies were thrown into the flaming clay oven and hastily prepared in greasy paper bags for the customers. Some were grumpy, some were yawning wide, and some smiling as they took their orders and returned to the next stop of their obscure daily lives. The sound of the clicking register and ripped receipts, the greetings and farewells, and crumbling bags – the economy was booming.

Then lunch hours were prepared with meat and chicken shawarmas, kibbehs, kabobs, white rice, brown rice, vegetable or meat rice, lentil soup, hummus, baba ganoush, falafel, shish tawook, kafta, tabouli and foutish. The working and middle class frenzy rushed in with empty stomachs desperate to be satisfied. Plates organized onto trays, trays given to customers, customers sitting at tables.

But at night the bakery was deserted and silent. The bakery would suddenly have that incomprehensible atmosphere one feels after being left behind in a place that was once bustling and intense. Nobody came unless it was late shift fathers picking up prepackaged pita bread and milk or young boys wanting a late-night sugar rush. But because it wasn't busy, Han could take as much time with the customer and even establish a proper human exchange. It's why he grew fond of working later shifts and closing after sunset.

Han thought that he would only be staying for the summer. But he guessed that he may as well continue, that nothing else would be different if he quit and looked somewhere else. After high school graduation, Han never saw his any of his friends again or anybody that was familiar from awhile back. He never really tried to reach out and some days he would plan on doing so, but just ended up either forgetting or losing interest. Also, he suspected that if he ever crossed anyone he knew, they would not remember him anyway.

Han watched the cars whirring by on the other side of the large tinted windows of the bakery each night. He would listen to hear the engines before the cars crossed the window and would play a game where he guessed the model or color. Or, he would imagine who was in the car driving and what kind of life they led. He would ponder whether they were young or old, rich or poor, unhappy or happy, heart broken or whole, married or divorced, or single, or where they were just coming from and where they were going to. He would also picture how they looked like and make up their distinct personalities, ambitions, ideals, or fears; a sort of God carving out plotlines of numerous human lives to his liking.

"Why haven't you done what you're supposed to?" his boss shouted behind him.

Han snapped back and responded quickly by rushing to his closing duties. He cleaned the floors covered with stale food crumbs, took out the trash, vacuumed the carpet in front of the doors, put the leftover food in the cooler, turned off the lights with the exception of the fridges, and finally the oven. He forgot to turn it off one night when he was new, and his boss had nearly fired him on the spot.

After, Han and his boss went out from the backdoor to the alley near the parking lot. Han's boss offered a ride.

"I got a friend picking me up soon. Thanks though."

"Alright, goodnight."

"Goodnight."

Han walked back home. It was not too far. But after standing for hours on end in the bakery, his legs said otherwise. Boss said that he had to be prepared for all customers at all times, so that meant no sitting or leaning. Then again Han had never taken a day off since he started, and it was getting to him. Maybe I should quit, Han thought to himself, just like every night he walked back home.

Once he finally got to the corner of his street, closer to his house, he was a little more joyful. The car was not in the driveway and Han's face became perturbed. He bit his lower lip to keep his anger from escaping. He walked inside quietly, took off his shoes, and black cap. He went to Mo's door and slowly opened it and saw him asleep cozily and all wrapped by the blanket. Han smiled.

He went to his room next door and sat on his bed. He didn't feel like changing clothes or getting ready for bed. Just planted his head on the pillow and lay there with heavy eyelids. But after a half an hour of trying to get himself to fall asleep, he knew that it wasn't going to be any different this time. His head started to get heavy and his eyes burned. Soon the shaking began, and his fingers and limbs vibrated.

Han got off the mattress and lifted it. He grabbed the rubber tube and syringe. And the zipped bag. Han was preparing it all in machine-like routine, like it was as simple as tying one's shoes. It was all ready and he brought it to the marked vein he punctured each time.

He wanted it so bad. His jaws tightened and exhalations increased in pace as his pulse rose. He could feel the blood rushing around his temples and sweat run down his body like an ooze. His shaking intensified and rumbled him to the core. All he had to do was push his thumb down and he could feel whatever lasting peace this world could offer him. Just one push and that was it. His heart punched, his limbs clinched, and the veins on his left arm were bulging as if they screamed for it. All his concentration was focused on the curved microtip of the needle and the background receded into a blur.

The doorknob turned and as it opened by an inch, Han was sucked back and instinctively threw the syringe aside and whatever could reveal him.

Mo had woken and was standing at the door holding his stuffed bear ripped at the neck. He squinted from the light and rubbed the crust from eyes with his small knuckles.

Han was trying to keep himself together. "Come here, little man," he told Mo as he sat on the bed and tapped on his knee.

Mo flashed with a smile and tucked under his brother's neck. Han held him and wrapped him with his arms.

"When did you last see Mamma? Was she here when you went to sleep, buddy?"

Mo indicated an affirmative with a nod that brushed against Han's chest. Han squeezed him at the thought of his mother. The thought of her fooling around, coming home late, or never even coming. It wasn't the same after Han's dad left around the time Han was close to graduating. She wasn't the same. Nothing was the same.

Han's entire body slumped against Mo like the despairing guitarist in that one Picasso. His head fell upon Mo's soft hair and at the corner of his eye saw the needle. He wasn't sure if Mo fell asleep on his arms, but it wouldn't have mattered because he couldn't hold back the tears building along his eyes. The more he tried to hold back, the more his emotions were ready to burst forth like an over pumped water balloon. Finally, he let them free and they travelled one after another to the edge of his chin and poured down like rain onto Mo's hair.

Sobbing like a wounded animal made him feel ashamed. He wiped his face and carried Mo back to his bed, tucked him in, and kissed his forehead. As he quietly closed the door, he looked through the slit to make sure he was asleep.

"Goodnight, little man."

# ANNA BARR

**Junior**
**Major:** International Studies and Spanish
**Reading:** Short Fiction

I like to write stories. I hope you enjoy this one. Thank you.

*Nominated by: Christopher Matthews*

# It Casts Odd Shadows

It sounds like someone is stomping up the double-steep stairs. You can almost see them brushing snow off their coat and tugging at their gloves with their teeth. The carpeting is stained and blue, damp with melted slush. Door number six is usually left unlocked. Inside, a low table from the thrift store, draped with a bleeding mandala tapestry, sits in front of a dingy sofa. Dishes are piled in the sink. The air smells of rose incense and cooking herbs, but the trash needs taking out. It's bewitchingly warm to someone coming in from the dark afternoon. The bed is so plush that when you lie in it hides you, the way your mother's did when you were very young.

They lie in the wrinkled linens, feeling a crashing bass vibrate through the blue wall. The sun filters through the blinds, casting stripes on their faces and hands. The neighbors are singing. They are letting sound loose from the chest, pushing their voices to screeching on the high notes. She turns to him and smiles, trails her hand over his thigh. He's staring at the ceiling, not noticing. He absentmindedly strokes her forehead with his open palm. The song is reaching a crescendo. She's considering singing, weighing if he would be made uncomfortable by the sound of her singing voice. She chooses to sing along. It comes out sudden and awkward. He joins her, unfazed, tapping the beat with his fingers on her skull. As the song is ending the woman pulls herself up from the bed. She leans on her hands, pressing them on the sheets behind her back. A fleck of dust is floating towards her, suspended in a shaft of light from between the blinds. She wonders what the man is thinking about. There's a pull in her chest like a magnet. When they aren't touching she feels like he'll melt into the floor, leaving only a fuzzy imprint of himself behind. She decides to stay in bed for a moment more, brushing her feet with his. It's already mid-afternoon.

The worry of being late again pushes her into the shower. As she's dispensing shampoo into her palm, the apartment door clicks open then slams shut. She stiffens and the gelatinous pile slips onto the tile floor. She shoves her head under the stream and twists the knob hard when she's done. Steam billows from the bathroom door and she's tying her robe around her waist, padding over to the stove. The tea pot is already full. She flicks on the burner and leans back. Yawning, she lifts the wooden lid of her tea chest and rifles through the little foil packages. Her fingers linger over each one as she weighs her decision, wasting time examining the designs on the packaging. She selects one and rips it open, inhaling the bergamot.

Bending one leg under herself, she lowers down onto the sofa. In the mirror on the opposite wall, she sees her reflection. Lines run horizontally across her forehead and folds of skin crease around her mouth. An urge to pull the sagging skin back overtakes her. She tries to smooth the wrinkles under her eyes with the tips of her ring fingers, pushing hard. The skin reddens. She quits touching it. As she holds the tea up to her lips, a shock of steam makes her eyes water. The hot liquid scalds her tongue. She twists around and is made anxious by the time displayed on the microwave. She grabs a pair of black pants, a lightly stained t-shirt with a name tag that says Karen, and a black waist-apron from the floor. She dresses disjointedly. On the way out the door, she rubs a smudge of red lipstick off of her slightly crooked front tooth.

The room is dim now, the macrame hanging on the window is casting odd shadows on the floor and the sofa. An empty wine bottle rots, forgotten in the crack between the mattress and the wall. You could hear a pin drop. Wind whistles over the exposed organ pipes of a church across the street. You can almost hear it. The fan still rotates slowly, shaking dust from its blades upon each turn. It falls gently onto the linoleum like snow.

After work, Karen sits in her Kia, smoking with the window cracked. The predominant memory she has from her shift is of stacking warm plastic cups. They were steaming from the dish sanitizer and the smell of bleach seeped into her rough fingertips as she stacked. She had to fish a bit of soggy bread out from the bottom of one and rub some chapstick off another. Droplets of water dangled in the baby hairs around her forehead. Holding an unwieldy stack, she kicked open the door to the main dining room and was sucked into the friday-night mass. It spat her out again hours later, dazed and spent. She mopped, cleaned the men's room, and clocked out, putting a cigarette in her mouth before she was out the door. Now, she is racking her brain for a Halloween costume. Her coworkers invited her to a party. They all sort of hate each other, but she hasn't been to a proper social event in a while. She flicks the butt out the window and starts the engine. She turns left out of the parking lot, not yet knowing where she's going. She's not ready to return to the apartment.

Towering, flood lamps line the five-lane avenue. The road is flanked by unending stretches of strip mall and distracting neon signs. It's late and the traffic seems out of place. Where are they all going? Karen feels herself turn into the usual drive and roll past the closed Panera and the vitamin store. Dollar General is blindingly lit. She stops the engine. The macabre whiteness of the artificial light glowing in the windows reminds her of an eye rolled back in someone's head. The automatic door clanks open sharply and doesn't close right away. A plastic skeleton hangs in the corner, reaching its arms out towards her as she passes. "Hey there" waves a middle-aged, balding woman behind the sticky green register.

Every aisle is trashed by this time of night. Plastic pumpkins and hockey masks spill onto the gray carpet. Flecks of green glitter mix with the dust and dirt on the floor. There's a woman staring blankly at some yarn a few feet away from her. In one hand she has red and the other yellow. She's not really seeing. You know the feeling. Karen runs her hand along some gauzy fabric dipped in red dye. She tries on the cat ears, but they make her feel washed up. The fairy wings will be irritating and she'll take a wig off as soon as she starts drinking. She settles on some fabric devil horns.

The woman behind the register has reading glasses on. They've slipped to the edge of her powder caked nose, held on her face by a thin metal chain with turquoise beads. She's leaning over a scrapbook, smoothing down a photo of an old man sitting at a picnic table. Karen notices that he's wearing tall, white socks with orthopedic sneakers. There's a jar of rubber cement open on the conveyor belt. She sets the devil horns down beside it. The woman pushes her scrapbook aside and scans the tag.

Karen returns to her apartment with her plastic bag and black apron in hand. The door hits her as it swings shut. Her shirt smells like garlic. She goes into the bathroom to wash her face. When she emerges, he's there, sitting in the corner tuning her guitar. His face looks dour, but handsome. He must have come in while she was shopping and found that thing in the closet. She hasn't touched it in years. It looks small in his hands. Karen feels like if she takes one more step towards him he'll evaporate. Why is it like this between us?

The thought of the word us makes her blush. She hops on one foot, trying to pull her wool sock off and hopes he can't read her mind.

Looking at him directly in the eyes makes her nervous. It doesn't help that he's pathologically quiet, responding only in grunts or the crack of another beer. She's unnerved by his silence and fills the gaps with anxious rambling. The monologue makes her increasingly breathless until he breaks her train of thought with a touch on her face or her leg. She doesn't know much about him. If he's been listening even half the time, though, he knows a hell of a lot about her. Her family and where she grew up. Her failed business. She knows she shouldn't burden him with all of this information at the beginning. Her mother would be horrified. This is what you do with your last shot Karen? Piss it away? But the catharsis outweighs the shame. He's not gonna hang around much longer anyways. She tries to stay available.

Even though her feet ache from her long shift, she rises from the couch to make dinner. The studio is small so the kitchen is only a few steps away from the couch. Sometimes, bits of grease from the pan she keeps on the stovetop splatter onto the beige upholstery. She likes to cook for him. She thinks it'll make him stay. The ground beef in the fridge is turning gray. There's not much else, though. The meat sticks to her hands as she rolls it into lopsided patties. The man puts Houses of the Holy on the record player and disappears into the bathroom. She only bought it because she thought it made her seem more interesting. It makes her happy to see him use it.

When he gets out of the shower, there's a cheeseburger and Doritos sitting on the table. Under the bun, Karen had squirted ketchup into a smiley face. Then, embarrassed, she had smeared it out with her finger. The condensation from the can of Busch is leaving a ring on the wooden tabletop. She feels silly waiting for him like this and doesn't know where to put her hands. She realizes there's probably an idiot smile on her face. He glances at her, picks up the plate wordlessly, and starts eating. It reminds her of feeding a cat. She wonders if she would feel less deflated if he had thrown the meal at the wall.

The gaping silence is encroaching yet again as he chews. In this quesy moment, she asks him to come with her to the staff Halloween party next weekend. Her excitement is thinly veiled. "You don't have to wear a costume or have to even come if you don't want to or already have plans or whatever." She's talking to the side of his face as he sips his beer. She shuts up to let him think. He shifts around and sniffs, then says "Why not?" He leaves after he's done with his burger, while she's doing the dishes. She stops halfway through, as soon as he's gone, flopping onto the unmade bed.

Each day extracts more from her than the last. She occasionally finds herself astounded by the fact that she's dressed and at work. Her coworkers are whispering with each other, speculating about the last time she'd washed her hair. They hope she won't come to the party. They only invited her because she was hanging around waiting for her shift meal and heard them talking. Karen is only vaguely aware of this. She feels it in her bones more than she understands it. Even the most delusional among us can't help but sense things.

On Saturday night, the restaurant slows down unusually early. She's closing with a teenage kid named Robin. Robin smokes joints behind the dumpster while taking out the trash. Karen knows, but pretends not to. She's much more efficient at restocking and putting away the dishes than her anyways. Her palms are sweaty thinking about the party. She's not sure if he's going to show. He hasn't been over at all this week. She goes over a script in her head, planning her nonchalant yet charming comments in advance. She braces herself to shoot whiskey, like the girl in that Carrie Underwood song. He can't ignore that.

When she gets back from work the apartment is dark and it's already 10:40. He's not there. The party started almost an hour ago. She pours some moscato into a mug and tries not to be upset. She's not really surprised. She texts him the address of the party punctuating it with the blush-smile emoji. Her full-length mirror leans on the wall at an angle that makes her reflection look short and squat. Karen grunts as she pulls a red spandex skirt over her thighs. It is ruched in the front and barely covers her ass. She examines herself, trying to tug it down. She chugs the wine. It's making her turn pink already. There's a red crop top on the bed that has "BAD" printed on it in glitter font. It made her feel hot when she tried it on, but now she thinks it might look chintzy. Too late. She squeezes into the shirt, adjusts her bra straps, grabs her purse and devil horns, and leaves before she can change her mind.

The Lyft driver drops her on the main street of a duplex subdivision. The houses are all exactly the same. She squints to make out the numbers hanging on the bricks in the dark. Her heels make a flip-flop noise on the pavement. She's already tipsy. Unit 42 has the curtains drawn, but Karen can see orange and purple lights flashing through them. Silhouettes stand around with shadow cups. That must be it. She approaches the door hesitantly, suddenly very aware that she is showing up alone. She takes her headband off and smooths her hair down in the back. Then, she walks in.

Get Low is playing. Robin and some girl she's never seen before are making out on the gray pleather couch. One of the delivery drivers, Tony, is sitting across from them. He's trying to hide it, but he keeps staring. A few other servers are losing their balance grinding on each other in the middle of the living room. No one seems to notice Karen. She checks her phone. He read her text, but he hasn't responded. She makes her way over to the white folding table. There's an open half-gallon of Captain Morgan, a two-liter of Pepsi, and a 30 rack of Bud Light. She opens a beer and takes a double shot of rum. It makes her sweat. Antsy, she stumbles out to the dancefloor. She keeps pulling at her skirt as she walks. She shimmies over to her coworkers and tries to make eye contact. They pretend not to notice. She dances by herself.

It's a long time before she takes a break. The liquor makes her feel pretty. Robin and her girlfriend have joined her. Being drunk with them reminds her of high school, the way they are giggling. It strikes Karen that Robin probably is in high school. Everyone else has left the room. She feels her head start spinning so he staggers into the backyard for some air. The girls don't follow. There's frost on the black grass outside. She lights a cigarette. The smell makes her gag. She tries to take a hit, but feels hot bile rush up her throat. She jerks over, her skirt hiking up, resting her hands on her knees. She pukes. It lays steaming on the lawn. Her vision is really blurry now. She spits and wipes her face with her shirt. Her fingers slide over her phone screen erratically as she tries to call a ride. It's two minutes away. She cleans her hands on the wet grass and tries to straighten her clothes. Then she makes her way unsteadily around the side of the house to wait for the car.

In the private darkness of the back of the Lyft, a few tears slip out of Karen's eyes. They cool her cheeks as they slide down. Still no text back. She feels silly and old. The car parks outside her place. She gets out. She fumbles with her keys for far too long until she feels the lock clank. The apartment is dark and quiet. She takes her shoes and shirt off, flopping onto the bed, still in her makeup. She pulls the sheet over her head. Just as she's closing her stinging eyes, she feels him press against her. She doesn't turn to look, but grabs his hand and holds it close to her chest.

# KRISTEN BOLSTER

**Sophomore**
**Major:** Public Policy
**Reading:** Fiction

I grew up in Monroe, MI. I enjoy writing slam poetry, realistic fiction, and prose. I'm currently part of the Comprehensive Studies Program as a Mentor and Ambassador. My love of writing started my junior and senior year of high school when I wrote my first novella and I've been writing ever since. When I'm not writing I enjoy playing volleyball and drawing.

*Nominated by: John Buckley*

# Thank You

Thank you for showing me how wonderful I am. How strong, and caring, and funny, and fucking great. Thanks for all the memories. For the laughs and the late nights and the music. You had such good taste in music, so similar to me, that I thought you almost knew me. I thought you understood who I was through chord progressions that we both loved. I understood the music, and you must have just listened. I sure hope you're listening now. Now that I am some intangible thing to you. Something you can only grasp through the lines on this page.

Thanks for the car rides and the coffees. You weren't supposed to drink coffee due to something wrong with your kidney, or liver, or some other part of your body. But you drank it with me, and I almost felt like I was enough for you to risk something. To risk anything. I was worth telling your kidney or liver or whatever to screw off. It was stupid I know. Trust me, I believed a lot of stupid things when I was with you. Thanks for helping me see that.

Thanks for dancing with me that one time in the parking lot when it had just snowed. My hair was covered in white water and my socks were soaked, but you lifted me up in the air and I wanted it to be winter forever. When you drew a heart in the snow on the hood of your car, I thought you meant it. I thought Christmas had come early, and I even thought you might have loved me too.

I want to say thank you for holding me. And I will thank you for holding me, when my grandma passed away. And I cried into the button down shirt you wore. That was the only time you bought me flowers in two years, and they weren't even really for me. Thank you for holding me steady. When I lost control and psyched myself out over classes, you calmed me down. The eye in the middle of my storm.

I give you too much credit, even now I act as though you helped, even though I made time to see you. Even though I was only something you had time for when you were free. Even though I was a side project in your life when you were everything to me. You knew that you had me too. You kept me waiting, and wanting, and wondering when I would be good enough. You kept testing my waters, diving deeper and deeper into me and I never resisted. I never resisted, and you thought that made it okay.

Thanks for waiting in my driveway. You always waited in my driveway to make sure I got in safe, and sometimes the lock would get stuck, and you'd have to come out and force your way in. You never walked me to the door. Do remember the night I ended things? When I slammed your car door shut right before the tears started rolling? When I dropped my keys on my porch steps because I couldn't get the lock to turn? How you watched me bang and bang on my front door from your parked car? Part of me wanted you to get out and help me one last time, the rest of me knew you wouldn't. When my mom finally let me in, did you think that was the last time you would see me? Were you surprised to look down at your phone after you drove back to find that you could no longer contact me, on *anything*. Did you even care?

Thanks for staying the fuck away from me. My friend saw you on tinder last week and thought I'd want to know, so she sent me your picture. You only look a little different. You changed jobs, just like I said you should. And even though it has been five months since I've looked at you, five good months, five months of trying to forget you, or at least trying not to think about you every day, you still somehow creep back into my life.

I will not thank you for holding me down. I will not thank you for not listening to me. I will not thank you for what you've done to me, and quite honestly it doesn't matter what I thank and not thank you for because you will never read this. And quite honestly I think this writing exercise is stupid, and quite honestly I don't think this therapist knows me well enough to do this. I will not forgive. I cannot forget. And I will not thank a man for hurting me.

See you never,
The ex you never dated

# SEBASTIEN BUTLER

**Junior**
**Major:** Creative Writing
**Reading:** Poetry

Sebastien Butler is a Junior studying English, and Creative Writing in the RC, from Dexter, Michigan. At U of M he is an active participant in theater across campus, as well as the RC Players. He loves movies as much as he does poetry. He has a fondness for the landscapes of Michigan, as well as Switzerland, of which he is also a citizen. He hopes to teach one day. This is his second Cafe Shapiro reading.

*Nominated by: Sarah Messer*

# Prelude

We'd wake and walk under sugar
stars, through matriculating snow,
meeting at the predetermined
spot without words, standing, waiting for

the bus to save us from the cold
as it had for children at the previous stop,
and the one before that—each
a small nativity scene.

Then in spring—storms at dawn,
the world through classroom windows
forcibly kept dark. The slap of thunder,
each child turned in their seat to see the reflection

of themselves in the glass—suspended—
until the lightning lacerated the image
and we vanished for a second, before being
brought back to the shock on our faces.

Then the teacher would begin his lesson.
By high school, we'd drive ourselves,
and I'd park at the furthest edge of the grounds,
prolonging my walk with the keenness of the cold

in order to see my breath hanging in front of me,
and the last stars ascending in the outermost blue,
whispering to me of Design, and the sun coming up
directly behind the school buildings, rose gold.

Then, graduation day, streets the smell
of gasoline and ice cream,
still in our gowns, we coated
the downtown patios, watching

the mayflies hatch and lather the storefronts—
their mass guppying for air—swaying
in the magic hour,
half of them already dying.

# Farmcat

I see much in my thin time, marking years on Fence Posts. When young Hawks hunt me, stealth and shadow save my skin. I hear Thrush's song, and I carry its head in my mouth like a banner. I see Fox bow to me. As it should, I am larger. I see Him walking about, attending to His labors, smoking His pipe on the porch. I stare in at His wheat colored rooms with only Stars to feed me. I stand watch by River, frost-cloaked, watching mud-frozen Toads beneath ice. I drink from Ditches. I hobble and grovel and hail Him for leftover chicken tossed out Backdoor. He sees my work. He is generous. I am his spectre. His servant. His sentry in rafters. Sinister survivor, in whiskered chainmail. I follow Him, pellet gun in hand, in Moth-thick midnight. I pounce as Barn Door is unlatched, His little flashbang, upon teeming mass of Mice. Nights with my showy ribs stuffed, the blood curdling edges of fur. At noon, I find Shed, and lick matted patches over my wounds. There, in immense sawdust silence, I weep for an hour. I lose an ear and several teeth defending His borders. I murder for His milk. I lay death at His feet. He is amused. He places the sweet bowl before me.

# At Sixteen

Our eyes October-wide, the cars crept down
country lanes lined in gnarled oaks,
to convene at the corn maze.

Prideful in our disregard for the shoe-boxed
dead bird we each kept in the eaves of our jackets.
The maze's childhood connotations long lost,

replaced by the death-rattle of the stalks,
the steady loss of light, the stars growing to match,
egging us on. The path twisted, turned,

and the girls giggled, squealed, clutched their necks
in ways the boys wished they could. Drunk
on transgressive darkness, feet fumbling, voices blurred,

and the stars stabbing they were so bright–
we found ourselves free, on the border of the picture,
startling something–a badger, no a coyote, no–

a couple making love in the grass. Frozen for a second
in the lights of a passing truck. The boy deer-dumb,
the girl cradling her hands over her mouth

to muffle laughter, or a scream. Their wet eyes
and bristling skin and rabbit haunches quivering.
And then the light slid off them, and they scampered off

through the brush. We laughed back to the road,
lapping up the rotting air, stopping
by where they had lain. The outline of a human body

pressed into the blades. We each took turns
running our fingertips over the after-image,
how the grass had stuck to the earth,

and laying in the mold, watching the sky shift slowly,
feeling where the warmth had just been. Then rushing off
to more salt and wrappers and playing with sleeves.

But our bodies jostled in unfamiliar ways,
leg against leg, shoulder against shoulder,
and I laid down on the bench as if a bed,

listening to my humming skin.

# Turning Five the Summer Bush Sought A Second Term

*after C.D. Wright*

Time we spent in staircases. Morning-doused sheets. A.A. Milne August. Days worn out like jeans. Houses and hostas. Leaf patterns on saharan cul-de-sacs. Throwing stones at election signs. Ethereal earth. *Mockingbird* schemes and scripts. Eavesdropping on the radio in my father's garage. Not knowing its math. Knowing the holes on his Kerry shirt better than the words. Algae growing in gutters. Losing light escapades. Chilled sweat. Chiggers. Grass cuts. The cooled tea of twilight. Apologetic upholstery. Week-old cake. Our first Olympics. My mother safeguarding the remote. Your mother's extra glass of wine with her in the kitchen. Honey dripping from our hands. Fingers unfurling like streamers. The residing heat in our tucked-in faces. The jugs of water, soaked towels, dog fangs. The bagged heads, zip-tied boys in Najaf. The unseen owls perched outside our windows.

# PANAYIOTIS CARDASIS

**Sophomore**
**Major:** Economics
**Minor:** Business
**Reading:** Creative Non-fiction

Pano is a Sophomore hoping to study Economics or Philosophy with a minor in Business. Pano has taken only one writing-oriented English class at the University of Michigan, so he was quite surprised to be nominated for this wonderful opportunity.

*Nominated by: Aozora Brockman*

# Listen as You Read

**Nirvana, "Lithium".** *Nevermind* (1991)

When I was six, my parents bought me and my brothers a SanDisk MP3 player so that we would stop bothering them to play songs that got on their nerves. It was our first experience listening to music with headphones. I would walk around the house and get the cord wrapped around a door handle every ten minutes while listening to my jams. Me and the boys would write song titles on a sheet of paper and hand it to our old man when we wanted him to download new music because we were technologically inept. He would take the device and plug it in to his computer and open LimeWire to bootleg the tracks. After about three years of free music, his computer caught a terminal virus from LimeWire and the old dinosaur Windows computer croaked. Should have seen it coming; phishing and trojans crawled all over that site.

One day, my father handed me the MP3 player after downloading all the 2008 pop hits I was hearing on the radio, plus some random rock song. *Lithium*, it read. My father snuck that song into the device, much like he did with Ozzy and Hendrix and the Doors. But this one was different. I had never heard so much sludge and reverb from a guitar in my life. I loved it. I ended up memorizing the lyrics after a couple hours of repeated listening. When the SanDisk died in 2010, I forgot about the song. It wasn't until I was grown and fully explored the grunge genre that I heard Cobain's mellow, hurting voice again. It was then that I realized the grunge was inside of me all along. I had a connection to it. *I'm so happy, cause today I found my friends. They're in my head.*

**Jimi Hendrix, "Voodoo Chile".** *Electric Ladyland* (1968)

My father drove me and my brothers to school from elementary to high school. His car didn't have a radio, so he had six CDs that we would alternate. For ten years, we listened to the same albums on the ten-minute drive to school: Paganini's *24 Caprices*, Electric Light Orchestra's *Classics*, Pink Floyd's *Wish You Were Here*, the Rolling Stones' *Sticky Fingers*, the Beatles' *Let it Be (Naked)*, and my favorite, Jimi Hendrix's *Electric Ladyland*. Hendrix was a genius, to put it simply. He could get these gritty, psychedelic, warped sounds from his guitar that no one had ever heard. Keep in mind, Hendrix came up in the 60s, when rock and roll was prevalent but not nearly as widespread as it would become. When he played concerts, he wore a headband in which he packed LSD. The LSD-infused sweat dripped down his face as he exerted himself. He would lick his lips when the beads of sweat reached his mouth. I sat in the back of the green Lincoln Mark VIII thinking about what it would take to rock at the highest level. I didn't want to simply listen to Hendrix, I wanted to live Hendrix. LSD in my headband. Fingers of God. I wanted to be the Voodoo Child.

## Slipknot, "Solway Firth". *We Are Not Your Kind* (2019)

*Here's an unexplainable one.* Metal has been integral to my music preference for about two years, and I cannot share it with anyone. It seems like metal is taboo because the lyrics are satanic and wrathful, and the guitar and drums are too fast for anyone to make out what's being played. Sometimes the screaming is so incoherent that it all sounds like one word over and over. To me, it's fine art. It's symphonic. Slipknot is the most raw, unadulterated, gruesome metal band out there. Nine guys who don't give a fuck if they die the next day and only care about tearing down concert venues and giving a big fuck you to the mainstream record labels. The band has been around for over twenty years now with six studio albums to showcase their talent. After six albums, year-long hiatuses, and tours across the world, they nailed it. *Solway Firth* is their Mona Lisa. Five minutes and fifty-five seconds of mastery. This one song encapsulates all twenty-some years of Slipknot's reign over the metal genre with superb lyrics, top-notch drumming and guitar, and aspects of thrash, nu, and core metal combined. It is the only song I know that gives me chills every time I hear it. *I haven't smiled in years* at the end is the icing on the cake.

*Today, up on this hill, I'm counting all the killers.* August of 2019 was when *We are Not Your Kind* was released, and the month I saw the Nine in person. A semicircular hill of 16,000 waited for the wrath to begin. As the sun set, the pavilion lights illuminated the crowd's impatient faces. "Knot! Knot! Knot!" the mob shouted. The drums kicked, a scream was belched, and all hell broke loose. I fell victim to the mosh and disappeared into the haze of people. Two minutes later, I came back to my brothers with blood streaming down my face and onto my Huf Worldwide T-shirt. "Dude, that's metal as hell," the boys said. When Slipknot called the curtain, the patrons left content and satisfied, talking calmly about how wild the show was. It dawned on me that these people are not just angry, dangerous, disaffected souls. This music is therapeutic. They came to rage and let out any burdening emotion for an hour and some change, and it worked. Metal music keeps me sane. It helps control my anger. Men and women of all ages and backgrounds conglomerated to appreciate nine guys thrashing about on stage and shouting expletives, and they even thanked Slipknot for leaving their ears ringing for the next 24 hours.

### The Beatles, "In My Life". *Rubber Soul* (1965)

*But of all these friends and lovers, there is no one who compares with you.* I've been told that I am the "Dad Friend" of the group: I float around many cliques with no tight circle, I offer water to anyone even if they didn't ask for it, and I give relationship advice without ever have been in a relationship. I mean, it all checks out. I came out of high school with three, maybe four true friends. I live with my brother in college and we are away from our friends which means it's the same-old interactions. Not that there is anything wrong with that, it just deprives me of making new acquaintances and trying out my people skills. I am a guy who loves to love. I have never been in an authentic and committed relationship.

For the longest time, I considered the negatives of giving your undivided love to a person. I'm too young, I don't have enough money, I'm still in school, I don't have my own car, I don't want to have that label and be unavailable to other potential partners. Solid reasons, yes, but am I truly happy? Do I force myself into something that I know will inevitably end in flames? I am stuck in my own head. I have been thinking about if I want to give my entire self to someone, but the thought never goes anywhere because I am too afraid of changing myself. But I love her. I love her madly. The Doors said it first, but I feel like I'm the one who has walked out the door 1,000 times before. I sit on the edge of the bed and tears fall while pondering my mistake of not taking the chance sooner. *In my life, I love you more.*

## A$AP Ferg, "Dump Dump". *Trap Lord* (2013)

*Bitch pop dat ass in the coupe.* It doesn't get rowdier than this. I am never in a bad mood with this song blasting. Absolutely meaningless lyrics slapped together over a kick-snare beat. But it fucking bumps. This track means acting like goons with the boys, raging, almost getting myself hospitalized, the usual rap stuff.

Back in high school, I was on the swim team. I never thought I was the swimmer type. As an underclassman, I was short and developed some early pubescent fat. I was ashamed of my image and I wanted to fix myself physically. I ended up swimming because I found myself hanging around the team during my free time, and I ended up selling my soul to head coach Marc Fazio by telling him I would join the team. It was borderline inhumane the stuff we had to go through. For three and a half months through the winter, I did not see the sun. I would wake up at 5am to make a 6am morning practice, get out at 7am, eat breakfast and go to school from 8am-3pm, take a nap on a science lab table, go to the second practice from 5:30-7:30pm, do homework, and crash at 1am. Rinse and repeat. No high schooler should be put through that.

Despite being run ragged through the whole winter, and even having two practices per day during Christmas break, my grades, social life, and attitude were excellent. As much as everyone on the swim team, myself included, dreaded every day more than the last, the boys were rowdy. The swim team had a reputation of being one of the loudest, most rambunctious sports teams at the school, and we took that pridefully. Our ribs would shake from the loud music playing at every practice, bus ride, and team gathering. We bonded over being thrown into the meat grinder of the rigorous work of swimming. "Trap Lord with about ten Jeeps, no telling what I might do"

### $uicideboy$, "For the Last Time". *Kill Yourself Part XX: The Infinity Saga* (2016)

Sometimes, you need to shut your brain off and bob your head. I got into the $uicideboy$ in late 2016, in the fledging stages of my disaffected, impressionable high schooler phase. This was the music playing when I was on my way to a soccer game or swim/track meet, frozen and mute on my buddy's couch, driving by myself, or doing homework. The mindless music with no chorus about drugs and murder and killing yourself just about summed up the thoughts in my head. I did not care about anyone's thoughts or what they thought of me. I did not need to hear about anyone's problems; I was self-absorbed.

When I was thirteen, my mother contracted ovarian cancer. During this time, I was in middle school, arguably the worst years of my life. I didn't know what to do with myself or my mother. All I could do was dissociate and sweep any cares or feelings under the rug. Ovarian cancer killed my mother's mother. It took a selfless, vogue, lionhearted firecracker of a woman and killed her. My mother was the lucky one. Her cancer was detected in its early stages, and her chemotherapy was supremely effective. The cancer was in remission after only one year of treatment.

It still didn't matter if the cancer was taken care of quickly, my mother had cancer and I didn't give a fuck about it. She went bald and wore wigs for almost two years. She is still trying to lose the weight she gained from stress eating. My stupid prepubescent ass was only worried about my appearance, which music I was listening to, which girls didn't think I was a prick. It wasn't like I had a parent who could have taken a turn for the worse and leave this Earth at any day or anything. I was too stubborn to think of how fragile life can be. Every week, my aunt would bring my family a big tray of food she cooked herself because my mother did not have the energy to prepare food. She had to use all her energy to fucking stay alive. My father had to drop off and pick up all four children from school and work his full-time job as a forensic psychiatrist. He even started to freelance his talents just to get some extra money to pay for the hospital bills. And I still didn't give a fuck. It haunts me to this day.

As mentioned before, I started listening to the $uicideboy$ in late 2016. Years after the cancer incident, thoughts of what could have been crept into my conscience. I turned to incoherent, disgusting rap as a coping mechanism. I shut off my brain when I listen to the $uicideboy$ so I don't have to be disgusted with myself. I have always found that my own thoughts are my worst enemy, simply because they are not usually good thoughts. I tend to dwell on the past because I beat myself up in hopes that I change. The $uicideboy$ have been the artist I listen to the most for the past two years. I always crawl back to the Grey boys.

Music is made from emotion, no matter the genre. I could be listening to rap music for hours and then overhear a sad song playing over a store's loudspeaker and be depressed for the rest of the day. Metal keeps me from getting angry, rap gets me amped, grunge makes me introspective. I am controlled by soundwaves through headphones. I listen to just about every genre of music; my taste is very diverse. I listen to so much music because my thoughts constantly travel in different directions and I must stay one step ahead. It's perfectly okay with me, I enjoy the love-hate relationship I have with music. Without it, I would be an empty shell of a man.

# VIVIAN CHIAO

**Sophomore**
**Major:** History and Creative Writing & Literature
**Reading:** Fiction

Vivian was born and raised in Ypsilanti, Michigan and evidently didn't move very far for college. Her parents overcompensated and now reside in Chicago. She has a passion for writing fiction, especially fantasy and sci-fi. Her hobbies include reading, playing video games, and overanalyzing movies.

*Nominated by: Christopher Matthews*

# to divine the province of the stars

Stella was born underneath Apollo, pale and bright Apollo, who blazed across the sky with the sun as his chariot. Apollo, who dictated augury.

I knew her for a seer as soon as she drew her first breath. Not because of her birth star – hundreds of babes give their first caterwauling cries under Apollo's light – but because I am always there, in the sick rooms and hospital hallways. White-robed as the doctors and nurses, I sit with the families of laboring mothers and disease-burdened grandparents, with the children who itch to slit their own wrists and the adults filled with police bullets and shackled to their cots. This is what people don't understand: I wait. There is no need to do anything else. Everyone comes to me in time.

In the hospital room of her birth, the baby girl kicked and screamed as I approached and brushed my fingers across her newborn brow. It was routine, interrupted. She looked up at me with cobalt blue eyes, stretching her tiny hand out as if to grasp my finger. I withdrew, surprised, and her irises clouded over into prophet-gray. I knew then.

So did the nurses who attended her exhausted mother. So did the doctors to whom the nurses whispered the news. So did the uniformed men stationed in the hospital lobby, who came so softly into the room and said, with voices full of quiet violence, for the mother to give them the child.

They had guns and her daughter's steely eyes promised nothing but trouble; she handed over the baby.

\*\*\*

There are certainly countries who hunt down gray-eyed infants to be put into sacks and tossed into the river, though they have a tendency to be wiped off the map by others with more guns and a willingness to gift Delphi's children money and fiefdoms. Stella's was a country that had surpassed such barbarism: they culled newborns from the visionless citizenry and put them into ivory towers and stone-walled temples, raised them isolated and loyal.

Men with guns plucked Stella from her mother's outstretched arms and placed her among rows of cribs in the mountain temple, each with a squalling infant. The self-styled guardians walked through the aisles. On the hour, they gave the babes bottles to suckle, changed diapers, and gave each child a perfunctory rocking – and then back in the crib they went, to be held again when their schedules demanded. When they got old enough, they were moved from the nursery to the dormitories and classrooms.

Stella squabbled with her seer-siblings, read the approved histories, played sometimes in the walled-in temple courtyard, where the mountain mists could reach but not overwhelm. She studied geography, astronomy, environmental science, and military tactics. She read the newspaper every day and sometimes had visions of newsprint text flying between her still hands on the kitchen table, bolded headlines of trade agreements and natural disasters flickering past. Her guardians recorded her fast-paced babbling with digital cameras before sitting down across from her at the bleached hardwood table as she recited what she remembered. The visions were transcribed, put into manilla folders, and shipped with her all her other classmates' predictions to the analysts in the capital. I don't read the reports; what ambiguities do I have to resolve about the future?

To be a seer is to live between the possibility and the resolution. To be a seer is to be nine years old and waking up in a pool of piss, screaming about the river, the *river*, pull me out, I can't *breathe*–

*The past and the future do not exist*, a clever human once said. *There is only the present.* To be Stella is to be a child crying in a guardian's arms and an adult drowning in river water, both of them true, both of them present, both of them forever.

\*\*\*

In the lull between wars and school lessons, Stella slipped through the temple gates and past the parking lot full of the guardians' minivans and pickup trucks. She was older, now, riding the wave of adolescence into a graceful adulthood. I hadn't seen her in a while, busy with famine and other seers.

She and her peers had chores, sometimes – today, Stella's was to courier messages. There was no electronic communication allowed to and from the temple.

She walked down the dirt road, headed to the Abbotts first, the family who lived on and tended the small local cemetery. The mist was light that day – Stella could see the small cottage from the road. Sitting on the front porch was another girl her age with unruly hair and chapped lips, one knee tucked to her chest as she scrolled through her phone. Stella stopped in front of her in the driveway, sneakers sending up plumes of dust in the soft sunlight.

"Yo," said the girl. "You here from the temple?"

Stella held up an envelope from the bundle she had under one arm.

"Gotcha, more graves to dig," the girl said nonchalantly. She swung her legs and bounced to her feet. Stella blinked, bewildered. The girl was in shorts, seemingly unbothered by the morning chill. She tipped her head to the side. "I haven't seen you around before. Got stuck with this job?"

Stella shifted her gaze from the girl's legs to her own shoes. "I'm taking over the job, I guess. I like it."

"Hey, that's good. I'm glad; I couldn't get up this early to walk to town if you paid me."

Stella smiled faintly.

"What happened to the last one?" the girl asked, taking the envelope from Stella's outstretched hand. "The tall, persistent fella – Marcos?"

Stella rolled her eyes. "Got caught opening the letters and nicking the cash meant for the grocer."

The girl laughed and held out her hand. "Well, here's hoping you don't fall so low, huh? I'm Tess."

There were rumors about the Abbotts, about disturbed graves and lunar calendars and runic circles drawn in the dirt. On my way to the temple, I sometimes saw Tess in the back of the cemetery at nightfall, chanting softly in dead languages to coax the new dead from their graves. It's impossible to know if Stella saw it too in some oracular dream, but she must've known the rumors. There is little else to do in the mountains but gossip. And seers, for all their dealings with me, are hardly admiring of necromancers.

She shook Tess's hand. "I'm Stella."

\*\*\*

Stella, grown by now into a young woman, lay in bed with Tess, sweat-slicked and searching for higher meaning like foreknowledge was found at the join of the thighs to the body. An oracle, one of the most blessed of her generation. If the guardians found Stella in her room at this time of night, with her skirts rucked up and her hands in the seams of the body of the gravekeepers' daughter – but these temple walls had seen a hundred trysts; Stella's wasn't even the most scandalous, regardless of her naive romantic impressions. Quite frankly, I've seen unluckier people.

Tess put her hands on her shoulders, head tossed back and her hair sticking to her face, and Stella was – consumed, overtaken, skirting the edge of something in the dark, lights off and her seer-white eyes closed, as if that changed the endless, unbroken *seeing*.

When they were done and curled into each other like commas, Stella laid a palm to her wet mouth, looking almost surprised.

"You alright?" Tess whispered, putting a hand to the side of her neck and pressing their foreheads together. "That was okay?"

Stella nodded, hazy and half-there. "It was nice."

Tess bit her lip, mouth quirked. "It was nice for me, too."

Stella closed her eyes. The rapids swirled and foamed behind her closed eyelids. She muttered, "You ever think things are inescapable?" Tess's fingers tightened on her bare back.

In the wake of the silence that followed, Stella slept, dreamless.

\*\*\*

War came, as it always does. Stella's country was proud, and it and its neighbor were hungry for land and battle, which would whet the appetites of the starving and the ambitious both. There was no need for a draft. The volunteers flooded in by the thousands; the army could feed a poor man and immortalize a rich one. I watched them sign their contracts with blood. Everyone always thinks they'll be the ones to cheat me.

In the mountains, a hundred seers sat in their white-walled room in the white-stoned temple, meditating.

Outside their doors stood the guardians in white robes, hoods pulled over their pale and sunken faces, ceremonial daggers in their belts. (They are imitators of mine; that is to say, pretentious.) They whispered to each other in a frenzy, about their troops retreating on the eastern front, the enemy now only fifty-odd miles away from the temple itself. What were they to do, evacuate? Give up their lauded fortress for some backwater government compound? There was the ivory tower in the desert to the west, where their counterparts raised gray-eyed infants to serve the state – but who among them would crawl on their belly to beseech those arrogant bastards for sanctuary?

Sitting in her room, Stella saw – ah, but here is the problem. I'm telling this story and there are some things even out of my reach. Perhaps she saw the eastern front, with its trenches and napalm, smelling of burnt flesh and rotting vegetation. Perhaps the northern regions, where famine drove families to eat dirt and fight over garbage at the dumps as food was directed away from the region and towards the army. (The army was always well-fed.) Perhaps she saw only the river. But I do know that when her vision ruptured, when she bent over retching, bleeding, nails broken off clawing at the stone floor, the men outside rushed in like flies on a carcass, voices overlapping in excitement-panic: *what did you see what can you tell us how might we fight them –*

Stella closed her eyes. Maybe she wished for Tess and her tender carefulness. Maybe she simply swallowed down the remains of her vomit and tasted hatred instead of resignation.

\*\*\*

Tess was the one who came up with the plan. This was not a reversal of the usual way of things: she was always the schemer between the two of them. Tess was born with human ambition. Stella, nursed at the breast of detachment like a good obedient seer, was not made of the same stuff.

The difference this time was that Stella had been the one who pushed for it. She'd been the one to observe the guardians' comings and goings, the one who worked herself to exhaustion spending her precious nighttime hours scrying instead of sleeping. Tess made the plan, charted their course; Stella was the one who talked her into it. After so many years, so many nightmares that were not nightmares – bloody war and the goings-on of a nation that starved its people to kill its enemies, violence that wore compassion into indifference, horror into nonchalance, shock into familiarity –

Tess was rebellious and righteous and devoted. Stella, I think, was simply exhausted. Like many seers before her, she reached the crossover point. Survival could no longer afford endurance. Flight was now the only option.

The night they left, Tess's mother and brother came out from their little cottage with mounds of blankets and armfuls of canned food. Stella and Tess took off in a car stolen from the temple parking lot, hoping to never be found.

\*\*\*

Months later and leagues away, Stella watched Tess raise the dead. It was midnight in the church graveyard and moonless. The only light came from Tess's hands and the glow of Stella's phone screen against the encroaching dark. Soft green magic sprang from Tess's fingertips and weaved through the air, twining around the first corpse and lifting it on marionette strings.

"Speak," Tess said, as gentle and sweet as when they were in bed together, her voice raspy and delicate as the play of her bare fingers in the air: the corpse raised its half-decayed face, bone showing through at the cheeks, eyes dark caverns of maggots and rot. Worm food. "Tell me about the murder, lovely."

Stella closed her eyes. Tess, half-bent over, hair cascading over her shoulders, lifted the dead thing's chin and brushed aside its lanky hair. Stella pressed record on her phone.

The corpse's voice hissed out of its broken windpipe, magic rushing through its vocal cords, and whispered the secrets of what its eyes had seen — back when it could see. Back when it had eyes. Tess always said, *only the body, never the soul*, but the body remembered, for a time, what it was like to live.

It was a run of the mill murder. Infidelity, jealousy, lovers bleeding out on the carpet — nothing important. But then, if I wanted importance, I wouldn't have come here.

"Thank you," Tess said, and the body flopped back into its grave, strings cut. She cracked her knuckles and turned to smile at Stella, who cracked one eye open as soon as the corpse hit the ground. "Not as easy as it is at home, y'know."

"Different land?"

"Maybe. Different ghosts, too." Tess turned to the next, black dress swirling around her mud-stained hiking boots. "Tell me what you know, dear."

Stella opened her mouth halfway. Closed it again.

I watched from where I was perched on one of the tombstones. When Stella turned her head and caught sight of me, I nodded to her in easy greeting. She didn't flinch. Seers never do.

* * *

For a while — after they ditched the stolen car by the side of the road and before Stella hung from the cypress above the river — Tess consulted for the local police department, dredging up bodies and uncovering testimony. This wasn't the life anyone expected her to have; her family ran the mountain cemetery. If Tess had thought to buck tradition, it would've been by moving to the city and going to college, perhaps retiring to the mountain only when she was old and gray. Then she fell in love with a seer and went on the run with her, and now she was going to spend the rest of her life ducking the authorities and lying about her real name. She didn't care. Regret wasn't part of Tess's vocabulary.

Stella stayed in their small cabin and minded the garden. Some days she didn't have visions, only pleasant dreams of frogs croaking and the tomatoes finally getting big enough to harvest, a dog they didn't own licking her fingers and a doghouse they'd never built taking up a corner of the yard. Some nights she had violent, screaming visions of hellfire raining down from falling airplanes and the gaping, sucking wounds caused by shrapnel. She woke up shaking from those, Tess's fingers in her hair – but they were getting fewer all the time. She read books banned in the temple. She ignored newspapers of the war. She learned to play the guitar.

For a while, they might've been happy.

\*\*\*

But things end. This is the truth Stella glimpsed during her carefully stolen liberty, in scratched mirror glass and the surface of still, algae-dense lakes, the thing that haunted her despite her best efforts. She caught glimpses of it in electronics store windows and the blank monitors of internet cafes, double-guessed herself in supermarket aisles full of snow globes. There was still the war – that was inescapable, even where she and Tess had hidden themselves at the far reaches of the country. But the thing that scared Stella was not the war, which visited in dreams, but something else.

She saw the white robe, the gray sheened blade, the hood shading the eyes – now tell me, am I talking about her guardians come to drag her back to the mountains? Or am I describing myself?

Stella didn't know. To be a seer is to live between the possibility and the resolution. This is why the guardians raised her apathetic, raised her detached. There is little use in a prophet who sees me in Baghdad and races to Samarra, not when I keep all of my appointments. Stella was one of the temple's best and brightest, once, because she knew that lesson so intimately. Now she was far from the temple, and full of malleable human things like fear, uncertainty. Would she be caught or be killed? And when? And could she avoid it?

Not all the things Stella saw came to pass – but most did.

***

Most seers are addicts. I know because I follow them when I can, those babes whose eyes clouded under my first touch. They turn often to distraction: the bottle, the herb, the knife, the flesh of others. I can hardly judge them for that. The human mind is not designed to know the universe.

I do not know where Stella found her absinthe: perhaps in books, perhaps in music, perhaps in the kisses Tess pressed so sweetly to her bare shoulder in the early morning. I know she spent most of her time alone once she left the temple, shading her eyes with a dark hood, always cautious of others knowing her by her gaze. I know that, near the end, she was sleepless, paranoid, waiting.

I was waiting too, by the river. Standing there, watching her hang on to the branches, the arms of that great sprawling cypress tree, watching her watch the water. If you have a nightmare for twenty years, is there gentleness to be found in the swallowing dark, those last moments before the brain exhausts its oxygen and the senses grasp nothingness? Is there relief in that surrender?

When Stella jumped, when she sunk seamlessly beneath the surface, when she gasped reflexively and began kicking, flailing, reaching for the surface –

They say a lot of things about me. But when I touched her face, I was so gentle. Her eyes were open and cloudy-white and when she saw me she smiled.

*** 

Tess came to me afterward.

She was a demanding girl, and consequently well-suited to her craft, which involved bending the remains of human bodies to one's whims. Contrary to popular opinion, I have nothing against necromancers.

But I do not enjoy being called to bear like a common imp, either, with pentagram and incense, gold coins laid over the hollow eye sockets of the white-washed skulls in her study. She summoned me hoarse-throated and red-eyed and with hands shaking — I went for the same reason I visited Stella: I was curious.

I stood in front of Tess plain and homely in my most intimate form — the white robe, the dull sickle, the bare feet. Intimidation is the realm of beings who need it.

Tess demanded, "Give her back."

I cocked my head.

"Now."

I sighed and stepped out of the pentagram, neatly skipping the line of salt and chalk meant to trap what is summoned. Foolish girl — all the books in the world couldn't teach her to bind me to anything.

She didn't back away when I walked towards her. Not a single step. Why would she? A necromancer lives in constant awareness of their own fragility. And Tess was bold, and bright, and terribly breakable.

"Give her back," she said, hand up as if to raise her human corpses.

I touched her cheek. Smiled.

"My dear," I said. "What makes you think it matters?"

# HEATHER COLLEY

**Senior**
**Major:** Literature & Creative Writing and Sociology
**Reading:** Short Fiction

My name is Heather Colley, and I am an English Literature/Creative Writing and Sociology double major. I'll be graduating from Michigan in May and hopefully pursuing English and writing at the graduate level next year. Thanks for supporting undergraduate writers at the Cafe Shapiro readings!

*Nominated by: Laura Thomas*

# Once On A Clear Day

The tree was only a tree, if it were only you, or even me, looking at it, albeit a very large and a very old one. And it was coming down. The way that Sheila felt when she heard about the tree's scheduled chop was something like what other people might feel once the airplane is smooth again out after that particular kind of threatening turbulence. The tree obstructed her view of the river. And this she believed obstructed everything else, as in, her general welfare, and her productivity levels, and her interest in remaining alive, and so on. It was always the goddamn tree. Her therapist disagreed. Her therapist, thought Sheila, was delusional. Ever since the issued notice of the death – *The tree on Riverview Avenue is coming down* – Sheila had been singing a lot.

She was seen, and heard, on her fastwalks down the road and back again, as she sung tunes she'd dreamt up in the night or in her daydreams, or both. At last she was dreaming again! The tunes had lyrics to them, original ones, oscillations between the same two or three notes, which felt right to her, and sounded not much like music to anybody else.

"The tree comes down," she would sing, "they all frown, I feel glee, I'll see the sea, bye bye tree, hello happiness..." There were other renditions, each of which alluded to the infectious fact that once the tree came down, Sheila would be able to see all of the Hudson River and beyond, right from her living room window. And on sunny days, even Manhattan. She would be able to distinguish the Empire State Building all the way out there, and it would look invincible, and so it would be invincible. And she too would be invincible. And this was what hope felt like to her.

She spoke to Jen on the phone, the day before the tree was set to come down. She sat in her living room, and gazed across the road. The leaves waved offensively, as if in knowing jest.

"See, Jen, once the tree is down the whole sky will open up. Sky like you've never seen it before."

"The sky is still up there," Jen pointed out, "Even though the tree obstructs your view of it."

"It may as well not be. While the tree stands I couldn't tell you the color of the sky. I'd be unable to tell you, Jen, if even it was a clear day out."

"Well," Jen said, "The sky is clear today. Blue and with no clouds."

"And starting tomorrow I will be able to see for myself, thank you, Jen."

"Don't you feel a sense of attachment to the tree, a little?"

"There are trees *everywhere*, Jen. I could go out to the trails and see as many as I please. It's that one that I want down."

"I dunno," said Jen. "I like the sense of nature that it instills on the block."

"Jen, I'm as into nature as the next. I could talk trees all day if you wanted. But *that* tree never spoke to me. It just never did."

"By the way, Sheila, it's starting to rain a little, I don't know if you could see."

"Yes I *see* the drops on the windows, thank you very much Jen. See you later for the tennis match."

"Bye, Sheil—"

Click, and Sheila's daydreams came back and reminded her of the coming foliage destruction and all of the things that she might see, soon, *finally*, in the nothingness of sky above her head.

The Scarstown School District Board of Education met in a historic mansion on the hill behind the high school. At present they dealt with a complicated case that had been recently brought to their attention. A sixteen-year-old boy was accused of soliciting nude pictures of a younger woman across cellphone channels and beep boop networks. These networks seemed to have diffused the photographs across the entire Scarstown student body. The girl's mother was furious. And the boy's mother claimed that her son's mental retardation had caused his lapsed judgment in the world of cellphone technology. The Board of Education right then was dealing with questions of morality, of youth sexuality, of modern technology and privacy, of individual rights, of the other kinds of rights that go with wrongs, of mental handicap, of justice and order.

It was nearing noon and they wondered what was for lunch.

This was a human resources circus. And all the while, the parents – the Board of Education was comprised solely of parents – round the table ached and itched to see the photos of the juvenile girl, out of perverted and nagging and nightmarish curiosity.

It was divine intervention when a more manageable case came along, and the Board of Education turned its fleeting attention to it when they heard: The massive maple on Riverview Avenue was set to come down tomorrow.

"It cannot be so," stormed Dana McCoy from the head of the table. She punctuated this with flashes of her gavel. She tended not to start or finish the meetings with the gavel but rather enjoyed hitting it about in the middle of conversation instead.

"I vehemently agree!" said Dylan Thomas, of the Thomas's. The Thomas's were an ancient townie family that mysteriously occupied a range of minor public service jobs despite nobody in town having recall of their election. They seemed to have migrated to certain places and remained there for lack of much else to do. Dylan Thomas's parents were not literary people. They spent a lot of time wondering why their friends and relations asked them so much about poetry. Could they not, the Thomas's wondered, just shut up about books and sonnets, and symbolism and romanticism, and get on with things that mattered, like education?

"I have a very personal resonance with that tree on Storm Avenue," said Dana.

"Wasn't it on Riverview?" said Dylan Thomas.

"What's more," Dana continued, "Is how the town's oxygen supply will be depleted if we lose it."

Dana McCoy, thought everybody around the table, is a forward thinker indeed.

"Think of the children!" said Dana. "They are our future!"

"And the bumblebees," said Thomas.

"The whats?"

"They're dying," he said. "And what if they lived in that Maple? The bumblebees? Their nests are unsuspecting."

Thomas, thought everybody, is perhaps even one step ahead of Dana.

"We must draw up an anti-action report," Dana said. Dana was the instigator of the drawing up and sending off of things. The question afterward was usually to whom they'd been sent, and what exactly had been written. Interestingly, Dana often forgot all about it, by the time someone got round to asking.

"It's time for my lunch break," said Dylan Thomas. "Nice work, team."

Everybody varyingly left. They wandered round during lunchtime and went about their usual work of thinking very highly of themselves.

And as they wandered they looked at all of the trees in town, for the first time. They'd been in that town for years and years, some of them now curled to decades. And they realized, finally and with redemption, how very much that tree on Riverview mattered.

You might wonder, and many did, although few asked, whyever a Board of Education might concern itself with matters of environment and the bumblebees. Once, but only once, a person asked them this directly, asked them why their sights were so horticultural all of a sudden. Here is what Dana said:

"Why not?"

And they were never asked again.


"The tree's soon dead, the sunset's red, the view they said, it'll fill my head...with the happiest sights of New York City," Sheila sang. She wondered if the Empire State had changed at all since she'd last seen it. The trouble was that she'd never seen it before in her entire life.

Sheila was in fact delusional. She had once had a nasty interaction with radiation, though has since forgotten all about it. But who could blame her for this, anyway? What person has not, at some point, lost his or her head in the belief that a new view of some great city might fix everything?

And now it was time for that fix. Humans have a remarkable capacity to turn anything to music if they think hard enough about it. Sheila did with the BRRRRRR and the WEERRRRRRR and the BUZZZZZ of the chainsaw. This was the Carnegie Hall Symphony Orchestra. These construction men were either geniuses or they were God. Even Sheila in her delusion knew that no one can be both.

Her euphoria atomized as the first branch was cut.

From down the road came a storm of human feet on a hurried pursuit of justice and future welfare. Dana McCoy led the Board of Education as they charged down Riverview Avenue.

"Stop this madness!" Dana shouted. "You bulldogs are shortening this town's oxygen supply! You are harming our children and their bumblebees!"

"No, Dana," said Dylan Thomas, running to catch up with her and finding himself short of breath, "*First* the bumblebees go, then the oxygen because of that, *then* the kids last of all."

"Excuse me – Men, chopping this tree will harm the bumblebees, then our oxygen supply, then our children, in that order."

BRRRRRRR

WEEERRRRR

BUZZZZZZZ

"Stop this heresy!" Dana McCoy shrieked toward the crew, who were clad in painter's pants and heavy boots and had brows that started to bunch up in her direction. She waved and pranced about their crane and their tools, and then Dana paused to watch Sheila huffily cross the road. Sheila said:

"What the hell are you doing? This is my happiness, that you're destroying, for some *bumblebees*?"

"Your happiness," Dana said, "For the children's *lives*?"

"What children? Whose?" Sheila shouted. "Yours?"


Lucas McCoy, the sixteen year old who'd solicited the nude photos of an unnamed fourteen- year-old girl, had that same girl in the backseat of his mother's black Escalade. The girl's name was Emily, though what with her being a minor, that information was not yet public.

Emily wished for a bit of harmless escapism. She wished even more to escape the Escalade. Lucas continued on with the same perverse actions that had driven him to trade her nude photographs all round town.

"You can't do this," she panted, as he successfully unzipped her jeans, which were embroidered with flowers. "Your mother is on the Board of Education."

"So what?" he said. "Try telling them. There is no way they're listening."

BRRRRR

WERRRR

BUZZZZZ

# SIERRA DANIELS

**Junior**
**Major:** Psychology
**Reading:** Fiction

I am a so-called "writer" from Vicksburg, Michigan – AKA, a "village" near Kalamazoo – who has been writing for as long as I can remember. Sometimes poetry, sometimes later-abandoned novel beginnings, but usually short stories or insomnia-induced-emotional rantings. I hope to eventually become a psychotherapist, and my love for human complexity (and simplicity) is a large reason for my passion in picking up a pen. Metaphorically. I usually type things.

*Nominated by: Jeremiah Chamberlain*

# Independence Day

The sirens are off, but the lights keep flashing; blue, red, blue, red; dull against the spreading sepia of the mid-afternoon sky. *Winter must be right around the corner*, Mrs. Alvarez figures from her spot in the yard. The dry grass looks like wheat in length and color, but cuts the folds of her skin when she curls her toes. She had been meaning to water it, and to clean up the junk everywhere: old food containers, her son's dolls, the cigarette butts she'd been tossing out on the doorstep. She now regrets putting it off for so long. The yard is in no state to be seen.

She looks past the officer in front of her, barely registering his condolences as she stares at her son's body, nestled under the white sheet. If it weren't for the blood stains settling in the asphalt, Mrs. Alvarez might have been able to convince herself that he'd mistaken the road for his bed.

Her husband sits in the back of the police vehicle, stunned but too drunk for the realization to hit quite right. Too drunk, or perhaps too high. After finding his equipment in the basement, Mrs. Alvarez can't be sure anymore. Not that she ever really was, except for when she smelled the beer on his breath when they'd argue. Which had been often, especially recently.

The minivan that her husband would always sleep in after those arguments has torn down the chain link fence, which hadn't been enough to keep the raccoons out anyway. Mrs. Alvarez isn't sure why she hadn't requested him to tear it down sooner. Probably because she knew the job would never get done, and she didn't want any more bruises should she have asked at the wrong time.

The tire tracks are burned into the asphalt, molded into the small body. She hadn't immediately looked toward the road when she'd stumbled outside, prepared to scold her husband for having missed picking their son up from school yet again. She hadn't been prepared for the sight she witnessed, but how could she have been? How could she have known that when her son mentioned he was going out, that he wouldn't get farther than a few feet beyond the fence?

"I'm going out, Mommy," he'd said, and she hadn't acknowledged him. Why hadn't she acknowledged him? It's not like he'd been easy to ignore.

When her belly swelled ten years ago, that hadn't been easy to ignore. She had been trying to be so careful, but she couldn't afford proper contraceptives beyond condoms, and her then-boyfriend neglected to use them a quarter of the time. It was really a long time coming, she supposed, but that didn't make anything better. How was she supposed to afford taking care of herself *and*  a child? Abortion wasn't an option; it wasn't legal, and while she might spend a lot of time in alleyways, she wasn't going to trust one with an operation like that.

It was easier to deal with her son as he grew older. He was a self-sufficient child, potty-trained by six through his own will. The Alvarez's were just too busy to help. Or too far gone. Still, Mrs. Alvarez made sure to read to him every night, so he was a smart boy. A smart boy who had kicked too hard in the womb, a tag team with his father. *Kick harder*, she'd prayed, *Get it out of me*.

There is a dark truth that Mrs. Alvarez knows. A truth that lingers like a malignant force amongst wishful thinking and denial. Birth is by its nature a destructive process, and a child is too incompetent to fix anything. But Mrs. Alvarez would like to believe that there is an afterlife, and that it is better than here, for that poor child's sake.

Mrs. Alvarez's tears leave tacky stripes on her cheeks as she stares at now-empty spaces in the growing dark, and for once in what feels like many years, she feels happy.

# Dividation

There's an almost orgasmic feeling when the hair separates from the roots. When she latches on to the ends and twirls them around her fingers like thread around a spool, feels the elasticity of the composition, uses it to measure the effectiveness of her most recent conditioner choice. She knits a pattern between her fingers, ribbons and spiderwebs, relishes the itch at the base of her dry scalp. She pulls sideways until just before the strands will snap, focuses on the spreading burn. She swears the snapping sounds like the beginning notes of her favorite pop song. It sounds like the crinkling of a flimsy plastic wrapper on the bottle of her diet pills, and she swears that she can feel the tingle from her scalp to the tip of her tongue.

The bare spot on the back of her head is now the size of a golf ball, having upgraded from its beetle-shape after the divorce, when she watched her father cry over a woman he had lost long ago. When she and her older brother watched their mother walk out the door and onto the motorcycle of the town's bewitching bartender – with his Barbie eyes and Ken body – wearing the dress she'd chosen to buy over her daughter's recital tickets. The scene was so laughably cliché that the six-year-old girl couldn't help but think it realistic, as it matched so many of the movies she had watched every night. That's why she didn't cry. Because that was the start of her film, where she'd develop the ability to talk to animals or befriend a fairy, and some prince would come along and buy her a stage that would be entirely her own.

But at that pivotal moment, the only prince she knew was trying not to fall apart on the couch, eyes rimmed red as he stared at the abandoned ring on the coffee table. He took his own off and placed it beside its match, the string connecting them leading to nothing but open air.

How far apart must she pull before the string breaks, she'd wondered. Is it already broken?

Months later, her father will pawn those rings for far less money than he had used to buy them, and she will understand that the string was just a phantom, a trick of the light. She could do nothing then, so she twirled her hair around her finger like the pirouettes she performed on stage and *pulled.*

The children at school bullied her once the blank spot became noticeable. At school, she wasn't allowed to wear the hat that the therapist had told her to wear. The one her father had practically fused to her scalp.

"Balding already, grandma?"

Such taunts followed her around the playground, where adult supervision couldn't steadily follow. From first grade to fourth, she had cried. She couldn't understand why she found comfort in pulling her hair, and she couldn't understand why the other kids hated her for it. So, she just pulled out more strands. Her father tried to complain to the school, but it didn't help. When it became apparent that the adults were being especially observant of her usual bullies, the taunts became less about her balding and more about her being a tattletale. The jabs became literal: jabs to her sides with an elbow, shoving at her back, tugging at her pigtails.

Fifth grade was a time of great physicality. With newfound hormonal strength, two girls shoved her down into the mud that had formed under the tree line of the playground. They jeered at her, yanked at the new dress her father had gotten her for being "such a good girl, such a brave girl," and pushed her back down whenever she tried to get back up. She pleaded with them to stop, to just *leave her alone,* but they just laughed.

"Hey, get lost, will ya?"

There had been a boy who spoke up for her. The new kid, the shy kid. They had shared crayons once during craft time. She watched as he bickered with the girls, shoved at their chests despite the fact that he was scrawny enough that the very wind could have posed a threat. The girls ran to the supervisor to complain that he'd been harassing them. That boy and her waited in the office while the principal called their parents.

"Why'd ya do that?" she'd asked, eyes trained on the principal's empty desk.

He paused in his eating of a small protein bar to glance at her. "If not me, who?" She didn't reply, just felt the gratitude sear warm in her tummy. She saw him tuck the half-finished bar away out of the corner of her eye. "Why do you do that, anyway?"

"Do what?"

"Pull out your hair." "I dunno."

"Does it feel good?"

"I dunno. Kinda."

They had left it at that, falling into silence except for a murmured goodbye when his parents had arrived to pick him up. When her father came, she had been ashamed of the pain that had crossed his face. He'd spent quite a lot on the dress that was now stained beyond hope. They hadn't had much money after her mother left.

When she returned to school, the boy became her unofficial bodyguard. She learned that his name was Evan. She and Evan became best friends, forging a vow to stay together through whatever hell came their way. She hadn't noticed that she wasn't pulling her hair back then.

That fact changed when she was fourteen. The spot became a penny when her brother hit a billboard, the condescending smile of the man on the toothpaste ad beaming down upon the wreckage. He'd been texting his girlfriend, apologizing for having missed their last date, calla lilies on the front seat. He'd always assured his love of her worth through flowers, compared her lips to their petals and her shape to their stems. At the funeral, the girlfriend dabbed furiously at her running eye makeup. The sister wore a baseball cap as to not offend, and her father scolded her for the inappropriate choice, but didn't force her take it off. Which does he find more offensive, she'd wondered. The hat or the balding? She couldn't provide her own answer, so she kept it on and cried. Her fingers had reflexively tugged on the hair falling out of her cap, and she spent the procession wrapping strands around her index fingers.

From then on, she tried to bury her head in music, in her studies, in the amorphous glow of television that she would watch flicker on the wall at night. She avoided looking at her father's increasingly despondent face, flushed and breath stinking in a way that had become familiar by then. She pretended not to hear his crying, politely blamed it on the high pollen levels of the spring season and not on the old baseball jersey she had failed to hide.

When she visits Evan's house one summer afternoon, unable to find the willpower to go home after class, she finds him alone. The house is eerily quiet, and she notices the half-eaten sandwich left staling on the counter. There is a retching noise, and she picks up on the smell like a trained bloodhound. That overwhelming burn of acid that churns your guts and makes your snot flow. She finds him, unprepared for her visit, bent over the toilet. She twirls hair around her finger as liquid twirls in the porcelain, looks him in the face as he stares back unblinking. She will blame the tears in her eyes on the smell, and will later watch him like a hawk as he eats that other sandwich half.

"I always thought it was unnatural how often you had to pee," she murmurs.

He looks up, laughs because it's the only thing he can think to do, and continues eating.

"Why?"

He struggles on a swallow, then gives a coy smile. "I dunno."

She thinks that is fair enough. She will not return home until she knows the sandwich has been digested. Her father will not call to check up on her.

She spends the next several years in and out of hospitals, clutching two men's hands as they spill their souls into toilet bowls. She eventually cuts her hair to dull the discomfort, hides it with the cap when she can. It doesn't stop the urge. She wears baggier clothes to let herself breathe, hopes it'll stop the constricting of her chest after her father goes comatose for the second time. She tears the strands out until there's two new spots to match the growing one, savors the control, refuses to acknowledge the definition of compulsion.

She will snap on her twenty-second birthday, the day when Evan doesn't wake up one sunny morning. She will take a pair of scissors in hand. She will focus on her breath as she watches the strings fall in clumps to the linoleum floor. Then she will take a razor to her scalp.

Her hand will shake, but there will be an insistence within the pressure she applies to the blade. A deliberation in the slow, even strokes that she will make. When her father wakes, he will click his tongue, shake his head, but will not be surprised. He'll clap her on the back, congratulate her self-control, praise her disinterest in public opinion.

She'll laugh, and feel pounds lighter despite having only lost grams.

# The Walls Were Orange

Twenty years later in the new public library, the walls were orange.

*Daddy's face is flushed and his breath is tinged with the staleness of the alcohol still rotting on the kitchen counter — she can see the fly buzzing around and inside of it within her mind's eye, twitching and rubbing its hands together like an eager audience or a nervous young girl wringing her hands as she explains, for the fifth time, that when she'd said "Daddy doesn't do much around here" it had been a joke, a drop of sarcasm in the pool of malted liquid in the sink, and it wasn't supposed to lead them here with her curled up between the bed and the wall with sweaty palms over her head, and Daddy's hand is sweaty too, as it tends to be, when it strikes her face, and his grip is tight in her hair, and his face grows redder against the pumpkin background of her bedroom — orange like the gone-mushy fruit on the kitchen table where Mommy sits, pulse jumping with each flicker of the magazine page and every bang a couple doors down, sweat congealing in the hairs on her upper lip like Daddy's as it slides down into the spittle on his lips as her head spins and her vision swims with tangerine stars, bright like the safety cones on the street, and heat explodes from her nose and streaks a sunset across the drywall like the one that is spreading across the hushed streets and that will remain there when all is done — as it is a constant like everything else — until it all fades to black outside, punctured by the goldfish glow of streetlights, and the room of fire turns into a room of ash until the sun rises and the embers glow again.*

Twenty years later in the new public library, the walls were orange. And so she left.

# KELSI DAVIS

**Junior**
**Major:** Communications and Media
**Reading:** Poetry

Miss Kelsi Lynn Davis was born in Kentucky and raised in Mackinaw City, MI.

She is total chaos covered in freckles and loves her work as an academic counselor.

She is joyously alive.

*Nominated by: Jeremiah Chamberlain*

# Hold Down the Fort

i have slow and steady dreams in which people speak a different language than i do. they're telling me something vitally important, grabbing me by the shoulders and shaking me until i crumble like a cheesecake base. in the morning, i stand in the doorway and wait for the motion sensor lights to feel me before i take another step, and they stutter alive, one by one. in the candy store, my shoes ever-so-meekly stick to the floor with the corn syrup or the brown sugar or just because the night shift didn't mop very well, and i feel the sugar thickening the air, too. I know a 12-year-old who doesn't speak, except to his brother, and only to ask for food. i haul 5-gallon buckets and watch military ads until i'm blue in the face, and people keep shaking my shoulders

# Walk Like a Man!

Oh, but walk like a man with your tits pushed way forward
I'm not afraid of a little bird shit or the spring ground, juicy with mud
Ah, but my elegant little kitten heels don't sink into it, and my hands
are immaculately clean

Where will my hallucinations and my fantasies of violence end up?
My descriptions of dismemberment will not arrive with Poe's, my
unnamable creatures far below Lovecraft's league

I'm hot and I sweat and I tarnish my silver,
you've all missed your chance to fix me so live with what you've got
I'd like to know who decided when I was too old to run around
shirtless in the house
I'd like to know who picked out the flower girl's shoes, and my cheer
dress
Who taught me to eat glass
Who's giving participation credit for the meanest shit I've ever heard
Who's in charge here, because it's time to start gouging out eyes

Let's have the gist of it
Let's not have it again
Get it down pat

Well just listen this once:
If I could do girlhood again
I'd buy a lot more lighters

# Save-a-Lot

My mother never shoplifted but I do
She says she raised two perfect daughters and
I make a liar out of her everyday
And so does my sister, up in the Great White North drinking like a fish

I once had a boss with disgusting birthmarks
Up the back of his neck and to his left ear
He told me he had done every drug known to mankind:
Lost in the desert for a week on peyote
Face down drunk in a superstore parking lot
Things I'd never even heard of with deadly side effects
Finally, he woke up one day on someone's lawn with police on all sides
He's the nicest guy I've ever met, never let old men hit on me
Giving everyone their fair chance and then some
Raising his perfect little child: a hyperactive six-year-old who only
wears green

I used to go down to the police station every year to wrap presents
And one Christmas when my boyfriend's kid brother opened his gift
I recognized it – I wrapped it, while his mother sat there in her
Clinique
So I stopped wrapping gifts

A coworker of mine, moved away now to Minnesota with nothing to
remember her by
Except the occasional picture of foot-deep snow
The only person not from my hometown who stood inside my brain
and spun
With her arms held out
She peeled and sectioned out my heart like an orange with her blunt
thumbnails

# The Moon's Got a Boat / Ailing

## The Moon's Got a Boat

And she motors around the sky on the hunt for her great white whale
Scraping across the surface of her cool, placid lake
Fishing poles with ocean lures trail off the stern and when she stops
She casts out a few more with worms

The moon's got long fingernails with dirt underneath them
And sweeping silk robes, with the edges torn up
Skin like glass, beading sweat caught in dark eyebrows
Say goodnight, she has to go to work

## Ailing

He rode a giant, mean ox through the thick purple cavity of space
Pierced the sun, broke it apart into shatters of white hot lightning
Careening towards Earth past his charred corpse and the ox,
His soul struggling to free itself.

The Earth's gravity such a delicious attraction for the splatters,
People saw them bearing down in their last moments and shot out
Their most honest words, ones that only God had ever seen
And it made things worse.

# Fat Pink Pigs

Pierce a hole through some denim to thread their grommets
Blood let and then let
The doctor put leeches down their thighs How
uneventful! How anticlimactic!

Oh all these little anklebiters clawing at my pant legs
As of yet, they don't regret
Claiming more land and more women What
do they want from *me*?

I've found my work in battue, yknow
Beating out the pheasants' bushes
To drive them towards their deaths by arrow
A profession usually reserved for beagles
"Rush dogs," they're called,
Faster than I, and scarier too
Sharper tongues with louder feet

But I am the chicken to the farmer, or wait
Better yet I am the chicken to the suburban mother with a 10
by 10 yard
Who has decided to fill half of it with a chicken coop and hens
that won't lay
There is no power for the hens and there's no power for the
suburbanite
How boring! And I!

I pierce a hole a puncture a wound a rift
To keep things clean, to make blood pudding
The ankle climbers see me as one hundred feet tall
And that's how I feel

# I Wanna Go a Little Nuts

I wanna go into the woods, find a nice silky black mole, dig him from the soft, wet dirt and eat his body whole. I'll slide him down my throat, digest him nice and slow, pick his teeth out from my stomach and wear them as earrings, oh! I want to take my clothes off, and rub sap off a pine tree. I'll cover myself in dirt and pine needles when I'm an evergreen.

I wanna burn my house down! Melt all my forks and knives! I want to taser my inner thigh and walk around at night! I want to cut my hair all off and I want to eat dog food. I want to run and run and run and never be pursued. I want to drown my boyfriend, a little, and free up my weekends. I want to scare him off and Lorena Bobbitt all his friends!

I want an Adirondack chair on a dock in eastern Maine, and I want to be a missing person that's never seen again. I want it to be April, when the ocean's nice and cold, and I'll slip into the ice water and I'll never get old. Let my purple body wash up in some God-forsaken spot, let the seagulls find me first, I want them to eat my rot.

Or, I want to dig my silky hair into black dirt and then get eaten. I want my world to forget every left and right I've written. I want big ugly claws, I want fur, I want yellow teeth. Only for those that exhume the earth am I something to reach. I want to disappear and I want destruction on my way out. I want myself as the only god to which I am devout.

# Dollar Menu

What is it in here that is making things
magnetic, and where have my earrings gone for the night?
I sign my bank papers and my car loans
With a green gel pen because my credit's screwed.
But they can't repossess until six months have passed,
And that's all we're asking because his new job
Is thirteen dollars an hour and it breaks his body and
She holds me accountable for things that I've said.
I smell like a dead dog rotting in the sun, or in VO5
So I give up what little reputability I have
In a last glorious fanfare, throwing up my hands, crying out,
Take all that I have left, and you'll find that I have nothing!

The promises and the little expressions of gentle love
are more than they look. Buying a drink with the dirty pennies from
The center console is comparable to a Sweet Sixteen's
Big red bow, and making room in a twin bed,
or a seven dollar air mattress,
or a layer of blankets on the floor
Is comparable to giving you all I have,
And I will give you all I have. There will come a time
When I sleep on your seven-year-old daughter's old crib mattress
In the living room floor.
I get caught up in the sleeping arrangements.

I am begging for momentum from an absent God, from
the people at the welfare office,
As my tires dig fruitlessly into an ugly beach.
I will do anything but that, I will board people in my house, I will give
    rides,
I will give charity. I will pull out the bottom of the barrel that once
Pumped blood in my body and give the last shreds that I can scrape
    from

Between the tendinous muscle. I will work the 12 to 8 shift at the
   Marathon,
I will let my teeth fall out. There is no other way.

The pharmacists know me when I walk in,
Before I can get a syllable out they ask
Who am I here for

# I Am the One Who Calls

I am the one who wakes you from your deadened sleep
I am she who aches and plots and tears my liver out so the bird
The damned bird can just eat it without bothering me

I am the one who knits hats
She who grieves and she who cooks white chicken chili are the same
And they are me

I am the one who is there when the light goes out
When the last sliver of sun falls and the candles are all black wax and
no wick
I am she who trudges my body across the unlighted, unsanded floors
with no hope of return to
        bed, who picks the high-hanging fruit, who gives up the ghost

I am the one who removes the festering corpses of men from
battlefields
I am the one who calls out when they are marching across the fields
I am taking a shovel and I cannot be stopped

# Red

I am a dog pushing my nose through the wires in a chain link face
And scrunching up my skin so much my whiskers might fall out
They can see how soft my fur could be
I am D's dog, and I live on West Etherington Street
I pull back from the fence and stand unhindered and large. I bark
There is a kid walking down the busted sidewalk eating a strawberry
    pop tart
Little chitlins like that always walk slowly past me, staring me down
They only walk fast when I can't see them but I know they do. I hear
    them
"Aakomaagwad!" the kid shouts, and he's right
The unmistakable stink of neglect radiates from me
When I was born, I was polluted with the dirt
It stuck to the fluid that left my mother's body with me
As I spilled onto the ground, blind, deaf, wet, alien
And confused
Leaves around me fall in the hot summer wind, dry and unwelcoming
The fence shivers, scared
Why does D keep that damn mean mutt around
This kid will be a drug dealer for D when he turns 15 and he will still
    fear me, that's why
And sometimes I taste the sweet flesh of dissenters in my teeth
My barking forms in the kid's brain as "maajaa, maajaa, maajaa"
This fence is getting ready to buckle at the knees
I will have my own strawberry filling when I sink my teeth through
    some poor soul's fingers

# Dear Everyone

DEAR EVERYONE I BECOME MORE IMPORTANT EVERYDAY
NOW I'M TWENTY-ONE AND I CAN TAKE FIREBALL SHOTS WITH MY MOTHER
I WENT TO NEW HAMPSHIRE AND BACK ON A GREYHOUND AND IT SUCKED
I'VE TALKED TO THE AMISH GIRLS AND THE BIKERS WITH NOT AN INCH TO SPARE
AND DRUG ADDICTS REFORMED AND DRUG ADDICTS IN THE WORST OF THE HABIT
I KNOW HOW TO PIERCE AN EAR AND MAKE A THANKSGIVING DINNER AND I KNOW
WHERE WHITE BUFFALO COMES FROM AND WHY I HALLUCINATE I'M TALLER THAN
MY SISTER BY A FOOT AND STEADILY GAINING WEIGHT IN MY HIPS
I CAN TELL THE STORY OF THE GREAT MOTHER, GOD DAMMIT, AND OF LAFAYETTE'S
SCALP AND OF PAUL BUNYUN'S GREAT BLUE OX
I'VE SMOKED WEED WITH THE POOR KIDS AND COCAINE WITH THE RICH KIDS I
SHOULD BE FAMOUS

# TYLER DITTENBIR

**Senior**
**Major:** History of Art
**Reading:** Creative Non-fiction

I spend most of my time listening to music—aside from a passion for photography and the arts. Writing is something that I have enjoyed for awhile now—something that once intimidated me, and that makes it all the more rewarding. More importantly, others taking an interest in my work—whether it is my photographs or my writing—is what makes the experience of sharing stories worthwhile

*Nominated by: David Ward*

# Death after Life

There we were, engaged in total silence punctuated only by the intermittent clicking of the furnace in the basement. She was sitting in the dark clay-colored leather recliner in the corner with her favorite possession in the world, her 7-pound bichon poo doggo. She never thought it was funny when I called Cali a poochon, but I did and so I used every opportunity I could to introduce her as such. It wasn't malicious, not mean-spirited, it was more a way of making light of it in hopes she would loosen up on the little things. Consumed by the fluff of the recliner, she sat holding Cali in her arms like the white teddy bear she was. Across from her on a couch – made from the same block of clay as the chair – was me. As with many things, I don't remember why we were in such frigid silence I just remember how it made me feel – not good. Finally, I cast out three words from my heart and for the first time in two years heard nothing in return. The words were hollow in the cold air, crashing into the walls before vanishing leaving me embarrassed to have broken the silence at all.

\*\*\*

I asked her if she still loved me, but she could only stare back at me with her intoxicating eyes. She was calm, too calm, she was cold. I could see that she had made her mind up and I knew she didn't want to be with me anymore, so I didn't bother asking again if she loved me or not. I chose not to look at her, instead I stared at the white curls of Cali's hair and occasionally her black olive eyes would glint, and I would wonder if she'd miss me. I couldn't bear to stay any longer and without another word I left not fully understanding that I would never be back again. I couldn't cry because I wasn't done being numb, but I could still be angry and as my grip on the steering wheel tightened, I turned over the fact that she had waited until now – that this was how it was going to end. I couldn't bear to question her; it would do no good to turn around and I wasn't so sure I had the energy to if I did.

The reality was tough to comes to grips with, but we tried to treat it like it was no big deal, hugging and kissing goodnight. But it was a big deal, made evident by my mom tucking a 20-year-old me into bed – something she hadn't done for a decade or so now at least. She turned out my light before closing my door with one last goodnight. Darkness and I, alone together once again and this time I wondered if we'd be together forever in the end. A heavy lead ball rolled in my stomach as my mind crept towards the edge of its understanding. I won't get an answer until it's too late, the anxiety freezes my mind in place, and I scramble to free myself from the existential abyss from which I have sunk. Shooting up in bed, I can feel the despair in my bones – its acid leaching into my muscles. I wanted to think wonderful things, I wanted to think about everything, I didn't want to ever stop thinking – but I couldn't stop thinking about death. I felt invisible amongst the darkness and eerie silence and for a moment I thought that maybe being a ghost wouldn't be such a bad gig. A sharp pain shot through my heart once more and I remembered that I couldn't fool myself for long, I had only a few hours to get rest and I was insulted by my body's pleas for sleep. After all, you can sleep when you're dead.

\*\*\*

I always enjoy a nice warm cup of coffee in the morning to wake myself up. It always becomes a race against the clock to finish my cup before it gets cold, accelerating with every sip. The less coffee in the cup, the quicker it cools. I don't know why, but I tend to lose interest in my coffee around halfway through a cup making this time trial one that I often lose with a mouth full of cold coffee – earthy and bitter. I woke up to the blue Sunday morning light filtering into my room through the curtains and the quickly realized disappointment of not smelling brewing coffee. Before beginning my morning ritual, I set in motion the slow drip of Folger's in the coffee maker. The rich and unescapable smell was my indication that the coffee pot was full and eager for pouring. I got up from my chair in anticipation of the first sip but instead I felt a hot blade being plunged into my back between my shoulder blades. The thirty or so steps to the kitchen was suddenly blocked by a paralyzing pain which brought me to my knees on the dining room linoleum. My lungs constricted as I gasped out loud for enough air to hopefully wake my mom from her weekend slumber. My attempts were futile and quickly I began to fear that I would die here. The smell of fresh coffee became insultingly stronger as it steeped on the kitchen counter just out of reach. Out of extreme determination, I rose to my feet again and stumbled my way toward the forest green carpeted stairs leading up to my mothers' room. I reached the top after a few minutes of crawling but quickly panicked when the hot blade in my back slipped deeper slicing into my heart. I was going to die, and my mom would find me like this – contorted and pale on her bathroom floor, covered in sweat and tears. In a split second I had to make the decision to wake my mom and hope she could call an ambulance in time or to dash for the medicine cabinet. Once again, I was brought to the floor by a searing wave of pain through my arms that extended up into my jaw where it began to feel as though it was being slowly crushed by a vice. I cried out once more, writhing in pain on the rug covered bathroom floor. As my vision began to fade, I became angry that I couldn't get my mind off the pain in order to reflect on my life. I didn't want to die like this, at the very least I wanted the movie-like ending with the chance to see my life flash before my eyes. Instead, I saw myself gazing back on the white porcelain bowl of the toilet as I succumbed to the darkness behind my eyelids.

\* \* \*

We had known for a while that something was brewing inside me, but I was the only one who knew what it was before anyone else even had a clue. I couldn't keep up on our walks in the park anymore, and I couldn't help her dad lift firewood into the back of his van. She knew, and so did her parents that something was wrong, and so when they finally asked me what I thought it was – I answered bluntly – it was my heart. She came to see me as soon as she was out of work, per my insistence that she not rush. The coarse, mint-green hospital gown did a poor job of keeping me warm in the freezing observation room. It wasn't so much observation, instead vampiric nurses cycled in-and-out with vials of my blood returning occasionally only to preface their leaching with pleasantries before disappearing into the depths of the hospital, my DNA in tote. Each vial left me colder and colder, until finally her eyes peered from around the curtain separating the outside world from mine, instantly warming my bones. She was there by my side when I learned of my imminent death. Her hand was the first thing my cold, clammy hands reached for – her eyes, the first thing I looked for to comfort me. I was scared for her, and for my mom who I still don't think could live without me. I didn't want to upset their worlds and I was instantly overcome with shame that I was about to put them through one of the most stressful experiences of their lives. They eventually left me alone to rest for the night and I lay awake on the plastic bed staring at the faint orange light of the corded TV remote next to my head. I didn't pray to a god or ask for forgiveness of my sins as a good Catholic boy should have. Instead, I lay awake imagining the world after me in much the same way a child imagines the world disappearing behind them when they look away. I hadn't quite convinced myself of a life after death, yet. I really didn't know what to think about life *or* death. The uncertainty of the next day was the only certainty I had to hold on to and I became grossly calm with the prospect of death as I felt its icy presence inside me.

\* \* \*

It was after midnight and the candle I had lit hours earlier was beginning to flicker erratically. The unpredictable orange spotlight was casting my animated shadow across the room like a dancing beast in a cave painting. I suppose that my rambling was just as primitive to her ears as was my gesturing. This was by far the latest I had willingly stayed up since the surgery and I was beginning to burn the midnight fuel. In my case, a blend of high-octane jet fuel. Her eyes were looking through me as she sat cross-legged on the love seat. She lazily fingered at her leggings trying to pick off the bits of orange fleece that my blanket had shed. She sat in silence as I struggled to translate the fear of existence into any meaningful language which only further alienated me to the dark recesses of my mind. It wasn't her fault that she couldn't see what I was seeing – she hadn't been brought to the edge, she didn't get to look over. I was deeply depressed and fearful that I could die at any moment. My circulatory system was compromised, or so said the test results and doctors. I had an auto-immune disease that no one had seen before, each doctor reacting with shock to my story. She knew it just as well as I did and just as the certainty of my existence in this life became unclear so did the certainty of my existence in her life.

# CEREN EGE

**Senior**

**Major:** Psychology and Creative Writing & Literature

**Reading:** Poetry

Ceren is from Istanbul and her family moved to and has lived in Michigan since she was in third grade. She began attending the annual poetry slam at her high school, to eventually speaking at and planning the event. She is pursuing an honors thesis in poetry, with hopes to submit a complete book to publishers at the end of this semester. Her work is heavily about her dad's cancer and her family's roots. After graduation, she plans to travel and spend a lot of time by water before attending law school.

*Nominated by: Sarah Messer*

# For Dear Life

My dad swings my four-foot body from side-to-side on the bed
he lies flat on his back        my fingers interlaced around his
knees        I hold on for dear life as he tries to throw me off the
bed        a giggle escapes as my hands slip        he catches me before
I fall        these were our amusement park mornings        our
cherry-jam and olive-spread toast breakfasts

For lunch I stand on my dad's feet        we make what he calls foot
sandwiches                he waddles first        then sways to Etta
James        our fingers interlaced together        he leans forward and
I hold on for dear life as my hair grazes the ground        this is how
I learn to slow dance

During lunch my dad walks me into my first day at American
elementary school shut behind us        I clutch his hand for dear life
down the yellow halls        he points to my teacher with his other
hand        he says        be kind to her        I will see you at six

We wait until six for dinner        this is when he comes home from
the hospital        we interlace fingers at the table        I put on his
white lab coat before bed and        ask him to hum        *Here Comes
the Bride*        he lifts and swings the bottom of the coat        singing
from behind

At sixteen I walk my dad into St. Joe's        he swings the footrests
of the wheelchair to the side        the doctor's fingers interlace with
Purell soap before she pokes him in the same spot        these were
our        chemo        afternoons        our        hospital        vending        machine
snacks        I don't know why they say he is        fighting        when
he cannot dance or        swing        or        eat        his hair meets
the ground and stays there

At sixteen I go to Costco for the first time by myself        Dad
needs Ensure and diapers        I hand my mom's card        they

say        she needs to be here        I say        she would be        I
say        she is pressing morphine under her husband's tongue
they are sorry        the highlighter man smiles at me

The last time I see my dad's fingers interlaced they are to each other
on top of his chest        he lies flat on his back on the bed        the
men in suits swing the stretcher open        I say        be kind
to him        they ask me to leave the room        I say        be kind to
him

# A Breath of Gray Air

It is the morning after
my hair is sticky from dry salted
sobbing and smells of cigarette
smoke because I slept on the sofa in the
basement where my dad's brother has been
breathing for the past month
and there are two ashtrays on
the coffee table next to the sofa
where I slept the morning after

It is the morning after my dad's visitation
and my dad died from lung cancer
and my dad's brother smoked a cigarette at
the visitation and my dad died
from lung cancer and my dad was caught
dead before he ever smoked

I'm taking a deep breath
like the one my mom took when
he was diagnosed and I'm
trying to think of what could
be a better motivation to
quit than to look at your brother
with a breathing tube a
feeding tube a
peeing tube my
dad is one fourth of his body weight and
the weight of his wife's hand crushes
his shoulder so they sleep two feet
apart

What about
looking at his two

eyes that have stayed
halfway open for the past two
weeks so his two
daughters who hold his two blue
hands talk to him because they're not
sure if he is blind or unconscious

The nurse said his hearing goes last so
how inviting is it to create your own language
where one blink means no and two blinks mean
no he stopped being able to blink three weeks ago
so how did you come into our home four weeks ago
with five packs of cigarettes and finish them in
six days

It is the morning after my dad's visitation and
I wake up in the basement to the sight of two
ashtrays on the coffee table and I take a deep breath
like the ones my dad took every time his daughters
or wife walked through the door and I am trying
to understand
how you can breathe
in cigarette smoke while your brother is
not breathing
how you can push down the butt of your
cigarettes into one ashtray
while your brother's ashes are in the other

# My Mom Used her Kohl's Cash to Buy her Husband's Picture Frame Urn

What I remember most from the nights is how they were the same as
his mornings.
What I remember most from his mornings is that they were still
coming. There is

no remembrance without pain. Pain from either the wish of re-living
it or the memory
itself. Sometimes when I want to feel alive I remember the dead. The
stillness of his

bones enough to use mine to run. The hollowness of his sunken chest
to stir rumbles in
my full stomach. He chose silence long before he knew he would live
in it. He

changed from what he chose to be into the only thing he would be. It
is one thing to lose
a blood love but it must be another to lose a love made by choice. My
mother put his

lungs in rice long before the doctors said to do anything. Left them
overnight to drain
the chicken stock his lungs have been sitting in for years of her
cooking. My father was

a simple man. He liked my mother's cooking and warm pastries. He
didn't buy anything
he didn't need and always woke up to give himself enough time to eat
breakfast. A man

called my father an honest man once. His sentence is the only one I
    remember from the
funeral. Or visitation. I am not sure which one we say it was when lying
    to his family

that he was buried when he has been burnt. His ashes rest in a large
    picture frame in
our living room. My mom used her Kohl's cash to buy a picture frame
    urn for her

husband. What I remember most from the mornings following his
    death is how my
mother woke with her wedding band for two years and counting. He
    wore his even

when his finger melted to the size of a smoothie straw. What I
    remember most from
watching his rest was knowing how much he wasn't there and how
    people aren't really

anywhere. I wondered which world his thoughts had him in or
    whether he had thoughts
at all. I wondered if he wished to be here or already gone, or whether
    he was waiting for

us to be ready. He waited until two days after his birthday, until we
    had all eaten a long
breakfast and came to sit at his side at noon. He had always been
    thoughtful that way.

# Reminders to Myself

He will miss me whether he dies tonight or
tomorrow. And whether I really slept over
at the friend's house I said I'd be sleeping at.
Or whether I kissed my mother goodnight.
Or helped Mother put away the spoons. Or
called his mother on Bayram. Or that I never
swam in college. He knows that isolation is my
craft, that death is a catalyst to introspection.
He will miss me regardless of which hand I
hold on his last breath, and he will miss me
even on nights I forget to turn off the lights.

# OLIVIA EVANS

**Freshman**
**Major:** Undecided
**Reading:** Poetry

Olivia Evans is a freshman in the Residential College from Northville, MI. She has currently not chosen a major, and is exploring creative writing and biology. Olivia has received First and Second Year Hopwood awards for nonfiction and poetry. She loves movies, literature, and music, and is very excited to read her work for an audience for the first time!

*Nominated by: Sarah Messer*

# Dandelion

These days, I am bitter to the root of me.
You wait in the dusk of something
undoable. You will break in a way I cannot
fix, and I do not know how to speak
of this almost-grief:
I am ruined, I am ruin, I will ruin this.
I know what you plan to do. I know,
and I sleep soft anyway. When I was little,
I dashed a robin's egg onto the concrete
because I wanted to know how strong it
really was. Years later I found a nest
abandoned in my backyard. I dug
a heat lamp out from the garage and
pretended I knew how to save something.
The end was the same; I will ruin this.

# Coyote Watch

When we were little, our mothers told us
there were coyotes in that wood

but all I remember seeing was the aftermath,
the little bodies soft and burning red against

the wet green. I never heard them howl
until long after you left. I wasn't afraid

until I remembered what it felt like,
the young jaws catching on a quick pulse,

the throat a gaping wound, a breeding
ground for the memory of violence.

Didn't you ask for it once? To glimpse her,
silver and starving under a shard of the moon,

and wasn't it everything you ever wanted?
To be small and hungered for again.

# Sleeping Bear

This story does not belong to us,
but we play-act anyway.
I, the youngest cub,
fleeing from a burning wood,
drowning in a lake as wide as the sea,
and you, the mother who
waits for me until the dunes swell
to smother you with all the
love you didn't know
where to put down.
I can't promise I will make it to
the shore unspoiled,
but the water has always been
a good friend to us
and in the end,
it will swallow the sand
and carry my body
to lay shivering at your feet.

# Late July

It is summer so all the old rules
Don't matter so much anymore.

We drink lemonade and interrupt
Each other at the dinner table,

Beginning with something new
Each time we open our mouths.

I track sand into the kitchen
And my mother only laughs.

# EMILIA FERRANTE

**Freshman**
**Major:** Undecided
**Reading:** Fiction and Poetry

Emilia is a freshman from Princeton, New Jersey in LSA Honors and the Residential College. She has been writing poetry and fiction since she could hold a pencil, and first "published" a now-embarrassing collection of short stories in second grade. She is a staff writer in the Arts section of the Michigan Daily on the Books beat, which means she gets to read books and review them (probably her dream job). She is also the co-grammar editor of the RC Review, the Residential College literary magazine. In her free time, she likes to sing, read Stephen King, and watch Criminal Minds.

*Nominated by: Greg Schutz*

# Excerpt from the short story "Explode"

The house felt empty without Tommy. It felt empty without all their stuff in it. It felt empty even though it was smaller than their old house. They only needed room for Irene and her mother, after all. The twin bed looked so lonely with no carbon copy on top of it. Irene and her mother moved around the house like polar magnets, like planets on orbits that would never collide. They were like ghosts, tiptoeing around one another, desperate to maintain the peace – or maybe it was silence masquerading as peace. It certainly wasn't peace for Irene, who woke up every night shattering the careful quiet with her choked screams.

Irene learned to navigate her world differently. She knew only the routes home that led them away from Wicker Lane, sometimes twisting and turning ridiculously to avoid the wreckage that, though razed, still seemed to smolder.

The house was destroyed. Not only by fire, but then on purpose, by men making it look as though it had never been there at all. They took out the skeleton of a house that still remained, the last charred remnants of childhood and sanity, and loaded it into a dumpster in the driveway. They poured new foundation, they filled the ground with cold and unyielding concrete. Irene watched them roll out sod like carpet. She watched a new frame rise from the ground, inch by inch, plank by plank. Like a phoenix from the ashes, or maybe like a pernicious weed. She watched the new house erase the old house, erase the flames that once burned there, erase her brother from the ground like he never even existed. She watched a new house come to life. A "For Sale" sign, then a shiny new car in the driveway, then lights in the windows and a swing-set in the backyard. Then you couldn't see the sod lines so clearly anymore because the natural grass grew into the little seams in between. Then the house started to look like a real house, no longer like a mask covering a grotesque secret but something even more painful, a smiling face stretched over rotting teeth that only Irene could see.

Her mother never explicitly told her she wasn't allowed to go back to the house, but Irene always knew somehow that she should never mention her little excursions to Wicker Lane. She never knew what she would say to her mother anyway. She and Irene crossed paths on their orbits too fleetingly for her to say anything, much less explain why sod, of all things, made her heart feel so heavy. So she stayed quiet.

# A Moment in the University of Michigan Museum of Natural History

To the dinosaur bones suspended
on fishing wire reigning supreme
still over museum stone floor;

To mammoths of eons past
frozen first in ice and then in air –

      Can you tell me how to
      make my words endure?

You wrote your stories in fossils and
sap and somehow, they lived forever
lasted through meteors and volcanoes
as Homer's lasted through cyclops
and Scylla so his rosy red-fingered
dawn still touches on an earth
untouched by a sense of oblivion.

Tell me, bones of velociraptor
skull of ankylosaurus you
eternal hipbones of
brachiosaurus, how do I
write a poem

# A Courtyard Study

Hair in wind  like seaweed in water,
late-summer air clings to skin.
Looking at their bare feet in grass,
my own tingle with  the remembered
sensation  of blades of green tickling
the spaces  between toes.
Faces stretched out into smiles,
their eyes follow each other,  and
my eyes follow them.

The air tastes like lemonade  left
out in the sun too long.

They stand in a circle  like a full
moon,  like the top of a
mushroom spore.

The sun is surprisingly strong in its late-afternoon laziness,
falling away from the courtyard in a solid line  that shades
in the grass with shadow.

# I, of All Places

I walked through my shoes, weary of my
hair and its tiny droplets. In rain that was
really mist air clung to my skin, clothes,
the building, the first thing I felt were my
feet and the first thing I heard was
singing. It was the door to climb the
stairs, which were beautiful in the way
stairwells are the most private place.
When I reached the top of the singing, of
the stairwell, it became everything. It was
making the whole world sound like where
he was singing making me a listener, a
trespasser of all places.
And when I opened up his song –
off-key, ethereal, terrible, wonderful
otherworldly – I asked him why he
was there, and he said He felt the
stairwell was his, not mine.

# Orpheus Looked Back and Ruined Everything, But When He Looked Up, My Mom Sang Him a Lullaby

Sara Bareilles steps back onstage for an encore
and when her lips touch the microphone her
voice becomes my mother's it's a grown-up
lullaby it's

my mother is telling me that she's done it all before,
that my pain is new to me but not to her or to the
world.
She sits next to me and grows
into the earth and tells me I
will too, someday.

//

We all miss the world we never had, the world
we thought we lived in when we were little and
we fell asleep to the sound of our mother's
voice and the glow of the moon-and-stars
nightlight.

//

I wish there was a word for feeling big
and small at the same time, feeling like
the entire sky but also like my mother's
voice.

I wish there was a word for a mother's voice.

I wish there was a word for the way it feels to be
hundreds of miles from home to look at the same sky
Odysseus looked at on his journey and know that he
missed his mom, too.
I wish there was a word.

**lull·a·by** / ˈlələ͟ˌbī/ *dew creeping*

*into the tent at dawn; always*

*knowing the last word for the*

*Tuesday crossword; the smell of*

*lavender and lemongrass; striped*

*shirts air-drying in the closet; little*

*ceramic houses covered in fake*

*snow, lit from the inside, for*

*Christmas.*

# Light We Took

Our shadow is not a constant thing,
rather it changes based on who
what where we are.
It's different when we're dancing
with our own animal our own
negative space. A little bit of it
loses shape in the twilight mist.
Sometimes it changes based on
when we're in the rain, and
becomes us when we are light
we took
we depraved, we far from homers,
we beloved, we travelers we grow
longer

It is dark and we dance and we are darkness,
lit from behind

# How to Leave a Dream

I step out into the meadow that is the
soccer field of my middle school.
Fresh cut grass and sweaty cleats No
shoes, grass between my toes.
It starts to rain

a sort of mist that doesn't really come from the sky
just seems to materialize in the air around like
water particles making themselves known creating
haloes around streetlamps because it's night and
I'm on the street now, one foot on each yellow line
slicing the asphalt in half. I see my house –
But it's not really my house, is it, because
I am not in it and

I look down again the asphalt peels
away to reveal green earth soccer
field which sinks away into the
ground and the house starts to shrink
away into the mist becoming the air
and I start to descend into the earth.

# MARIA GHALMI

**Sophomore**
**Major:** Creative Writing & Literature and Microbiology
**Reading:** Poetry

Maria is a sophomore double majoring in Creative Writing & Literature and Microbiology. She was born and raised in Dearborn, MI . She is interested in video games, poetry and the distinction between protists and fungi. You can find her at the Sweetwaters on W. Washington St. anytime of the day.

*Nominated by: David Ward*

# Fertilizer

A canary (or two) died to
remind hundreds of men
what it meant to grow
old (above ground) while
said canary chokes in the
mine that collapsed years after
because nature can only give
so much before it finds other
ways to kill hundreds of men
who think the Earth like a
canary–better dead than
alive because money doesn't
grow on trees but *from*
them and nothing–nothing
is more important than the
number of commas in a net
worth–even as man's
legacy is to become fertilizer
for the Earth as they share the fate
of a canary in a coal mine.

# Esraa Ghaleb, 21, of Bethlehem

Esraa. I repeat your name for as long
as your screams remain echoes in my head.
Esraa. I scream in that cave that I am sorry,
sorry your name is a hashtag to an honor killing.

Esraa we only want to remember the good,
As we expunge the sunset
of your bruises
with the light of you cast on this ungrateful Earth.

Esraa.
Esraa.
Esraa.

I honor you like the clouds honor
the Earth. With rain that I cannot keep in.
Esraa. What law did you violate with a smile on your face?

Esraa. What have you done?
What have we done?
What have women done?
What have women born in this life done?
Esraa.
You. Esraa Ghaleb.
Esraa Ghaleb of Bethlehem.
Esraa who needed a family.
Family:
What is a family?
Family: your murderers and the last faces you would see.

Esraa.
I do not know what made you laugh,
Or what music made you most at peace.
And still I will be your family.

Family:

What is a family?

Esraa.

Family: we will love you and keep you in our hearts

For as long as water evaporates from the sea.

For as long as the law takes to stop your relatives.

For as long as it takes to see honor killings become just a memory.

# La Grande Poste, Algeria, 1960

Cats do not have political
affiliations except when
drowned

French soldiers give politically
affiliated scratches
behind the ear    who
knew colonizers to
give

Algerian rebels hate cats who
stink of berets and
baguettes    they miss
the smell of couscous and
*mahaajib*

My grandmother had two
hearts    one for her *blaad* the
other for *son beau chat*    who
knew war to allow love to
coexist

Colonizers found joy in my grandmother's
cat and visited her home in la Grande
Poste where rebels refused to share
Algerian blood so *son beau*
*chat* was filled with Algerian
water

Cats do not have political
affiliations except when
drowned

# Untitled (for now)

America wears a hood
ignoring the wires
coiling around its dick
and the Middle East raises
the voltage until the line
between eyeballs and
fire is blurred like the
line between compassion
and imperialism.
The fire is larger there
than anywhere
as petroleum replaces blood
and capitalism.
Where are the saviors?
Where are the saviors?
The ones that raped
boys in front of their
fathers as fathers were
penetrated with broken
brooms. Next door people
were afraid of bathrooms.
Where are the saviors?
Those who waterboard
for sport and take
selfies as though they
kill Iraqis just to pass
the time as time is running
out. And as Bush watches football
fourteen years after the
Abu Ghraib prison was
refurbished from Saddam
Hussein by the United

States, the seven thousand
four hundred ninety people
imprisoned there
suffer as if fourteen
years was only yesterday.

There are no saviors.
There are no saviors
to protect the world from
the United States.

# Toys

An antique rocketship
sees no deaths

A manic snowflake
watches children
drop because metal
toys sometimes
hit them and maybe
the child didn't study
hard enough: how to be

bulletproof, which in
and of itself is proof
that toys don't kill
and kids should say
goodbye—

their decade long
life will come to an end
any day now and that's okay
smaller coffins are cheaper anyway

# MATT HARMON

**Senior**
**Major:** International Studies
**Minor:** Playwriting
**Reading:** Poetry

Matt is a life-long Michigander, born in Kalamazoo and raised in Royal Oak. While he can't wait to share some poems tonight, he is also a Playwriting minor and is often buried in script revisions for the stage. He is also a photographer, musician, and is profoundly inept at making pour-over coffee despite being a barista. He loves you all.

*Nominated by: José Casas and James Cody Walker*

# For Elijah

I heard from an article in the Times who heard
From his wife that Mr. Cummings, Elijah, the
Iconoclast who clashed with Baal, the bombastic ass, who
Told Baal to fuck right off, who willed fire from
heaven, singeing the soles of soulless, supremacist
Sociopaths, who called the rusted, racist spade a spade, died
today.
I heard from an article in the failing Times
who heard from his wife that, before Mr. Cummings
Made his grave at the John Hopkins Hospital in Tishbe,
Maryland, his attendants wheeled him to the roof so
He could see his constituents, his city, his sun one last time.
"Boy, have I come a long way," he said, according to his
Wife and the crooked journalists at the Times.
It's all hearsay anyway.

Don't tread on me, Baal,
For my body is weary and tired
Of your shit. From now on, I tread
On you. Your foam swords do
Nothing but bounce across my breast. My
Words bludgeon and bruise when
I choose to use them on you.
My words are inked in history, endowed
With Elijah's righteous animosity. Yours
Are Gotham Narrow and sent into
The Twittersphere. I saw a crow peck
Out a tweet of yours on YouTube in
Return for seed.
He added a comma you forgot.

# The airport is a liminal space

The airport is a liminal space.
The hum of conveyor belts,
The pointed splash of a penny breaking the skin
Of the fountain, the slack-jawed
Hawksters peddling pulsating neck pillows
While fighting to keep their eyes open.
All signs point to liminal.

The airport is a liminal space.
There is limited air in the liminal air-
port. It is sucked out by the carbon fizz
Of a lemon spritz. Balloons burst
When you dream of Paris before you fly to
Texas.

The airport is a liminal space,
Says the bird who rams his wings
Into the ceiling. Two hits. A cavernous thud.
It dies while begging
To reunite with its aluminum alloy allies.
To the bird, the airport is no longer a liminal space,
Now, sleep.

The airport is a liminal space,
Says the tarmac laborer who
Spends his nights playing air drums
With his glowsticks. The planes turn whichway to the rhythm—
The pilot is dozing too!
Engines blare but the tarmac employee has no need for
Eardrums.

The airport is a liminal space
Until you take-off on a red-eye,
Looking out the window at

The neurons of metropolis
Like an airborne urban planner.

# s m a l l a r m s

We have small arms.

We have small feet that leave chaotic mobs of tracks from games of tag in the dirt.

We have small hands that catch pigeons and cradle them like our younger siblings.

We have small fingers that slide into safety scissors.

We have small hairs that fall from our bangs as we give each other horrendous haircuts.

We have small smalls of our backs, made for Mommy's clammy hand.

We have small elbows that launch basketballs into the sky, eclipsing the sun.

We have small ears that hear the alarms.

We have small eyes that spot the planes that took our house away fly overhead like crows.

We have small brows that furrow when we watch boxes of food sway from the plane.

We have small mouths that ask why they chose the same model plane to drop food and bombs.

We have small arms and they have big arms.

We have—

# Smith and Baker

Domineering dusk, your weight sits
Heavy on my creaking chest as
I fall back in melancholic
Grime that coats my clothes and soaks my bones.

Wallow! Wallow! yells the dusk. Oh
Well, OK. I Bottle Up And
Wait for my own Vessel to Ex-
plode to tunes of midnight echoes.

Elliott and Julien are
Bars that I wander Between. They
Turn Out Lights by whispering their
Odes of loaded– No, I know this road.

I traveled it the year before
And learned its luring curves. I Waltzed
Along the paths their words have made
And bid A Fond Farewell to dusk,

Which wanted me to dwell on Brittle Bones and Big Nothings and grim-
ly painted canvases. I stand
My ground and stare him down. "You leave now."

My Elliott and Julien
Console me, wrap me, let me know
That I am not an island here
Where Everybody Does Rejoice.

encompassed by his calloused hands
and lips that have yet to harden
lain down on his jacket to protect me from catching cold.
I wanted to tell him that night,
And the gnomes we sacrificed to would have blessed it,
And the cats, too,
But we say it every day now,
More than once, or twice, even,
And I think that's what the lake had in mind:
For us to be the lovers
Greater in strength and beauty than had Hephaestus and Aphrodite
More powerful than the meeting of the sky and the earth
Louder than the fall of a great oak
on the ears of the tiny animals and insects
around to hear it.

I don't stir,
I don't move
anything but my thumb over the lines of his palms
warmer than my own;
possibly the only warmth I've ever known.

# Peace is a Conceit

Peace is a head injury
Either it is, or it could be
A horse with a broken leg
Shot in the rest of his limbs
Twenty five dollars short on rent
and I still have enough for a bag of chips
A young deer shot dead in the woods,
Not meaty enough to harvest.

Peace is a fossil
Pulverized to fuel industry and destruction
A small hand checking the temp of a doorknob before proceeding
The meditative moments in line at the 7/11
Hoping they'll sell me cigarettes without asking how long I've been
here for
Like it matters
A brother's punch in my eight year old gut
The nine month anniversary of a love that has existed for eons
Tears and being held in the bottom of my DXM trip.

Peace is more sound than silence,
Maybe the soft melody of *Stairway to Heaven* playing inappropriately
as Roger lays, arms crossed, unable to object.
Laughter as I remember good times,
and laughter as I remember sorrow.

Peace between my thighs and under my bottom lip
Peace in the red panic lights and peace in the soft dark.

Peace where I can find it;
Either I can
or I will try again tomorrow.

# EILEEN KELLY

**Freshman**
**Major:** Elementary Education
**Reading:** Fiction Short Story

Eileen is from Freeland, Michigan and is a freshman in LSA with plans to major in elementary education. In her free time, she enjoys writing, playing the clarinet, making zines, and reading. She loves cats, dogs, and plants, and someday, she would like to write and illustrate a children's book. She is also in the process of editing her first novel.

*Nominated by: Greg Schutz*

# Flow

Maybe it was a sign—getting expelled from Westshore High made Charlie reevaluate every detail of his former plans for the future. He was going to graduate somewhere smack-dab in the middle of his high school class, go to whatever college offered him a scholarship, and get an arguably safe, predictable degree in computer science. He'd probably end up working in a windowless lab for the rest of his life, and that was fine with him.

But it was like this: Charlie hadn't *meant* to hack into the school district's network security system. Well, maybe he had meant to, but he definitely hadn't planned on getting caught. It was just for fun, some lighthearted Friday night experimentation, until he was called down to the principal's office over the PA system during second period on Monday.

To say that his father had been upset was an understatement, like saying that the universe was "big" or that the ocean was "deep". He had given Charlie two options: transfer to the military prep academy that he himself had graduated from or get a job and move out.

And Charlie, though quiet and nerdy and the kind of kid to sit in the back of class and never say a word, was nothing if not stubborn. He had spent his whole adolescence avoiding and opposing even the very idea of going to the school, and he wasn't about to back down now. So, he had done what any other teenage delinquent would do: persuaded his uncle to take him on his annual spring fishing trip to Alaska and hadn't come back. He had been picking up sandwiches for the two of them to have for lunch when he'd seen the sign at the local deli counter, pinned to a corkboard on door that looked ancient, more holes than cork. "Help Wanted", it had read, scrawled in forward-slanting black ink. "Steward- Commercial Fishing Vessel. Starts Immediately." Charlie had torn a slip from the bottom of the advertisement without a second thought, dialing the number listed at the payphone down the street.

As it turns out, "Starts Immediately" was a pretty good way to get out of that return flight to Florida and the military school acceptance letter that he knew his father had paid good money to ensure was sitting on his desk at home. The next morning, while the sun was just starting to creep above the horizon, Charlie found himself aboard an emerald green fishing boat that looked like it should have sunk in the last century.

The remaining weeks of Alaskan summer were spent getting his sea legs, learning the ins and outs of life on the ship. Charlie's only previous experience on the water was one singular airboat ride in the Everglades when he was five. The way the Alaskan sea was so different to the Florida coastline surprised him, even after a whole year—the ocean here was cold and dark and lined with evergreens and rocky mountains, a shadowy contrast to the sandy shoreline he had played on as a child. Early one morning, an older deckhand- well, they were all older, to Charlie, who had faithfully told the captain that he was eighteen on his first day- had asked him over oatmeal about his life back in Florida.

"Well, do ya got a lady down there? Are ya going back to visit her for the winter?" The man had asked.

Charlie had almost spit out his cereal—a little stale, now that the crew was nearing the end of their trip. He had shaken his head, violently. "No, no. Nothing like that. I'm not going back this year. I'm going to get a factory job, if I can." He knew that the other men on the boat worked canning fish in the winter.

The man had rolled his eyes. "'If I can.' Charlie, these days, they'll pay ya just for walkin' in the front office of them fish cannin' factories. If ya want a cannin' job, ya'll get a cannin' job."

And so it was settled. Charlie had spent all fall and winter cutting open and gutting fish in a crowded assembly line with other out-of-season fishermen, wearing blue gloves that reached to his armpits and a yellow latex rain coat that did the best it could do protect him from the sprays of briny water that shot out when he sliced into a fish.

Working in the canning factory wasn't nearly as bad as Charlie thought it might be, all things considered. The worst part wasn't getting covered in stale seawater every day or even the smell of fish guts that he could never quite wash off of his hands. It was sharing the tiny onebedroom apartment that accounted for half of his weekly pay with Mark and Olly. The only time Charlie wasn't sandwiched between the two other boys was when he was on the toilet, and even then, he could hear every movement that was made in their apartment, and the one above it, and the one below, and the ones on either side. Their twin beds were pushed so close together that every time someone rolled over in the middle of the night, Charlie woke up. He missed the bunk beds on the ship, the white noise of the boat's engine that masked any other sounds. They were shoulder-to-shoulder at the assembly line, too, Mark yelling over the chatter and clank of machinery in Charlie's right ear and Olly shouting right back at him in his left.

Charlie had grown up being crowded, sandwiched between little cousins and neighbors on the merry-go-round at the local playground and in the backseat of his mom's rusty burntorange pickup truck, hot and sticky and sweaty in the humid Florida heat, rolling the windows down and sticking their heads out like dogs until his mother noticed and reached back to pull them in. She always had little kids running around—she had owned a daycare when he was little, and so he had always had built-in friends.

Charlie's mother had been a stark contrast to his father. She had been friendly, almost never without a smile, with crooked teeth and a face covered with freckles, framed with curly ash-blonde hair that reached to the middle of her back. His father was always stoic, strait-laced, an Army veteran with a chip on his shoulder, always thinking that he was entitled to the final say in any family decision. What had always surprised Charlie, from the moment he was old enough to notice, was how much his mother still loved his father. She'd pack his lunch every weekday with a colored-pencil heart on the bag, she'd fold his laundry while he watched Saturday football. Looking back, maybe she hadn't really loved him at all. Maybe she'd just been doing what she was told.

Eighth grade had come with the dawn of "Important Decisions", a phrase that his father always said like it had capital letters, decisions about Charlie, not decisions for Charlie to make. There had been an argument, raging on like a hurricane for weeks and weeks on end. His

mother said that military school was no place for a boy like Charlie-
*like Charlie*, meaning quiet and crafty and unobtrusive, who would
hide in the locker room to get out of gym class and always turned in
his math homework a day early. His father had been *mad*. So mad that
his parents had had the biggest fight that Charlie ever remembered-
his mother stormed out wearing nothing but a blue sweatshirt and
some pajama pants, bare feet, and drove her rusty truck off down
Mango Lane, just to "get some air".

And she'd gone and crashed the thing right into the Spanish-moss-
covered tree at the end of the road. No airbags. The doctor had said
she'd been dead on impact. Charlie had never been able to get the
image out of his head: his mother, the most *alive* person that he had
ever met, imagining what her wild hair must have looked like as she
flew forward, propelled towards the steering column as it forced itself
through her chest.

Charlie hadn't realized how much his mom had been the rubber
band that pulled him and his father together until she was gone. She
had been their interpreter, the commonality that had allowed them to
coexist under the same roof. After that day, Charlie didn't even know
how to talk to his father. It was as if they spoke different languages.
Everything that Charlie said made his father angry, and everything
that his father said to Charlie made him feel like screaming, blowing
up, throwing a fist through the drywall.

Of course, he never did. Because, like his mother had said, he was
quiet and unobtrusive and couldn't stand to be an inconvenience to
anyone. But that didn't mean that he wasn't appalled and frustrated
over and over and over again at every mention or threat of military
school if Charlie didn't get his grades up, win his heat at the swim
meet, *get up* and *try harder*. How could his father hold it over his head
like this—the very reason that they couldn't communicate, the reason,
really, for his mother to have driven off that night, became the only
topic of conversation that he would have with him.

Charlie hadn't talked to his father since the day he left Florida.
Charlie doubted that his father even missed him at all.

He was happy when summer finally came around again. Happy to get back on the ship, happy to meet the captain's stern stare from across the deck as he collected his crew uniform, even happy to receive a few friendly punches in the arm from his cabinmates.

On the first day back on the ship, Charlie met Marie. Marie was the captain's daughter. She was young, pretty, dark-haired, smiley—and Charlie was viciously warned about her the first time one of his crewmates caught him even glancing in her direction.

"That's Marie. She's off-limits. She'll try to draw ya, in talk your ear off- but you can't do that. Ya hear me?" the man next to him had hissed in Charlie's ear.

And Charlie heard, but the warning, although well-intentioned, was unnecessary. Charlie didn't want to get with Marie—he was just *fascinated* by her, the way she managed to fit on the ship like a puzzle piece and yet at the same time look so out-of-place, always carrying a laptop and a clipboard and at least three notebooks, her glasses sliding down her nose and a pencil tucked behind her ear.

In mid-June, Charlie approached her for the first time. She was sitting on the deck, legs crossed, and he attributed his sudden bravery to the fact that it was three in the morning—the captain had the crew working nearly around the clock this time of year, when the sun never dipped below the horizon for long.

She had looked up as he approached, smiling. "Hello!" She stuck her hand out towards him. "I'm Marie. As I'm sure you know."

He nodded, shaking it. "Charlie. What are you working on?" he asked, gesturing to the computer and notebooks that lay in an array around her.

"Oh, it's just research. For school. I'm studying the ocean. Last summer, I went to Greenland to study." she paused to hit a few keys on her keyboard, and Charlie got the impression that even while she was talking to him, her mind was on her work. "Charlie, do you know anything about entering data tables?"

"Oh, um, yeah. Yes. I do."

"Great. You can help me, then?" Charlie went to look over her shoulder, glancing up at his fellow crew members dazedly winding nets, half asleep. They didn't seem to have missed him yet.

Helping Marie with her research became a regular occurrence, much to the disdain (and jealousy, Charlie presumed) of the other men on board the ship. He'd sit with her in the dining room after dinner when he was off, plugging in numbers that didn't really mean anything to him into data tables. It felt a bit like the coding he'd done back home, plugging in letters and numbers and crossing his fingers that everything worked out the way he hoped it did when he pressed "enter". Or, in this case, the way that Marie hoped they did. She'd actually clapped with delight as they made the final click, making a series of lines and colored boxes appear on the screen.

"What does this mean, exactly?" he asked her.

"It's a map of all the ocean currents." she explained, already enthralled in her notebook once again, her pen scribbling furiously.

"Oh. Nice." Charlie watched the map on the screen move, feeling the ship sway from side to side as he followed the lines—the currents—as they swirled and wove their way around continents.


It was a few days before Charlie truly spoke to Marie again. They'd pass in the corridors, sure, and talk between mouthfuls of dinner in the dining room, but they were always rushing off in opposite directions—Marie was working on a project that she just simply *couldn't* tell Charlie about just yet, and Charlie was always just working`. He was rigging nets, laughing on the deck with his crewmates, long conversations fueled by boredom at repetitive tasks, punctuated by aching arms and exhausted backs.

He finally saw her again after dinner one night, lingering at the table across from one another. She had gotten up to go to the bathroom, or to sharpen her pencil; looking back, he didn't really remember. All he knew was that something made him reach for that notebook, the one with the purple cover that she was always scribbling in. He flipped the pages: charts, graphs, vertical columns of color-coded numbers that he couldn't decipher. He wasn't sure what he was even looking for—"secret project" she'd said, and what did that mean he would find? A magical, gold-foiled map? He was about to slide the book back across the table, flipping the pages back to where he had found them, when he came across a note, paper-clipped in.

It was a list, scribbled in a pen that looked like it might have been almost dry, a list of items- food, water, blankets, a raincoat. Quantities—*one can of coffee, seven cans of tuna.*

Marie came back, then, squinting at him over the glasses she wore when she was reading.

She asked him what he was doing.

"Nothing. Just looking at what you've been working on. Sorry." And he wrestled with his brain for a moment, trying to squash the nosy curiosity. He was unsuccessful. "What's the list for?"

Marie sat down on the bench next to him, her back to the table, her ankles crossed. "Okay. Well. I have this, well, this *idea*. It's for my research. But you can't tell anyone, alright?"

Charlie didn't know what he was agreeing to, really, but he nodded anyway, reflexively. "Okay. So. I want to take a lifeboat out. Tomorrow night. And if all my mapping is correct, and the currents are where they should be and going the right speed and the right direction, I should make it back to port at the same time the ship does at the end of the week."

Charlie raised his eyebrows at her. "You're serious?" Marie nodded. "You know that we're, like, in the middle of the ocean, right?"

She rolled her eyes at him then. "Oh, really, *Charles*? I had no idea."

"What if your map's wrong?"

She shrugged. "The lifeboat has a motor. I'd be fine." A pause. "I'll leave my dad a note. But I *need* to do this. I need to show him that what I've been doing is more than just data and spreadsheets."

Charlie studied her face, dead set on this plan, not even willing to consider the possibility that this might not exactly be the best idea she'd ever had.

"You're not kidding, are you?"

She fixed him with that same look she'd given him when they'd first met, when she'd asked him if he knew how to make spreadsheets, all steely and serious and making him feel like she knew what he would say before he'd even opened his mouth.

"No." And she'd picked up her notebook and her computer and left.



Charlie lay awake that night, thinking about Marie and her plan. How did she know that the weather would be alright? What if she slipped and fell and hit her head and got knocked into the water, unconscious?

But when morning came- slowly, and then all at once, as it always did on the ship, with the stamping of feet in the hallway and whoops of the early shift headed up to the deck, Charlie had made a decision. He passed her in the corridor, giving her a steely look of his own, one that he hoped looked the way that it had when he'd practiced his line in the mirror that morning. "I'm coming with you." he said.

She didn't even protest. "Alright."



And so that night he met her on the upper deck, with a bag that held a rain jacket and some clothes, waiting for Marie with the supplies that he'd found out she'd been hoarding under her bed in her cabin. He could hear the voices of the crew on the deck below and hoped that nobody would glance up and see his rubber-boot-clad feet sticking out from under the stack of lifeboats. Their shift would end soon—Marie had memorized the timetables. They were to slip away while everyone else was at dinner. This was Charlie's last chance to get out of this- he should call the captain now, preserve his job—and probably his life, if he was being realistic.

But maybe he should have heeded the warning that was given to him on the first day. He couldn't say no to Marie if he tried.

Then she appeared—out of nowhere, with a bulging backpack on and carrying two blankets. She was smiling, grinning, even, and any thought that he had of backing out was gone. She tossed one of them to him. He had to reach out over the edge to catch it, making him stumble a little. "Shhh!" she said.

The voices dwindled from below them, finally ceasing with the slam of a heavy metal door. "Okay." Marie said, sitting down inside the boat. "Let's go."

Charlie wondered when the lifeboats had been tested last. He and Marie pulled themselves downward, hand over hand on the rusty chain, pulling it over the pulley system, staining his palms and making them ache. Finally, the boat hit water with barely a ripple. Marie unclipped the hooks, letting the cable fall away. Charlie looked up at the ship, at the circles of light that illuminated the dark water from the portholes above. The boat was silent—nobody seemed to have missed their presence at dinner yet. He and Marie sat silently as the ship slowly drifted away.

"Alright. Now what?" Charlie whispered, foolishly. Nobody was around to hear them now except some mayflies that had gathered on the edges of the tiny orange boat.

Marie smiled. "That's the beautiful thing about currents, Charlie. You don't have to do anything for them to work."

"So we just...sit here?"

"Well, I'm going to sit here. You're going to go to sleep, so that when I wake you up you can take a turn recording data." She pulled out that same purple notebook, encased in plastic wrap, and a tiny navigation device out of her bag—Charlie thought that it looked like nothing more than a glorified compass. They were out here, floating in the middle of the ocean, with nothing but a *compass*, and Marie wanted him to sleep?

He thought that it would never happen, laying there on the hard plastic bench of the lifeboat, the waves rocking and making his stomach churn in ways that it never had in his time aboard the ship. But he must have drifted off at some point, because he woke to Marie nudging him with the toe of her shoe, the sky lighter on the horizon.

They went on like this for a full twenty-four hours. Marie would sleep while Charlie was left with strict instructions not to take his eyes off of the compass—as long as it was pointing east, towards the mainland, she was happy. Charlie wasn't sure how she knew *where* exactly they would end up on said mainland, but she was so sure of herself, not to mention *asleep*, that he couldn't find it in him to ask.

The second time Marie woke him up, it was to pull him over to the edge of the boat. Charlie gazed down into the dark blue water, penetrated by the early morning sunlight. "What?" he asked, half-awake and irritated, rubbing the sleep from the corners of his eyes. She had just pointed in response, a hand in the center of his back pushing him to look over the side. And suddenly he wasn't asleep at all. A huge dark grey shape moved under them. "What is *that*?" Charlie breathed.

Marie smiled. "It's a whale." And they had stood there at the rail watching it under them, easily six times the size of the boat they were in, moving through the water as smoothly as birds glide through the air. Suddenly Charlie understood, a little, why Marie cared so much about the ocean in a way he never had, even growing up six minutes from the beach. Here in the open water, the ocean wasn't just a streak of blue on the horizon or a place to pull fish from. The water was alive and breathing and here they were, just floating on top of it, tiny and so, so *ordinary*. It was on the second night, when they were both awake together, staring at a distant light spot in the sky that Marie claimed was the port. A wind had started blowing, making her dark hair whip across her face—they'd laughed about it. A few raindrops fell, then, the big, fat ones that land on your head and almost hurt, announcing that a storm is coming.

Marie waved them off—just a sprinkle, she said. But for the first time, Charlie saw a flicker of what could have been concern dance across her face, gone as soon as it was there, making him wonder if he'd even seen it at all.

Marie was right, as usual, about the rain. It didn't do more than leave some circular prints on the thick rubber of the boat, not even enough to make them dig around to find their raincoats. But the wind didn't leave, didn't lessen—in fact, it only picked up as the sky got darker. Charlie soon found himself sitting across from Marie on the floor in the center of the boat as it whipped around them, making her black hair twirl in the air, up and blending with the night sky. There was a flash of yellow out of the corner of his eye, and Charlie turned his head sharply. It was Marie's jacket, flying through the air on a gust of wind. He stood, reaching for it as it drifted towards the edge of the boat. His fingers had just closed around the slippery material when a second gust hit him, propelling him forward, over the railing, the weight of his boots dragging him down

down

down.

He thought he heard a muffled yell from above, although it was impossible to say- his ears were filled with water, and he had gulped a mouthful of liquid instead of the air he had intended before plummeting below.

The saltwater got colder, and he wondered, paddling furiously towards a surface that only seemed to get further and further away, if this is how everything would end. His body would sink to the ocean floor, decompose and become food for tiny fish, and maybe there wouldn't even be a funeral for his father to attend and not cry at.

He thought of his father, how he'd taught him to swim as a kid, and how it certainly wasn't much use to him now, sinking slowly towards the bottom, his lungs burning. He hadn't thrown him into the pool like most dads did, hadn't watched him struggle and gasp for breath until he inevitably figured out how to doggy paddle. He'd held him, instead, when he couldn't have been more than three, in their backyard pool, telling him to *kick* as his mother sat on the edge with a huge straw hat and a glass of lemonade.

And so Charlie kicked.

Something grabbed his arm, then, and he was pulled upward, his head breaking the surface. He coughed, finding himself clinging to the edge of the boat, Marie climbing in beside him. He absentmindedly noticed that she was barefoot. Smart.

She pulled him in, throwing a blanket at him. "Don't you *ever* do that to me again." she said, angry on the surface, but it was Charlie's turn to see through her and extract the relief that he saw behind her eyes.

"Sure. 'Course." he said, wrapping the blanket more tightly around his shoulders and pulling off his boots with numb fingertips. She turned towards the helm, then, the navigator held in her hand tightly with white knuckles. Charlie caught her glancing back at him every few minutes, to where he was now laying on his back on the floor of the boat, as if to make sure he was still there. Charlie was sure that even if everything inside the boat decided it was going to blow away, he was going to stay put.

They reached the port that night. The storm had pushed them back out to sea, but Marie had been right, as she always seemed to be, the current leading them almost directly into a slip near the land.

A spotlight shone on them from the shore as she was tying them to the dock. "Marie!" someone bellowed. She looked up, confused.

"Dad?"

The captain barreled down the dock. "Marie! What did you think you were *doing*? You could have *drowned* out there, you could have sunk the boat." And he pulled her into his arms, hugging her even as she tried to squirm away.

"It was fine, dad. I knew what I was doing."

Charlie looked on at them from where he stood in the boat, hearing Marie, the way she wasn't even realizing how worried her father sounded, his graying hair tangled as if he had been running his fingers through it since she left three days ago.

And he pulled on his still-damp boots, tip-toeing around the reunion that was happening behind him, unobtrusive, up the dock to where an ancient payphone was mounted in the ground on a tilted metal pole that looked like maybe someone had backed into it with their car.

He picked up the receiver and dialed, listening as it rang once, twice, three times.

"Hello?" said a voice from the other end, crackly with static.

"Hi, dad." he said. "It's me. Charlie."

# FRANKLIN LASSEN

**Freshman**
**Major:** Creative Writing and History
**Reading:** Poetry

I am a freshman from Redford, Michigan and I've been writing my entire life. Poetry has come to mean more to me than almost anything during my first year at the University of Michigan. Writing helps me through hard times and has granted me a vehicle through which I can discover more about myself.

*Nominated by: Laura Kasischke and Leslie Stainton*

# Us: The World

There were seven of us
And we walked for seven days
Or maybe I was seven
Years old?
Or seven people?
Or I am everyone on
This godforsaken bus
This bus that we ride and ride
On the hottest days
We ride
On the earliest mornings
There we are
Still riding
Always riding

But the bus,
It lurches to a stop
So unpredictable
As one, we lurch forward
As one, we lurch backward
Even,
The lady
In the cast
She holds her baby and
It's five AM
How strange
Just moments ago it was
The peak of the hottest day
Of the hottest summer

But now,
Five AM we ride this bus,
Lurching along

Sweating and lurching
As one
As a child reaches out his hand
Reaching for the purse we all hold
You know this child
It's the child we've all met
The child who holds curiosity
In the palms of his hands
Always reaching,

The way we reach
Towards the sky as
Lightning strikes the water
We swim, taunting
Every lesson we ever learned in school
We know we will never die
So we need never be careful
Even as
The pain, sears up,
The pain we all feel
Searing up our legs as we swim
Lightning coming down around us,
Still we swim

Off the coast of Florida
You know the trip to Florida
We've all been there
All been somewhere
We had no business being
Stuck,
Wishing we were home
But knowing
We never will be
Not so long as we are alive and
We will always be alive

Always reaching,

(Remember? Like the child?)
Reaching for the large drink
Slid across the counter in the hands
Of the ex we hate so much
We've all had the ex
The one we cannot stand to see
We know him
And he knows us
He gave us this large
When all we wanted was a small
How does it feel,
To give more than asked and
Still always fail?

We are always failing
As we search,
Still searching
For that one friend
You know that friend
The one who gets kicked out
Of all the best parties
Just when you need him the most
The greatest disappointment
Of all,
The friend you depend upon
The one we all depend upon
We are abandoned,
In a cornfield
Next to that great staircase
Looming, even though we all know
It leads nowhere

Except maybe
Las Vegas?
Mom, Dad, you're in Las Vegas?
How could it be
That the ones we trusted the most

Have gone to Las Vegas
Leaving us alone,

The ones we trusted the most
Bringing home this red,
Angry, crying baby
Telling us it is our sister
We don't want a sister but
Just as we will never be home we
Will also never get what we want
It's why

The police officer,
He's just doing his job
Protecting the children
But,
We remember what it is to be those children
We remember the anger,
The frustration,
Of being denied the simple pleasures
Like watching the sun rise

Or being the red power ranger
On the greatest night of the entire year
We all remember
How it feels to show up dressed
In the greatest costume
Only to find we are not unique
The way we showed up to homecoming
Only to see we were not the only ones
Who shopped at Forever 21

Just the way that police officer
(You know, the one doing his job?)
That police officer is not
The only one to deny

Or to be denied
Is not the only one to make mistakes

The way he opened the door to the house,
That glowing red door,
Only to find,
Instead of the screams that
Torment us
(Remember, how the screams echoed?)
Instead of the screams,
He finds the
Most beautiful music,
He remembers how it echoed through the street
He's sad to have to deny us
He wishes we could've had our fun
Wishes we could've heard that violin
The way he did,
The way the notes mixed with the night air

The same night air
That hugged our family
As we sat, silent in our grieving
As we listened to that ocean
(Remember the ocean? The way it stung)
As we sat in our company
But also,
Alone

Alone above the world
We can see everything from here
Don't you remember how it felt?
To see the world laid out before you and
To know it was not yours?
Which hurt worse,
The fall or the truth
That this world was not ours
Would exist without us

The world did not care
About the stick,
Pierced through our leg
The world
Was too busy piercing
Through our innocence

The same innocence that was
Broken when we met that woman
You remember that woman, right?
The woman who almost changed everything
That woman
Would have erased us from
The world that hated us so much
That woman
Who loved our father
Once upon a time
Don't you remember,
How the light glinted
On that ring
The ring so big it was
The center of the universe
For a few short hours
How is it that one woman
Could have had so much power?

How that wedding,
(The one in Ecuador, remember?)
The wedding, so foreign,
The language swirling around
Us, holding us
Reaching
(Like the child, remember?)
Reaching and pushing
Pushing us to the bathroom
How despite
The strange world around us,

The one thing everyone knows,
Sleep,
Is still there
Waiting for us,
Welcoming us with open arms
How even when the world rejects us
Even when the world lets us know that
We are not special
Sleep,
No: Dreams
Dreams are there for us
Welcoming,
Like an old friend
As our eyelids begin to grow heavy
I start to remember,
Yes, I, because I
Am not the world
I am only
Listening
To it

# Myself

My skin is shiny pink
Like that of a newborn's
It speaks of resistance and
Persistence

I told myself I could never go on
But my skin proved otherwise
It died and came back alive
It persisted

When I look at that raw pink
Shiny and new
I see God
And I believe

In myself

# A love letter to the girl of my dreams

When I look at you, the first thing I see is wild,
the second thing I see is sadness.
I wish I could wipe some of this sadness away
like I'm scraping your windshield clear of snow.
Except,
you don't have a windshield,
or a car.
You're just a child
stuck in that horrible, awkward time of life.
Nothing to protect you from the winter winds
blowing, knocking you over.
You were always so small
and they never let you forget it.
I wish I could have been that shield to protect you
from both wind and name calling.
Wish I could have been a little bit stronger when we met,
strong enough to help.
People like to say they were in love but the timing was off.
To me, that sounds like an easier way of saying you weren't in love
but with us, boy was the timing off.
I remember something my mom used to tell us,
that it won't hurt when the pain goes away.
And when we were together, God, how much it hurt.
An aching only growing stronger by the hour
until some days it was unbearable.
But now that that pain is gone I can't help but want you back,
even though I know,
when you left, the pain went with you.
I still see you in my dreams,
a ghost of who you were

if you were ever anything more than a ghost.
I hope the pain you took from me doesn't continue to cloud your own
vision,
hope there's clearer skies wherever you are.
Where it doesn't snow
and you don't need a windshield.

# Two-Headed Calf

maybe i am just
a two-headed calf
my body
barely sustains me and
i am too much for the world

but it doesn't matter
because right now
the stars are doubled
and, in two days
i'll be dead anyway

# DELANEY LEACH

**Senior**
**Major:** Film, Television & Media and Creative Writing & Literature
**Reading:** Fiction

Delaney is a senior studying Film, Television & Media and Creative Writing & Literature. When she is not writing, she enjoys participating in theater, watching movies, reading, and drinking as much coffee as possible.

*Nominated by: Laura Thomas*

# Keeping Time

She wasn't used to moments like this, existing alone with someone else. Winter was finally taking shape; the snowflakes falling outside the boy's window were no longer an uncommon sight. The girl couldn't decide if she thought the world outside was captured in a snowglobe or if the two of them were. A study date had turned into a study nap which turned into not waking up from the nap which turned into staying over in the boy's room because it was already two in the morning at that point. She woke up while the moon was out and the boy was still asleep. This was the first time she hadn't been able to sleep through the night beside him. It had her wondering why.

The last time studying turned into sleeping, she took advantage of the unfiltered access to watching his face. She liked to monitor his occasional twitches and snores. He was a heavy sleeper, tested by the moments she dared to touch him, gently running her fingers along the seams of his t-shirt which was worn but not soft, skimming the ends of his hair. His hair was shaggy enough that his mother would tell him to get a trim if she saw it, but the girl liked it. She had to stop herself from thinking too much about what motivated her to look at his face for so long. Even so the answer was unavoidable. She loved him now. She hoped that he knew that she loved him. If he knew already, she wouldn't have to tell him, and that was easier. Once you tell someone you love them the only way to take it back is pain. And even then the words could never truly be taken back. She wondered if he loved her. She hoped so. She thought so. She didn't trust herself. She worried that she would not be able to maintain her love. She looked at his ear and wondered if she would burn out on loving him before the clock on his desk ran out of battery.

But what would she do if she couldn't come back to this room at the end of this evening to tell him about her day? How would she manage walking alone down the stretch of hallway between his room and hers at the end of the night? Was she getting carried away? Could she fall asleep without a body beside her? But would she ever wake up alone again? Was there anything of her own anymore? Had she given all of the open space in her heart to him, like giving him a drawer at her place? Would anything happen to her that she wouldn't feel obligated to report? Not out of the sensation of finally being known, but the fear of what it meant to intentionally withhold information?

She found herself looking at the ceiling again. Smooth and blank. She breathed sleepiness back into her body slowly and curled against him. There was no equilibrium for her beyond the here and now. He looked at her for too long. He got close enough to touch. He did too much. He was there. She was running out of energy to lie to herself, to resist the pull that made her want to curl against him. It's stupid, she thought, it was nothing. It didn't matter. But she wouldn't have been thinking about it if it didn't matter. It was so small. It happened when they were still studying. She had been bent over a notebook, scribbling down information. He had reached over and brushed away an eyelash that had landed on the top of her cheek. He held it out on his pinky finger just below her nose, in front of her lips. *Make a wish.* Her racing studying thoughts shuddered to a halt. The moment rang in her head. She covered her extra intake of breath by using it as fuel to blow the eyelash away. She tried to blow the feelings that settled into place for her in the moment away. It didn't work. It would have been so easy to not bother with this line of thought if she didn't care so much. She couldn't keep up like this. Lying in his bed, she tried again to blow the feelings away.

To occupy her mind she closed her eyes and visualized his small dorm room in her head. She started at the door, dark wood with a sticky handle made to look bronze or gold or nicer than it actually was. Heavier than it looked. Good for leaning on when she was pretending to try and leave at the end of the night, or before class, or whenever she wanted to stay longer but shouldn't. She trailed an imaginary hand along the cinderblock wall drenched in white paint. Better to touch than to see, in her opinion. She got caught at the refrigerator. When she first met him, she didn't understand why he had bothered to get one when he barely seemed to use it. Her own was rarely full, but generally stocked with some sort of snack or drink, even leftover dining hall food if she could manage (she usually couldn't). She liked to fill it for him. Play the provider. Since the two of them moved past being too afraid to admit that they meant something to each other, he had begun bringing her coffee regularly and she considered the leftovers she retrieved, and the cold sodas she brought for him to stow away, her repayment.

The refrigerator brought her back to the window on the adjacent wall. She liked it for its inclusion of a quiet stretch of campus: strong trees that would be lush if it weren't for the season and the backsides of stately brick campus buildings. If framed correctly, she bet it could be used on a brochure. Although, fall would probably be a better time for a publicity photograph. She decided she liked winter with him. She liked running into him on campus and walking each other to class. That way they could catch each other if they slipped on ice, or their arms would brush together and bounce apart from the cushion of their heavy winter layers. Maybe if she spoke up, some winter day with him her would tug down her scarf just a bit so that his lips could reach hers, but only a quick brush and then scurrying into class to not be late. She wondered if it would feel like she didn't need all of her layers to keep herself warm. She liked winter. She was getting off track.

The rest of the wall was uneventful, and the one after brought his bed with it's gray-blue comforter and flannel sheets that she assumed his mother purchased after he shrugged his approval. It was the standard twin that could be found in each room in the building. To celebrate a month of classes (which she secretly marked as a month together) she snagged two glasses (plastic cups) of (boxed) wine with which to toast. The first time she fell asleep there, they had just been talking. She woke up groggy. She didn't want to remove herself from the bed and have to deal with the stiffness of sleeping in her normal clothes. She worried about pillow wrinkles on her face, all the more reason not to pick her head up. Waking up next to him was a treat, not an expectation, and it still was.

She opened her eyes to take herself out of her imaginary walk around the room. She found herself still in the bed she had just been picturing. She untangled the worry and excitement to find the body and heart that held it all. The boy was still asleep. He would likely stay that way until his alarm or some other outside force decided to rouse him. He kept an alarm set at all times for occasions like this. He used his phone and not his desk clock. He was a sleepy gangly thing who couldn't be trusted to stay awake at any given time. One of his snores startled the girl, but he turned on his side, facing her through sleep, and the noise ceased. She looked at him again. Not reassessing, but rather grounding him in her mind. She tried to match her breaths to his. In and out and in and out and in and out. Slowly and methodically, she tried to lull herself.

She worried that it happened to easily. It was a simple process: she found him and she stuck around him. After careful consideration she decided that she didn't want to leave. So was she done now? Could she say that she loved him and call it a day? Would he say it back and they would be set? When was it too late to change your mind? Could she turn around and take him out of her life if she decided that was what she wanted instead? She'd put so much time into this thing that wasn't quite something and couldn't be put away as nothing. She fretted over when it was too early to wonder if you could change your mind. She conjured up problems that didn't exist at night, but she didn't usually have to face them like this.

The girl was running out of hours to sleep. Outside, the sky was reaching peak darkness, after which light would soon follow. There was no frame of reference for what spring would bring. Whatever she was caught in had blossomed as everything around them was dying in autumn. Nothing could forecast what the birth of new nature would bring. She chided herself; things weren't so simple and blameless. This wasn't merely something she was assigned and she could opt out at any point. She couldn't control the world around her, but her hands were her own. When she ruffled the boy's hair with her fingertips or traced the seams of his shirt or brushed his hand or held the cups of coffee he brought her or blew an eyelash from his fingertip she was the one to be held accountable. No one could pull words out of her mouth. She just had to say them so that someone could hear.

# DEIRDRE LEE

**Junior**
**Major:** English and Psychology
**Reading:** Fiction

Deirdre is a junior double majoring in English and psychology in the College of Literature, Science, and the Arts, and she's currently studying abroad at the National University of Singapore. She's excited to use her study abroad experience to diversify her fiction stories, since she loves writing stories that focus on culture, history, and psychological processes to highlight the stories of various groups of people across time. Aside from fiction, Deirdre is very interested in investigative journalism and hopes to use her writing skills to bring awareness to historical and current people, places, events, and issues.

*Nominated by: Patricia O'Dowd*

# Lady Grey

Marmalade-colored flames licked the inside bricks of the fireplace as if they were peasants groveling for the last morsels of banished food scraps from the bourgeois. In the glow of the flames, two delicately crafted cups of herbal tea rested on the coffee table that graciously separated us, each cup placed within arm's length of where we were seated. From each cup, wisps of aromatic heat whispered soothing reassurance, perhaps to the fire, perhaps to me, or you, or nothing or no one in particular.

I chose to sit closest to the fire, finding solace in the flames' turmoil. They did little to light the room. Darkness had already slithered through the windows, successfully performing the bidding of night, and in the light flickering in the hearth, a rather unsightly shadow was cast across your face. You settled into the leather armchair opposite mine, your body deflating into it with ease.

Earlier this morning, I had merely asked you to join me for evening tea, to which you eagerly obliged, even offering to prepare it. With my lack of resolve, I hadn't been able to properly execute my final decision, and your earnest haste was single handedly your most brilliant action. How could I deny you? I hadn't for the past eleven months we'd been married, but now, because of your offer, I placed the fate of our one year anniversary in your hands; it all depended on the type of tea you were to give me. How funny to think a beverage would carry this much weight.

And now, the sweet, blood-colored liquid sat proudly in front of me, secretly signing a contract you were excluded from. I sighed, placing the dainty cup in my hand to absorb its warmth before sipping it. You watched me with intent, probably analyzing my every movement. I was used to this by now – your gaze was an unending succession of papercuts, the kind that just broke the surface and healed within a few days but caused enough pain to induce a looming sense of trepidation.

In the beginning, your stare had me feeling like a ghost had latched itself onto me, ready to haunt me if and when I were to agitate it.

When we met, your threats were merely bluff, but too quickly did they materialize, each strike decorating me with a colorful medal only you could give. There were rare times, though, when your eyes would actually show traces of humanity, each eye glinting as green as mint leaves in a mojito; in those moments, it was impossible to not get drunk off of you. That – that break in character you had – complicated everything, persuading me first to date you, and somehow, you even managed to swindle me worse than a street peddler into marriage. In a harrowing way, it was a little impressive.

Amid my reminisces, you, being the impatient person you were, grew exasperated with a lack of attention and proceeded to ask if I loved you. That question enough startled me out of my thoughts, yet before I could answer, you laughed as lightly as a freshly inflated balloon, so confident in our perceived relationship status. The silvery tone of your voice unsettled me, for few things elicited such a cheerful response. Two explanations were plausible: Either you weren't sober, which, surprisingly, you did seem to be, or you had been in bed with another woman earlier in the day. If it were the latter, bless her soul.

My primal instincts kicked in, and a strained smile stretched my lips apart in an upward fashion. Apparently, I put too much effort into this simple expression, for the air had grown thick with an unrequited tension. You reached your hand across the table, your fingers strolling toward mine. Mine remained quite still, while yours, unshockingly, pushed through mine until your fingers curled around my hand. You pulled my hand with enough force to indicate your intention while still remaining playful, as your eyes darted to the corner of the room to our bedroom.

Evidently, if you had been with a different woman, she clearly didn't satisfy you. With that in mind, the possibility of spreading my legs for you to avoid a worse consequence for another night was out of the question. I told you I wanted another cup of tea first and that yours had grown cold, as it was untouched. With lustful eyes, you nodded, making a vulgar expression that prompted a small amount of bile to rise to my throat.

Swiftly, I stood up, gripping the edge of the armrest for stability. As if on cue, again without me initiating it, you asked for me to make your cup like mine, as if that would flatter me and entice me to become intimate with you. I nodded happily, assuring you there wouldn't be too much sugar in it. You smiled, your eyes following me like an assassin stalking their target as I moved to the kitchen. It took only a few moments for me to return.

You reached for a cup, and holding tightly onto the one in my left hand, I handed you the other. As I nestled myself back into my chair, you took a large gulp, the impatience of your sexual desires obvious. Within a few moments, your breathing intensified, quickly growing haggard, as your limbs began to seize. You stared incredulously at me with a look of pure hatred, but it was too late. In its powdered form, sodium cyanide looks remarkably similar to sugar but takes only several minutes to end a life. You were too infatuated with sex to realize we had two different cups of tea – yours was the herbal with a dash of chemicals, while mine was a perfect cup of Lady Grey tea, the type of tea you should've brewed. I told you this aloud as your pupils dilated and then rolled back in your head. While I basked in the delectable taste of my black tea, your body really did deflate this time, slumping into the chair like a popped balloon.

# LEEANN MANTTA

**Freshman**
**Major:** Undecided
**Reading:** Fiction

LeeAnn is a freshman from the small town of Houghton, which is located in the Upper Peninsula of Michigan. Hobbies she enjoys are hammocking, snowshoeing, donating blood, correcting the pronunciation of "sauna," and training to be a Zamboni driver. LeeAnn tends to write whatever comes to mind. That's all you need to know for now, so hang on for the ride.

*Nominated by: Kelly Allen*

# A Trip to Funky Town

It was going to be the biggest party on the block, and all the kids from school were going to be there. It was Timmy Hopper's 8th birthday, and his parents would not let this celebration go without the extreme absurdity of all their other parties. After all, who else turned eight years old on August 8, 1988? Clowns were making a comeback that year, so Timmy's parents spared no expense at making sure there was a hoard of clowns to make even the most fickle guests entertained. Along with these prized entertainers, there were plans for thousands of balloon animals, a few piñatas, a ball pit (with rules of no prime puke candidates allowed), eight birthday cakes, a life-sized chocolate fountain, and 8,888 golden wrapped chocolate coins to celebrate this surreal golden birthday.

Now, by no means were Timmy's parents rich, but if they were rich in anything, it would be spirit and family values. They prayed each day for a miracle to happen for them to pull-off this outlandish party, but it seemed to get further and further out of reach. Of course, they hadn't planned anything last minute because they knew that they may struggle with this financially. So while they continued to pray, they set out with collecting packets of balloons and interviewing and enlisting future party clowns. Everything had to be perfect, so one could say there was no clowning around when it came to Timmy's party.

Timmy was a third grader in Barkell elementary school and was one of the brightest among the class. In his parent's eyes, he was an angel. His soft brown eyes could melt you into a puddle in your shoes. But he knew this and used it to his advantage. While he was always doing his homework and regularly put in the time to volunteer at a soup kitchen to keep up this facade, he was also involved with the smuggling of acid from state to state. Undisclosed to the public, this share of wealth he got was used to finance whatever frivolous plans his parents wanted to take on next. Usually, he'd put a small loan of $4,000 precisely under the loose left floorboard closest to the front door in their front porch. He'd angle it just enough so that the corner of one of the bills would be apparent enough for his mom to see it when she went to unlock the door. Even with different parties, it would always be planted at 5:04 pm for his mom to discover when she got home from her 5 pm shift at the local hospital that was a six minute walk away. So while he was involved with terrible things, Timmy still had a good bone in his body, even if he sometimes spit in the soup he was serving.

While Timmy wanted this to be a birthday to remember, he was also aware that he was in a dangerous business. Trying to keep his head down low, he communicated with his cronies to provide him protection at his party. Since it was *his* party, his parents made sure to include him with the enlistment of all the party entertainment. With each accomplice interviewing to be a clown, Timmy would give an enthusiastic "Yes!" and rant and rave about how they were even better than the last clown they hired. With his parents feeling pleased that they were able to provide a small glint of happiness within their son, there were no arguments or questions about who was hired. Not even the man with seven face tattoos, a bald head, and missing an eye. He was the last to be hired, and Timmy just about went nuts with excitement for Toes McGee.

You see, Toes McGee was known as the ringleader of the Dissolution Gang. He knew the business better than he knew the back of his hand. Of course, that might have been in part from him losing part of it from tripping too hard when he tested out his product. No more right pinky for him. What a shame, that was his favorite finger to pick his ear with. Toes McGee instilled within his gang that there was to be no man's back left uncovered.

He would always say, "We're playing a dangerous game here, boys. See my eye? I lost that in 'Nam, but it was because I was left behind. I did what I had to do to survive, but it wadn't pretty. I care fer each of ya more than I ever would for that bastard. That's enough lovey-dovey shit, get back ta work."

Although it was dangerous for Toes to be out in public, he still felt like he needed to be there for Timmy. While he wanted to protect him, something seemed to say that there was more to what Toes let on. He treated Timmy like the son he never had, constantly giving him scraps of bubble gum as well as an assortment of pocket knives. One time, he even offered Timmy the pocket knife he had as a child.

Anytime the other members of his gang would question him about his bond with Timmy, he'd always say, "You try being eight, and in the acid business. That shit can take a toll on ya."

See, the entire reason Toes was so protective over Timmy was because the opposing gang, the Dry Pancakes, were ruthless in the business. They had a history of scamming people, as well as intentionally sending them to the hospital. The way they worked was giving their customers a taste of the good kush for a few sales and then completely switching to some "home remedies." These ranged from PH strips soaked with cough syrup, to pieces of confetti glazed with concentrated hand sanitizer juices. They sold this strain of acid with its name being "Tuesday Night Club Vibes," since your heart rate would rise high enough to match the energy given by the club "going up" on a Tuesday. This was pretty serious shit, given the fact that literally no one goes to the club on a Tuesday, so if they did, it had to be some serious energy. So with starting a child off young in the acid dealing business, it was much easier to train them in and keep them around for the long haul– that is, the amount of time it would be before they got caught or killed. But then again, once you're in the business, you learn the trade pretty quickly and learn what to do and what not to do. With Timmy being one of the brightest bulbs in the box and so inconspicuous, he was a hot commodity for any drug ring.

The way that Timmy joined the Dissolution Gang was really through pure luck. Timmy had just finished his shift at the soup kitchen. Exhausted, he sat down on a bench outside of the shelter to wait for his parents. They were always running late. Mom just *had* to leave after she had listened to "Meditations Before You Commute: Jesus Take the Wheel." The CD of a woman talking in a voice used for babies and tiny animals lasted precisely 34 minutes and 12 seconds. Then the ride there would take approximately 17 or 23 minutes, depending on the traffic. Timmy considered going back inside to the welcoming atmosphere of warm air, even if it had a slight scent of stale piss.

Before he could though, a taller man dressed in glorified rags with enough stubble to clothe a fly approached him.

"I see what ya been doin' there behind the counter. How many loogies ya put in the soup today?" asked Toes.

Timmy, trying to show off, replied "Only nine today. Normally I'm able to get at least 13 without worrying about getting caught. Don't worry, I didn't spit any gross stuff in your cup of chicken noodle."

"I woulda ate it regardless. Soup is soup. A little extra protein can only benefit the soul," said Toes.

"Wow, you're a real trooper there. I don't think I could ever," said Timmy.

"What's your name, son? I can change that if you're up for it."

And with that, Timmy was in and Toes was there for the ride.


On the day of the party, Timmy was the talk of the entire school. He was the buzz word that teachers had to treat like cussing. Classes seemed to fly by, and everyone was anxiously awaiting the fun that was a measly four hours away. The party was scheduled to start at six, but with the block closing and limited parking, everyone was bound to show up at least an hour early. While Timmy's parents rushed to get all the food and decorations ready, the disguised clowns began to file in, one-by-one, to provide entertainment as well as protection. Finally, Toes McGee walked in, face lazily slathered in white paint, a bruised tomato for a red nose, magazines for a collar, and an old jester's suit with a few cigarette burns on the chest and thighs. His shoes, though, were a vibrant red pair of wide-toed clown shoes. Famous for his name, he decided to dress the part.

Soon enough, a crowd of people formed at the door, demanding to be let into Timmy's party. For the parent's sake, it was a merciful plea to just shut their kids up for a minute. Happily obliging, Timmy's parents wrangled the kids in and started them at the food table that was unsurprisingly overwhelmed with cheese pizza. Although it wasn't Timmy's favorite, he compromised because he was aware that most kids, and even adults, didn't like anchovies, peanut butter, sriracha, and pineapple on their pizza. But Timmy's parents placed a separate order for him and saw that only Timmy and Toes McGee were devouring the pizza. Other than greasy cheese pizza, the table was filled with spaghetti, sloppy joes, hot dogs, cookies, cupcakes, and whole pickles.

For drinks, there was a single bowl of punch. The bowl was as large as a doctor's office aquarium, unrelated to the fact that Timmy's mom worked as a receptionist for Dr. Bigby. The clowns thought the punch was the best thing since sliced bread, so they often came back to refill their cups within five minutes spans. Unfortunately, when Bongo the clown went to fill his cup for the eighth time, 19 tabs of acid fell from the inside of the greasy sleeve of his clown suit and into the punch bowl. And even more unfortunate, all the guests at the party were parched from all the sweets they ate for dinner. It's a good thing that the punch bowl was large enough to concoct a less concentrated mixer of acid and red Hawaiian Punch. Even so, all the children downed at least four glasses of punch before too eagerly going into the ball pit. The adults on the other hand, passed around a flask to put a little more "love" into their drinks, unaware of the tablets that had already fallen in. Oh, were they in for quite a surprise.

In the ball pit, Timmy had begun to feel the effects first. He had an irrational disgust for cotton balls, and as he put it, "I hate cotton balls because they make the nastiest sound ever. Ugh, get them away from me." Transforming before his eyes, the small plastic balls began to turn even smaller. In a matter of seconds, Timmy was surrounded by thousands of plush white cotton balls. And in a matter of seconds, Timmy was frozen in fear and let out a scream that could curl your nose hairs. He didn't dare to move in fear of sinking deeper into the sea of white and hearing the screaming of cotton coming in contact with one another. Beginning to feel the effects as well,

Suzie from Timmy's math class tried to muffle his scream and pushed him face down in the sea of balls. She ended up falling with him, the balls transforming into thick mounds of blue cheese. Suzie was terrified of mold, especially on food, so she started to thrash around and eventually grabbed onto Jerry, who was afraid of ice cubes. Before his eyes, the balls began to turn icebergs, causing Jerry to pass out due to a double whammy of the fear of ice and things that were bigger than him.

Unfazed by all the screams coming from the ball pit, the adults were too crossfaded to distinguish any need for help. Besides, they were too entranced by the piñata and balloon animals. Stumbling to their seats by the punch table, the adults watched as the balloon animals danced across the floor, making their way to the piñatas. The piñatas then stretched their legs, almost as if to show that they were sore from having to stay in one position for so long. Together they began to conspire about how to escape this hell they were destined to.

"You know what they were planning to do to us! We can't stay here for any longer." said a few piñatas.

"I'm sick of being a one time pleasure. I deserve to be loved for more than a birthday party. I know I'm just a piece of rubber, but that doesn't mean that my emotions are as flexible as my body," said a balloon animal.

Together, the piñatas and balloon animals exclaimed, "We have lost too many brothers in the path of being lucky enough to get this far in our lives. Today is the day we finally break free!"

And with that, the balloon animals and piñatas began to rush towards the door, taking out four of the eight cakes on their way. Covered in cake and beginning to fall apart due to the moistening of their cardboard, the piñatas soon realized that they were too short to reach the door handle. In fact, both the balloon animals and piñatas *severely* underestimated the distance from the floor to handle. But with quick thinking, they soon started to climb and stack themselves on top of each other. But it was too late, the weight of piñata on top of piñata caused the base piñata to cave in, sending everyone else toppling to the ground. Screaming and writhing in pain, each able-bodied animal tried to pick up their fallen brother, bringing them to the chocolate fountain to give an honorable death. Stunned by this series of events, the adults just stood there with their mouths gaping open. Some began to scream, some rubbed their eyes in disbelief, and some shed tears for the beauty within it all.

Staying away from the punch for the entirety of the party, Toes McGee stood guarding the door. Worried from not being able to locate

Timmy within the party, he abandoned his post at the door and moved from attraction to attraction, hoping to find him. When he made his way to the ball pit, Toes saw Timmy face down and unmoving. Moving fast, Toes called out "Timmy!" and swan dived into the ball pit to rescue him. Tossing the other children aside, Toes swiftly picked up Timmy and threw him over his shoulder. Wading through the ball pit, he then sat on the edge, Timmy in his lap.

"Are you okay, son?" Toes asked.

Timmy, unable to respond, let out a small gurgle, and a small amount of foam dripped out of his mouth.

"I swear ta God, if Bongo spiked anything ya touched, I'll fuckin' kill that jackass.

Fuckin' sticky-fingered prick," said Toes.

While Toes was saving Timmy, the leader of the Dry Pancakes, Tendy Boi, snuck through the door and surveyed the situation. He knew the effects of acid when he saw them, and this was no different from a cesspool beneath a nightclub. Immediately, he found Toes just by his jazzy red shoes. Walking over with the grace of a model and the attitude of a soccer mom, Tendy Boi stopped shortly before the two, spitting a thick mound of chew on Toes' left shoe. Toes looked up and saw the biggest pain in his ass.

"What da ya want?" Toes asked with clear annoyance.

"I want the boy. Give him to me or I'll kill both of you," said Tendy Boi.

"Fuck off ya commie," said Toes, "Timmy's too far gone already."

"Let's settle this like real men then," said Tendy.

"Tarps off it's tilly time?" asked Toes.

"Tarps off there, bud," said Tendy.

With a sigh, Toes set Timmy down and stood up to face Tendy. He then proceeded to unbutton his jester's suit and yanked his crusty old white t-shirt off, getting out a switchblade and being sure to move Tendy an ample distance away from Timmy. Walking over to the chocolate fountain, Toes motioned for him to follow. The two were stationed in front of the three-tier chocolate fountain now, with Toes making the first move to splash Tendy in the face with lukewarm chocolate. From there, Toes lunged at him, aiming to strike him in the gut, but missed due to his lack of an eye. Toes went stumbling past him, with Tendy catching and spinning him around. Disoriented, Toes went to slash again, but Tendy was too quick for him. In one swift motion, he sent Toes flying face-first onto his blade. However, even though disoriented, Toes managed to throw his blade out of his hand in the knick of time and directly into Tendy's shin. Screaming in pain, Tendy fell and tried to grab onto the fountain for support. But veteran Toes had just enough time to tackle him to the ground, being sure to twist the knife once he was on top of him.

Once Toes had full control over Tendy, he roughly picked him up and sauced him into the chocolate fountain. Tendy passed out from the slight twist of the knife, his "all talk no action" attitude put to rest by a mere stabbing. What a loser.

Quickly, Toes ran back to Timmy. They sat there, Timmy in Toes' arms, for about four hours. Toes didn't move an inch. Heck, he might not have been breathing, he sat so still. And after the passing of time hit four hours on the head, Timmy stirred just the slightest in Toes' arms. When he finally managed to open his eyes (a stressful 13 minutes and 42 seconds later), Toes gently moved him from his arms to the ground, making sure to place Timmy on his side in case he turned into a prime puke candidate.

"Toes, what happened?" Timmy asked with a groan.

With a sigh, Toes responded, "Tendy came an' went. You and everyone else took a bad trip. There ain't much more ta say."

After two more minutes on the cool ground, Timmy managed to push himself up enough to sit side by side with Toes.

"I love you Toes, thank you."

"I love ya too, squirt."

And with that, they sat in a warm hug, waiting for the crowd to come back to consciousness and watching a single piñata escape through the ajar door.

# NINA MOLINA

**Junior**
**Major:** English
**Reading:** Poetry

Nina is a junior transfer student from the suburbs of Chicago. Her writing days began in her first grade diaries, also commencing her frightful relationship with spelling. Nina is studying English and political science. In her free time, she enjoys reading literature and nicknaming people she has just met.

*Nominated by Greg Schutz*

# To his silk flower in my desk drawer

I try trading you for the honeyed jasmine that
tumbles over our yard fence in summer, yet you
press your needy face into my dusty desk corner,
refusing to leave, you silly thing.
Your milky plastic petals perform as
lenses to my histories,
rewinding memories like film reels,
downloaded stories,
shift-command-z.

A pimpled, mirth-eyed boy
plucked you from a bouquet of plastic stems
in a high school cafeteria line,
smirking at the lunch lady's frown, while
falling into a deep,
gallant bow, to push a small
silk flower into my palm,
reducing me to pliable joy in his hands.

I try trading you for my brother's fifth grade sandstone
ground down by guzzling water and beating air,
summer sun over
damp leaves over
snowbanks over
moonlight,
of climate and earth,
born of soil,
something real and steady to depend on.

I try trading you for a snowy Ferris wheel ride,
soaring slowly across a starred skyline,

or a boy browsing Salinger on the L train,
anything to shun your white plastic,
synthetic cloth tapered edges that bite
down with the sharpest incisors,
gnawing the hollow wood of my skin,
chopping me away, chip by chip,
till you reach the stump of my heart.

I try trading you for the January deep freeze,
August floods, mosquito bites in May,
viscous hot marshmallow hissing on October nights.

I tied you to his eager hand,
his simmering eyes, gleaming grin,
the short curls pinned atop his head.
I twisted your petals' pleasing seams,
plucked and pruned just for me.
I turned my calculus book to page 219,
while, under my desk,
sanding your essence into my palm,
searing his scent into mine.

I try trading places, little flower,
you for me, so I stick my fingers,
slide my palms against the desk drawer's wooden plains
my warm flesh to replace silky,
cold-hearted,
manufactured you,
to dethrone him,
to throw you,
at last,
into the trash bin.

# No name.

Her forehead pressed against the train window and the afternoon sun was too bright. The cold had returned, a friendly reminder of the off-balance nature of the life she led with anxiety and depression. It hit her when she became distracted from reading the Keats ode for English class. She locked eyes with a boy sitting in the section past the doors, Hispanic with dark eyes and thick eyebrows. A nanny spoke to two children in French as the doors welcomed more riders.

She tried her own ode, one to a feeling you can't place that is nudged between anguish and deepening emptiness. The building on the right side was firetruck red, a storage space playfully colored with gaudy signage. She wouldn't ever get to move away like the others. At 20, she tried to master the choreography: fold your arms into your stomach, smile at family parties, say the prayers loud enough at mass, clean the toilet, fold the clothes, be there for those you need you. To expect or hope for otherwise was plain ungratefulness. What about your cousins in the Philippines with no money, huh? No money for panties or two pairs of shoes, yeah? This is what happens when "laki sa dito", when the kids grow up here in the States, they become white, Americanized, independent, cruel, selfish, greedy, atheist, gay, disrespectful, distant.

The choreography became heavy as her limbs slowed and grew cold, detaching from her body, useless extremities flailing around, failing to portray normalcy. She craved something more, felt guilt for wanting the more, and eventually crushed by the reality of never achieving that more. Or, maybe she was one of those people who would be eternally dissatisfied. Or, the problem was being the rope in the tug of war between familial and cultural expectation and the white culture of freedom and self-sufficiency and "my". What a selfish word, my. The other end of the rope claimed "my" was what "ours" used to be; "my" got lost in the flattery, gluttony, sin, distance in the clean walls of America.

The train stuttered to a stop and beeped over the intercom, "We are momentarily stopped because of signal problems. We will be moving shortly."

She turned around to find two twenty-some year-old hipsters eating raw spinach out of bag like potato chips. They were white and the boy had his light brown hair in dreadlocks. She tried imagining what it would be like to never think of race, culture, or ethnicity. To be like the tv show Girls and only have to confront it when you sleep with someone not white. She wanted to own her culture, to shout it like she saw some black and Hispanic girls do, wearing hair scarves and traditional clothes. Being unafraid to call themselves strong, brown and black women.

Filipinos pass along this collected feeling of poise under oppression. They keep their heads down, do good work, remember never to grow a chip on their shoulder, never assume racism. They blend in and scowl at the other minorities that try to stand out and complain about prejudice. Too many titas wash their face with whitening soap, clutch fake Prada belts, and buy the largest, newest iPhones for their children. To be white-washed, literally. It always made her laugh because she remembered she insulted a white guy for being pale once. In the Philippines, it would have been a compliment, a byproduct of Spanish colonialism and mestizo culture. It was residue from the oppression of 500 years that led into Filipinos preferring to be white. White meant prettier, richer, well-connected, well-off, well-fed.

She admired the Hispanic boy with the headphones across the car. He bounced his head, red Beats crumpling his black curls, rich brown skin bathed in the afternoon sun. The couple was still munching on the bagged spinach and the thought made her stomach churn.

Right now, her parents were cleaning the house like the family was going to lick the floors and sleep on them naked. That's how thoroughly Swiffered, Cloroxed, Febreezed, and Shamwowed the house was. She was coming home to the chaos that wouldn't calm until the family left- supposedly six months from now. Unless, they tried to stay, under the radar, like many do. With ICE hunting and knocking on doors, it might not be such a good idea.

They would be coming and if things didn't already feel suffocating, she knew she was about to feel like the sarcophagus at the bottom of the Egypt exhibit at the Field. But sadly not as bedazzled or gold-leafed, she would be smothered under emptied Balikbayan boxes, baby cologne, spicy sardines in glass jars, plastic wrist rosaries, an already-blessed miniature Santo Niño, overacted Pinoy dramas about wealthy Chinese-Filipinos, K-dramas, a new karaoke chip with pop songs from 2013, shell jewelry from Cebu, wooden crosses to hang above the beds, kitschy Hello Kitty paraphernalia from the Seoul stop-over, a new puffy Filipinana shirt for the Ethnic Fair, a concert DVD of Gary Valenciano, Tita Carla's fake Louis Vitton purse, Rika's manga version of the Bible, Tito Pet's booklet of places he's been, and Lola's word search puzzle from the bookstore at the airport. Try breathing under that, she thought. In. And a stuttering breath out.

# Third person
# self-portrait-Nina Molina

Nina is 21, and according to her 8th grade graduation gown measurer, 5'4", a fact she maintains even though the doctor argues otherwise. She is Filipina and has sported the same haircut her father used to give her while teetering on the barstool in the basement bathroom. She has brown eyes, as so does the rest of her family. She also does not care about eye color, as almost every Filipino also has brown eyes. She has many moles, some potentially malignant, however she will not get them checked. She has light pink glasses. Her favorite shoes are her shiny black Docs because they remind her of lake waters at night or something dipped in a fondue of ink. Her hair is thinning due to anxiety, to the point that she is just now anxious about being anxious.

Nina had a good childhood. She grew up in one of those towns orbiting Chicago, pulled in by the city's gravity, only relevant because of its proximity to something actually important and interesting. She used to live on a dead-end street where they were the first minorities. Half of Chicago is Polish and so were their neighbors, her family devouring Polish cookies and chocolates during Christmas and waving to the Polish neighbors at church.

Her best friend Nadia moved in next door when Nina was in 2nd grade. They first noticed when Nadia's father mowed Nina's front lawn, a burly black man charging across their weed-infested grass. Nina's mother ran out to give him a glass of water and the girls became the first people to tell each other anything.

Nadia's father died of a stroke in the master bedroom of their house next door. Nadia, Miguel, Nina's older brother by 17 months, and Nina watched Disney channel original movies and watched Lola make oatmeal while Nadia's mom settled the house and cried. Nadia moved away in 4th grade and Nina lost her book club co-president and co-conspirator against Miguel. Nadia lives in Pilsen now and takes great Instagram photos, according to Miguel who follows her.

Miguel is Nina's kuya, older brother in Tagalog. She jokes that she never grew up calling him that because he doesn't act like one. They used to share a bedroom with matching blue plastic bear beds (the headboards sported the face of a smiling bear that Nina finds creepy in hindsight). On Saturday mornings, Miguel and Nina would lie in their beds and create family trees with extreme superpowers – like barfing toothpaste or farting instead of laughing. Miguel drew people with large heads and small bodies and ripped paper napkins when he got mad. Nina read for hours on her stomach, often tearing through two novels a day in the summers. Nina used to make her Barbie's nuns that had adventures with the stuffed animals and Neopets on their beds. Miguel played along and reminded her to take care of them.

Nina rarely thinks of childhood anymore. When she has to look back, she only sees the past six years clearly. She let her friend Lian read this and asked why she didn't write about the present. So, here's the short version of 2012 to 2020.

Nina's old. It's the joke of her current friend group that she doesn't get their Vine/TikTok references. She graduated 8th grade in 2012 and moved from a relatively diverse and mixed-income middle-school to a competitive, affluent, majority-white high school.

In general, Nina should have studied more. Instead, her first two years of high school saw her completing the library's ultra-marathon competition of reading about 40 books between October and May. She had ulcers at 15. She was told to pray and exercise to relax. She tried.

Nina regretfully writes that the tipping point of her mental health was a boy, a boy she thinks of whenever she peels a Ricola or creates a new dance move. He only stayed at Nina's school for junior year, but they packed a lot into that short time. By the end of junior year, Nina stopped going to class. She'd been cold for a while now. Nina barely graduated, mostly by the leniency of her teachers and her sighing counselor. The next fall she worked at a popcorn store that was in competition with Nuts on Clark and Garret's, two names never to be uttered in her boss's presence. She popped butter popcorn and scooped cheese from white buckets while the Cubs won the World Series, her friends moved away, she started therapy, and Trump was voted in.

The next spring, Nina started commuting to a school in the northern-most neighborhood of city. She didn't have much of a choice other than community college. She went two semesters, took another semester break, and then another two semesters. The whole while, Nina saw a psychologist and needed medicine but wasn't allowed to have any. Finally, she got some in the fall of 2018 behind her parents' back. Then, she applied to transfer behind their backs. Then, she had to tell them the truth about everything. They didn't talk to her for a while. Now, they're talking again, and she moved her entire life to Michigan. She made real friends for the first time since high school. She still sees a therapist and takes medicine, and the heaviness still creeps in anytime she's overwhelmed. Driving from a day in Frankenmuth last semester, Nina pinched herself that she was still alive, since she didn't think she'd make it to 20. She's 21, older than ever, and finally has the distance from her old life to write about starting a new one.

# ABIGAIL NUTTER

**Senior**
**Major:** Creative Writing & Literature and Psychology
**Reading:** Fiction

Abigail Nutter is a Senior in her last semester at the University of Michigan. She will be graduating from LSA and from the Residential College. In her time at Michigan, she has enjoyed polishing her writing and finding her own voice. She leans towards lyrical fiction and enjoys writing from odd points of view about dreamlike worlds. She also enjoys hiking and music, things that, like writing, encourage reflection and joy.

*Nominated by: Laura Thomas*

# We'll All Be Fine

It's Autumn, and the leaves have started to change. They're beautiful, like a gentle sigh as you fall asleep. You stare at them in a trance, realizing at the last minute that you've begun to drift into oncoming traffic, and yank your wheel back to the right. You clutch the steering wheel tightly and ignore the blaring horns by staring at your pale knuckles.

When you pull into your driveway, you realize that you received a text from your father. You read it, then read it again, then turn your phone off and sit there with the car running. The pine tree in your new driveway is turning brown, you realize; it's dying.

It's the first hard snow of winter, and you decide it's not a good day to drive. You were meant to head home and see your parents, but you can't get the image of sliding off the highway into a pole out of your mind. You've seen ten glowing ambulances and four accidents since Fall began. You run your tongue over your gums and they taste salty, metallic. From your bedside table, your phone buzzes and announces the third call you've received today. You turn your back to it and pull your blanket over your head. It's hot underneath; you imagine that if you fell asleep under it, you might suffocate and never wake up.

Christmas comes around and you can't put off visiting home any longer. You pack a small duffle bag, just enough for three days and two nights and something nice to wear to church, and take the long highway home.

Your mother meets you in the driveway and holds your hands, says some things, *I know it's hard but it's important that you're here with him while you still have the chance*, but you just stare at the tiny clouds she births from her lips. Up they float into the sky, masked against the spread of grey. She says your name again and you look back down at her, but you swear she's only looking through you with those dark blue eyes.

When the two of you head inside you feel weak and realize you must be hungry. You drop your bags by the door and go to grab something from the fridge. You aren't quite able to ignore the lists of specialists and the medical invoices with your father's name on them, stuck over old high school pictures of you and your brother.

The inside of the fridge is nearly bare. You guess you'll make some eggs. Five minutes later you're pushing them around on your plate while your mother stares at you from the living room, holding a tissue to her face.

Night turns to day. It's Christmas Eve. Your brother has just been dropped off from the airport – he *could only take off Christmas Eve and Christmas Day, sorry it isn't longer,* – and your mother has decided that you're all going to kill a pine tree. This hasn't been a big deal since you graduated high school, but you all pile into the truck anyway.

You and your brother sit on the fold up seats in the back, knees facing inwards towards each other, bumping occasionally. To your right you can see the icy road speeding towards you; to your left you can see the rusted bed rattling like it'll make a break for it at any moment. Two or three inches to your right you can feel your father, right on the other side of that chair, and God it's weird to think it but he doesn't smell like he used to. He's dustier, maybe, or more chemical, but you can't see how both are possible at once. You can see his veins through his skin, just a bit, like rivers, like frozen rivers. You imagine that the blood underneath is like deep water under a frozen river. It must be just as cold. You feel cold being near him, so you stare down at your phone even when your mother clicks her tongue at you.

When you get to the nursery, there aren't many trees left. While your family scours the rows for anything acceptable, you wonder at the fact that it's even called a nursery, since every tree born here is destined to die. You never used to think this way. You wonder when you started.

Ahead of you, your brother is holding your father's elbow. The two of them talk quietly as they make their way through the snow. You drift, stop, stare at this poor crippled tree in front of you. It's not even as tall as you are, much shorter than the one in your driveway, but its needles are already browning and falling in a pick-up sticks pattern around its base. You jump as your mother places a mitten-shrouded hand on your shoulder, suddenly at your side. *Is this one calling to you?*

*Should we take it home?* You're puzzled, a bit angry, and your cheeks burn against the snow.

*No, it's shitty. It would die before we even got it home,* you tell her. You turn and quickly walk away so you don't have to see her face.

Your father is the best man you've ever known, but he never was a religious person. Once your brother graduated high school and was out of the house, you and your father started letting your mother spend those hours in church without you. On Christmas Eve you'd all dress up and take a picture, but then your mother was the only one of you who made the cold pilgrimage to mass.

This year is different. Once the tree is up and the lights are strung – you're all a bit too tired for ornaments – you all bundle into the car, all dress shirts and ties and shiny shoes, and fishtail your way to church. You only see one accident on your way, a minor one. Your brother points out the woman standing outside her car, taking a picture of a dented bumper. *So what,* you say. *It's not like anyone even died.* Your brother starts to say something to you, but you see your mother shake her head at him through the rear-view mirror, and he stops, takes a deep breath, and looks out the window.

You sit next to your father during church. You don't intend to, but you swear your mother refuses to enter the pew just so you'd have to sit next to him. You stare straight ahead at the curly white hair of the old woman in front of you. She has a red poinsettia sweater on and she seems to know all of the hymns by heart. When it's time to hold hands and pray, you're surprised to actually feel your father's hand, warm and solid, and you realize fully for the first time that he's standing next to you. You feel his whole body trembling ever so slightly and you hold on even tighter to his hand, although you can't bring yourself to look at him.

Mass is long. By the end of it you're exhausted and feel wound tight like a ball of yarn. When you get home, you rush past the Christmas tree and into your room – at least, what used to be your room – and collapse into bed. You learned long ago how to cry silently, but your pillow still gets soaked from the tears and snot. It isn't until you stop clenching your hands that you realize your nails have left red crescent moons in your palms.

There is a tentative knock on your bedroom door. You hold your breath, try desperately to clean off your face and look natural just sitting on your bed, and the door opens. Your father comes in, walks over, sits on the bed. He reaches out a hand and sets it on yours. You look away, but you leave your hand there. He says some things in a gentle voice. *I know this is scary, but we'll get through it together.* You stare at the boxes piled in your room. Since you've been away, they've started storing all sorts of things in here. *The doctor says the odds of recovery are good, we caught it early.* One box is labeled College Textbooks. The idea of your parents being in college, being young, is so abstract. *I don't want you to worry about me. I'll be fine. We'll all be fine.* Back when he was your age, did he ever expect this to happen to him?

That night you can't sleep – maybe you're still trying to catch Santa in action, picking your lock or slipping open a window – and you hear him. The door to his bedroom opens. You hear quick footsteps into the hallway, panting. Your father is having a panic attack in the living room. You stare at the ceiling, listen to the tell tale sounds of furniture moving. You hear your mother leaving the bedroom. Her voice is hushed as though you can't hear her through the paper-thin walls. His voice, rising like some wailing animal. The door to the bathroom opens, clicks closed. You hear your mother knocking on it quietly, repeatedly, but the only response is a retching sound from inside. It continues like this for a long while. You fall asleep from sheer exhaustion before you ever hear him flush.

The next morning there are no stockings, but there are a few presents wrapped and under the tree. You wonder when anyone had the time to do that. As you take a seat on the couch in your pajamas you realize that the TV is up against a different wall than it was yesterday – it's visible from the kitchen now, like it used to be when you were little.

Your brother comes out from his room – he looks like shit, with bags under his eyes – and sits near you on the couch. You exchange the silence as you wait for your mother and father to come out of their room. Five minutes pass and your brother grumbles something, stands up, and walks into the kitchen. You slide sideways and curl into a ball on the couch. From here you can still hear and smell the pancakes he begins to cook and keeps cooking for twenty minutes. When he comes back out to the living room, he sets a huge stack for you on the coffee table and sits next to you.

The pancakes wobble balefully. You begin to cry, covering your mouth, your shoulders shuddering. Your brother hugs you, holding you up, and pats your head. After a moment, he claps you roughly on the back and says *Eat now, cry later.* He cuts into his own stack and starts to eat. You rub your blurry eyes, wipe your nose on your sleeve, and cut into your pancakes.

When your father wakes up and comes into the living room, you force yourself to look at him. He's already gotten dressed in jeans and a holiday sweater. His hair is thinner than you remember, but then again it had been thinning since you started high school. His sweater seems a bit baggy, but it isn't as bad as you thought when you'd seen him out of the corner of your eyes. You can't see his veins from here. A pattern of red and green light falls over his face. He looks tired – he *was* up all night – but he smiles gently at you when you meet his eyes. Your brother scoots over on the couch and you pat the cushion next to you. With a slight huff, your father settles down between the two of you. You lean on his shoulder.

Your mother joins you, red Santa hat tugged snuggly over her head. She always used to dress up like this, back when you and your brother were kids.

You and your father and your brother sit on the couch while your mother brings you all presents and squeezes your shoulders gently. For a moment, it almost feels normal again.

# MADALYN OSBOURNE

**Senior**
**Major:** Psychology
**Reading:** Poetry

Madalyn is from Grand Rapids, MI, and would eventually like to pursue a doctorate in Clinical and Community Psychology. She is particularly interested in the public health implications of psychology research, criminal justice reform, and the intersection of the two. Her writing is inspired by family histories and the complexity of memory.

*Nominated by: Sarah Messer*

# What Use Is Remembering

We leave behind bare walls and sprawling windows
frozen calculations and starched resentments
stubborn defenders and weak *I'm sorries.*

We leave nineteen guitars, an electric drum set
a nest of amps, each artifact
more precious than us.

We forget his business trips to Tampa that
never were never really business trips at all
what we understood, but wouldn't say.

We remember coconut-scented tanning oil
his precious salt water pool and
the predictably slimy house guests.

We ignore the acupuncture and chiropractors
flushed prescriptions
in our names.

Though hooked on sleeping pills himself
as he nods off to sleep
his face is kept lit by the salt-leaking TV.

We forget clicking dress shoes
too much cologne
from any time we'd leave the house.

We remember loud music, good music
kale and garlic and Mexican sausage
toasted almonds and chili.

We give up the fat, trembling house that quaked every time
our dad dropped cast iron balloons in the basement
built as a bomb shelter during the second World War.

We leave decades of collected Dwell magazines
drawers of treasured ticket stubs hundreds of
CDs, alphabetized and autographed.

When he wasn't home
I'd run my fingers across their plastic spines
wishing to map a way in.

We remember cowboy coffee
thick enough to chew
only ever burnt.

And sipping morning orange juice out of
a light-up shot glass he forgot to hide
from the night before.

We forget five moldy bathrooms that no one cared to
scour because we never meant to stay as long as we did.

We remember dark rooms
as products of his demands to save electricity
despite proclaiming climate change as a liberal ploy.

And saved egg cartons for farmers
we don't know
nine years later and the ceiling-high stack just keeps growing.

I Wonder If They're Still There

I stare at the blank walls he is hostile to drive a nail in
because we're leaving soon
but I barely hold my breath.

# Stevens Lake, off Ole White Drive

Guided by domino-stacked pines
and condemning billboards: *Lust
drags you down to Hell.* We passed
taxidermists, whippy dips, the
Soaring Eagle Casino. Passed the
flaunted Confederate flags of
people who forgot: this state was
never Southern. July, Northern
Michigan, and we were nineteen.
Cans of Monster and white-tailed
deer lit the roadside. We ate
salmon, sang opertically to Mario Spinetti, and droned
on about the dreadful Roger Stone.
The sun had set. Now, floating in a
freshwater spring, shielded in a
thicket, illuminated only by the
stubborn moon. We left our clothes
inside. Braless, we bobbed down all
121 stairs, caught our breath on the
dock, and glided into
the soft glass molt. Baptized by
the stillness, panting in rhythm,
holding afloat our long bodies,
forbidding the spring to enter us.

# Blood Beat

1.

On Saturday mornings, we'd cross
the street and wander through the
Catholic campus in search of the
cafe, a taxidermied moose head
on the wall, where we bought
Oregon Trail chai and lemon
poppy seed muffins, $3.75. We'd
split them both, though never
evenly. I always ate the
sugar-crystaled cloud on top.

2.

In the summer, we'd cross the street and
go back to the campus, stained towels in
hand, to collect hundreds of fallen
mulberries from sky-scraping tree tops.
We ate most of them before we ever
returned, all half-smushed and smeared
from the tiny squirrel
paws that trampled our tart jewels.

3.

The same nestled patch of
land swaddled my gentle
grandfather from the Irish hills
of Kentucky. Where his
Southern kindness met my
God-fearing grandmother.
1963. Where they found
routine skipping beneath the

neon excitement of the only
city they would ever live in
before returning to their village
of Merrill, Michigan
Population: 700

4.

The campus captured my parents
too. They raised their family
across the street. Did they walk
past our red-brick bungalow as
dumb, skinny collegiates? Did
they admire her? Did they notice
her quaint yard, her heavy
door, or embroidered windows?

5.

Later, I would spend many nights
dancing on our shared driveway in
my silk nightgown. Where I scabbed
the pads of my toes and swung too
violently on our neighbor's antique
porch swing, clutching a melted
piece of blue chalk, my hand swollen
from the heat
of the Midwestern summer.

6.

If luck had its way, just before the sun
flopped, I might make out the hum of
bagpipes on the campus. 8:05. It was
always me who heard it first, and always
me who willed our slew to schlep across
the street. Prancing around the pensive
Irish man's wool-wrapped ankles, I

rejoiced in what I later learned is the
hymn of my grandfather's blood beat,
but not until after his heart stopped
in the driveway in the snow 200
miles away from our campus.

7.

January 5th, 2005 and I
forgot to thank him.

# An Abbreviated Family History

Born of a secretary of an
envelope manufacturer, former
seamstress, shoe salesman,
traded, now, for a diabetic.
Sprouted from brain-zapped
Betty, still trembling six feet
under. Deemed witchcraft, had
she been born less than a
century earlier.

Now, one of us makes prosthetic
bones on an assembly line, the
other cuts sheets of metal during
third shift, the next working
overtime in the salad dressing
factory poisoning the river that
segregates their hungry
hometown. And my favorite
uncle: a musician turned magician,
yet sugar-laced cancer
took his last breath.

Despite routine arrests and stolen
cash from the ones who love my
mother's brother most, we
inevitably hum a rush of endless
patience and hushed forgiveness.

Why does he do it?
Like clockwork, it
seems.

His mother
fled to Iowa on Thanksgiving Day.
Took everything precious, but forgot
them. Years earlier, she'd left infant-
him swinging above the bathtub, his
steady rhythm clanking
against the pre-cracked porcelain.

Yet, we mustn't deny: we all come
from her pulse—a rhythm now
saturated with poison. Our first
touchstone.

Years ago, she carried on the
predictable pattern of a
maternity wedding
dress. *Loose Ladies*, they
repeat, again and again.
But soon she'll lose the
part of her that sustained
us, nourished us, loved us—

If only the magician were
still here: might the tumor
evaporate? Born of dust,
and back again.
Though how could
he learn to save his
mother if he
couldn't even save himself?

We knew work
was rhythm and
so was love. It
was all the
same—or so we
prayed.

# CHELSEA PADILLA

**Freshman**
**Major:** Political Science and English
**Reading:** Creative Non-fiction

Chelsea is a freshman majoring in Political Science and English from Grand Rapids, MI. She's been writing all kinds of stories in notebooks ever since she learned to write. Aside from writing, she spends most of her time reading and watching cooking videos.

*Nominated by: Leslie Stainton*

# Tight-lipped Smiles

I was born American. For some time, I grew up thinking my mother was somehow born American, too. It was a logical assumption to make: everyone I knew appeared to be born here, so where else could she have come from?

I eventually learned that my mother was not born American. The evidence lies in the pictures she brought with her when she and my father immigrated from the Philippines to the United States in the nineties. One, in particular, shows her with a group of her college friends. She sits on the porch of a *bahay kubo* – a house made from bamboo and thatched mangrove palm, raised up on hardwood stilts to avoid the effects of flooding during the monsoon season. She's dressed in a loose white T-shirt and high-waisted, light wash jeans that are carefully cuffed at the ankle. Her entire expression seems candid: the movement of one of her hands is blurred as it reaches out towards the camera, her head is tilted back, and her jaw is open slightly in laughter. In another picture, she stands at the top of a flight of stairs with her fellow med students. She wears a crisp white lab coat and skirt, and her dark hair cascades neatly down her back. Her chest puffs outwards, and she beams at the camera with a wide, toothy grin.

My mother doesn't smile like that for photos anymore. Now, her smiles are a bit tight and closed-lipped, and sometimes, you can hardly tell she's smiling at all. Even in person, she tries her best not to show her teeth. In conversation, she has a habit of obscuring her mouth with her right hand when she speaks. My mother has mastered the craft of making this gesture appear natural. Instead of placing an entire hand over her mouth, she hovers her thumb, index, and middle fingers just above her lips. Occasionally, she gestures with her fingers to give the illusion that she isn't deliberately obscuring her face.

Once, I asked her why she doesn't smile showing her teeth and she said, "My teeth are too ugly." When I disagreed, she pointed to her bottom right incisor and slight overbite to prove herself. "See? This is not straight. It would look bad."

The change in her smile, it seems, happened as early as her move to Chicago. Looking at my parents' pictures from their first couple years in America, I see my mother's big, toothy grins become less and less frequent as time progresses until they are practically nonexistent and fully replaced by the small, tight smiles that hide her teeth entirely.

People didn't care about dental care where my mother grew up. In the Philippines, her own mother had decided that her children didn't need their teeth to be fixed, despite the fact that they had enough money to do so. My mother said it just never seemed like an issue – her teeth weren't necessarily unhealthy. They worked. There were more important things to worry about.

But when she moved to America, she saw people with perfectly white, straight teeth everywhere. America seemed to be obsessed with having a flawless smile, and teeth, it seems, became a source of insecurity for her – so much so that she projected her concern for teeth onto my brother and me. When our first permanent teeth started growing in, she insisted that we try to make them straight by pushing them into the "proper" positions if it seemed like they were going to grow in crooked. I wasn't convinced that pushing my teeth would do anything, but my mother was adamant.

"You *have* to take care of your teeth," she told us. "You don't want them to look like mine, do you?"

The day my mother got her green card, though, she ignored her tight-lipped smile principle. I was perched at the kitchen counter when she discovered the envelopes containing her and my father's green card documents in the mail.

"It's here," she said. Her voice sounded oddly hushed, as if it were the middle of the night rather than late afternoon. I looked up at her. She was staring down at the envelope in her hands, and she stayed like that for a few moments, just staring until she tore into the envelope with a certain, desperate ferocity that I didn't quite understand but was too afraid to question. She emerged triumphant with several thin papers and a single, pale green plastic card.

I never really understood my mother's struggle with her smile when I was younger. I viewed her reminders of "Wear your rubber bands!" and "Floss your teeth!" as nagging. I thought her closed-lipped smiles meant she was perpetually serious. But I never thought that either might've come from a place of insecurity about her own teeth. After all, mothers always seem invincible.

As she held that card, my mother's face broke into a smile – one that was wide and bright, teeth and all.

# ALEX PAN

**Senior**
**Major:** Dual-Degree Triple Major: Business, Organizational Studies and Psychology
**Minor:** Quadruple Minor: Writing, Playwriting, Music and Gender Race and Nation
**Reading:** Fiction/Short Story

Alex is a dual-degree triple major and quadruple minor Senior at UMich. He is an avid writer of fiction short stories and theatrical plays who enjoys exploring the universal theme of loneliness in his pieces. In his free time, he enjoys composing music, writing, and creating other art. With goals of breaking into both screenplay and writing/composing his first musical theatre play this semester, Alex is excited for what will come ahead!

*Nominated by: José Casas*

# Life is Like an Unfinished Performance

Life is like an unfinished performance. We change how we act and talk–how we wear our clothes and speak our words–so we can be loved by others. Eventually we change so much others don't remember who we are anymore. And *we* don't remember who we are and what we want.

There once was a beautiful, young girl whom I knew; not a woman, mind you, for she enjoyed playing with my emotions like a daughter does with her doll. Ah! How her name still so delicately rolls off my tongue: Anya, like a guilty bite of sweet cherries. I can still feel the warmth of her breath, as I buried myself in her gaze on multiple starry nights. We were never romantically involved–but I yearned for her.

In one evening as the sun fell, so did her voice lower... whispering to me what she loved in a man. As any ill man plagued with love would do, I played the role she wrote. I became that man, hoping to win her heart. But night by night, she would revise her dreamt man, making every night with her a new audition to test me.

But then when the sun fell and her voice lowered again during another night, she whispered to me she had found a new lover for herself: perfect for her role. Yet she continued to toy with me, still inviting me to share darkening evenings with her and watching the sun fall again as she would lower her voice... whispering to me again with never-ending desires to which I tirelessly followed and changed myself for her.

But then a wondrous evening came, when the sun fell yet her voice did not lower–nor did her warm breath whisper. For when the sun fell that night, from Anya's gazing eyes there fell a tear. She had found her lover unfaithful to her. We laid on the grass in silence. Once the night turned black and the only thing I could see were the whites of her eyes, I turned to her and whispered: "I have always loved you." We touched our noses together as our innocent lips became one.

I can still feel her soft palms.

Then she spoke.

"But I have not always loved you," she said. "You are not the same man I first met long ago. You have changed to something else. Who are you but just a sculpted replica of the same man who just broke my heart?"

And she was not wrong.

For at that point, I knew she would never love me.

When one completely changes, there is little one can do to undo it. She could only enjoy me as her performer with a mask she constantly revised, and I would change to fit every night so I could entertain her...

What a sad life it is, to change oneself so much beyond any recognition so one can be vainly loved. And yet, to have no one with whom to truthfully confide my deepest secrets, happiness, and events of the day...

With great confidence I can say, up until this point all I have wanted to become and ever will want to become is... nothing.

For the more we attempt to change ourselves, the further we lose our minds on what we truly want.

# The Romanticist

A poet revels in such writing that learns to capture the people's life and the people's world, and then by some form of creative deception translating it into the people's language. Never have I believed this to be within my possibility, for the fair poet just as well can be the heavy-handed writer. A plenty time I have received praise from fickle friends for my poor poetry, but the profession of sharing stories is rarely a profitable one. I ponder little about such concerns, the chasm that separates my strong thoughts from my weak words, as I exercise my craft in poetry purely as a pastime.

And then life lulled on toward loneliness—it was inevitable. For I lost little in leisurely time from other affairs beyond writing weary words. And now I continue to write and only write, never escaping either to my unforeseen adulthood and independence or from my torn adolescence and lost love. My adolescence struck its end once my heart fell to ashes from the most childish of romance. I now live within the fraying string of maturity hoping to settle upon true love before time disintegrates me.

So I have tasted the sweet cherries that oh-so cleverly hide in this sour world and also know of the terribleness that will eventually poison them all. I have seen it all—the people's life, the people's world—but have yet learnt to tactfully write the people's language. Too many thoughts did I have infecting my sanity, though no pleasing language by which I could express them. After all, the forgetful poet must create writing before they have forgotten everything they have seen.

This prompted my joining of a local literature club—not any group that I fancied more so than another. Though my thoughts quickly filled with regret; stepping afoot upon this literature club was the most interesting of experiences. My writing perhaps cannot fairly portray such a scene as this with deserved artistry, yet I must comment upon the sheer number of eclectics that populated the room. They all crowded atop their lanky stools in the dark, closeted space—a scene that reminded me of nothing remarkable except for the plainness of my own washroom. I would have otherwise assumed I had arrived at a funeral and soon expected a eulogy.

Ah, but my strange collection of first thoughts quickly dispelled upon hearing their voices: the jumping contours and laughing melodies that bounced between the tight walls. And these eclectics' colourful fashion too! The ladies adorned rose petals woven into their dresses and full roses braided into their mermaid hair, none of such vibrant flowers resonating the true colours that could possibly exist in nature. I had hoped to practise my literary commentary regarding the stylish appearances of the gentlemen present in this miniature room too, but the literature club casted only women before me—many a kind of women though, from soft-speaking and tender lips to frivolous greying and sparse hair.

And then there was one crumpled man who sat with his spine curled. His stature was not so much from his old age but rather for guarding his immense focus on locking his fragile fingers together, his entire body shivering in the rather warm room. Without breaking my walking rhythm, I compelled myself to approach the stoic old man with hopes to befriend another lonely body. I seated myself to his right side. By his left side was a vacant seat as well, though he had planted atop the stool his coat and claimed the land his own.

I politely offered a handshake to the old man, erecting my hand and forcibly interrupting his focus upon his wrapped fingers. He did not appear too startled, for he gradually glanced up at me like a curious animal and soon became possessed with a wild smile and desirable eyes that posed nothing but the most primitive of happiness from seeing my kind gesture. He gently baited his right palm upward and outward—barely moving with his shy elbow still tucked in beside his body—and awaited my hand to move forward to complete the exchange. The old man did not move his delirious eyes away from my own, never once glancing at my hand.

I immediately grew uneasy with the old man's behaviour. But I drew nothing of significance from his rabid peculiarities, assuming it was simply my isolation that overcame my fair judgement of the outer world—socialising is not an easy feat, after all. I knew well of the people's life and the people's world as a poet, but perhaps not so well of the people themselves.

I considered the thought of motioning forward to accomplish my handshake, trembling the joints and veins that wrapped around my hands. Like an unsatiated animal, the old man pounced upon and consumed my hand with his own stiff fingers. His unsettled eyes mimicked his shivering body which moved down to his quivering hands and then to the bony tips of his jittery fingers, finally giving way to my weak heart, pulsating ever faster. Though it was a warm handshake—and sincere at that. But by the gods I feared yet more so lusted to know what terrifying thoughts were jumping in this man's broken body.

"Look around you, young man," he snarled. "Do you see them?"

"Why," I started. I diverted my attention to explore the room, hoping to find something of interest to feed the old man. "—Why, yes. Before us there lies a plethora of eccentric women, young and old, who wear roses from head-to-toe upon their hair and down their lovely dresses." I returned to face the old man and felt disturbed by his comfortable yet unnatural silence. I fled my attention to scan the room once more, looking again for something notable to mention. "As well, we sit here in a literature club. So these women's thoughts must flourish with fantastical inventions, much like the passionate roses that bloom upon their beautiful bodies."

Upon hearing this, the excited old man became a disappointed old man. "Are you a poet?" he asked. I cautiously nodded. "Then surely your creative mind can see the grotesque creatures that chant and mock us right before our eyes," he gently proposed.

My fear of the old man's madness subsided as I found my thoughts lost in trying to capture his intentions. "Do you refer to the women?" I asked. He looked over his shoulders and returned to worryingly stare at me. He silently nodded.

# THERESA PHAM

**Junior**
**Major:** Economics
**Reading:** Non-fiction

Theresa is a junior studying Economics. She is from Grand Rapids, Michigan. In her free time Theresa enjoys cooking, exploring local restaurants and traveling. She'd like to thank her parents, particularly her mom, for inspiring her to write this piece.

*Nominated by: David Ward*

# Language as a Barrier

"Bao! Đi lấy thêm thịt bò," my mom ordered as she pointed towards the freezer, "Mẹ không có thời gian!"[1] She brushed her disheveled dark brown, wavy hair out of her pale face. Deep, purple bags formed beneath her sharp and determined eyes. When life got busy, she is one to sacrifice sleeping and eating. She vigorously washed the various vegetables from her garden all while keeping a careful watch on the boiling *phở* broth. Like myself, my mom kept her life busy. From working a full-time job, in addition to weekly volunteering and maintaining a side, she rarely had leisure time—yet she didn't need it. Cooking was her outlet. The act of mass-preparing intricate dishes was necessary after a long week of work. My mom was an expert at preparing traditional Vietnamese recipes, skilled from years of experience. My mom effortlessly seasoned, sliced and simmered each ingredient for dinner that night. Each meal demonstrating the passion she has for cooking. My mom became known for her cooking within the family which was why she hosted and prepared the main course for every family dinner.

I'm not sure when such dinners became a thing but for as long as I could remember until even now, each week a family would host the dinner and all my relatives would pack the house with laughter, gossip and the meals they prepared from home.

"Uhhh..." I trailed off as my mind worked to think of the phrase, "Where did you put it?". My Vietnamese was never great. My pronunciation was off, I didn't know how to read or write. I was equivalent to a first grader, probably less. "Ugh, cho tôi lấy."[2] My mom rolled her eyes and pushed me aside. Intuitively she reached for the frozen, red cuts of beef beneath all the other meats and vegetables hoarded in our freezer.

1. Bao! Go get more beef, I don't have the time!
2. I'll do it myself

As an immigrant from Vietnam, my mom spoke little to no English. Living in Michigan for nearly 30 years, I believe she knew more than she let others knew. However, she rarely spoke English, ending conversations short or having my dad translate. My mom has never been able to spell in English. For as long as I could read or write, my mom would enlist me every time she had finished decorating her cakes. No matter how many cakes she creates, for each one I always write out "Happy Birthday" or "Congratulations". I used to believe she just never bothered to learn, but I figure now she's unconfident in her language skills. Like myself, she was embarrassed of her mispronunciation in her second language. Her English carried a heavy accent that indicated her life in Vietnam and labelled her as an immigrant. When she speaks English, my mom is timid and quiet; she keeps to herself. When she speaks in her native tongue however; she's talkative, loud and full of life.

For years I've wondered who my mom was and how she became the person she is today. I've lived with her my entire life, yet still I am unaware of how her experiences have shaped her. The reason I aim to understand my mom is because of how entwined our traits are. I'm always told that I am exactly like my mom–the good and the bad.

*The disparity in our languages is an invisible wall.* Neither of us can express ourselves clearly to one another, often getting frustrated due to miscommunication and interpreting each other's words incorrectly. Despite this, we learned to express ourselves in non-communicative ways.

＊＊＊

My mom dusted the counter with flour before rolling out the rested dough. She then unwrapped a neat block of butter. My eyes watched in awe as she wrapped the soft, fluffy dough over the cold, hard butter. Overlapping the dough and butter, one would think that she is making delicate, French croissants. Yet these are not the delicious pastries from France, but rather the Vietnamese alternative: *bánh patê sô*. They are purposely sturdier, and filled with savory ground pork.

My mom argues that these are more complex than croissants,

admitting that even with her skills; she has trouble perfecting the dough. Yet, my mom is not one to easily give up. She will always keep on trying to perfect new dishes, even if the results are disastrous.

My mom has been cooking since she was about twelve. At the time, her father was sent to re-education camp, his punishment for serving in the military for South Vietnam. During this time, her mother was left to care for her five children, including my mom. My mom, being the only daughter, could not join her brothers working in arduous fields. She was taken into a family friend's bakery, where she learned to bake all sorts of pastries. Her childhood was very different than mine. She didn't have the freedom and carefree attitude most twelve year olds have. She didn't have the education or even basic necessities. Like most children in the aftermath of the war, she starved each and every day, struggled to even have enough for a small portion of rice.

The house feels warm from the baking pastries in the oven. The air mixed with the aroma of fresh, buttery pastry intermingling the garlic seasoning of the beef. My mom pulls out the *bánh patê sô*, luckily they look perfect. They are golden brown, glistening with the brushed butter on top. Cinched at the edges, the pastry is puffed in the middle, stuffed with the delicious, juicy ground pork. My mom cuts the pastry in half, carefully inspecting her work. Steam rises from the center of the browned pork, laid beneath the multiple flaky layers of golden perfection.

She subtly smiles to herself. Hiding the pride she finds in her puffed creation. She blows on the pastry in attempt to cool it down, and hands me one half. Every time my mother makes *bánh patê sô*, it yields the same flaky, delicious result.

Her life has never been consistent. Growing up, she's moved from various houses. Been in and out of school, and seen her family be moved around. Yet she is able to find stability in cooking. That's probably why her food always has the same flavor and depth. She has been cooking and baking for decades, and while other factors of her life may be changing, her recipes never fail to remain the same.

I am not entirely sure the exact moment this occurred, but I was sick. Sick enough to convince my dad that staying home was worth more than studying. My body was exhausted, succumbing to the enticing warmth and comfort of my bed. I managed to get my way downstairs and towards the kitchen counter. A pot of cháo gà, or chicken congee was stewing on the stove. The slow boil of the thick broth filled the kitchen with the aroma of tender chicken, soft and disintegrated rice, and the broth seasoned with the intense umami flavored fish sauce, garlic and pepper.

I set the bowl on the counter near the stove. I fill it with the thick congee. The congee is off-white from the seasoning of the chicken broth and fish sauce. Tan, shredded chicken hide among the porridge. A bowl of pre-cut cilantro, scallions, and onions is set aside. I carefully garnish my congee with a generous amount. This meal is warm and delicious. Every flavor blends and compliments one another perfectly. Each ingredient is carefully chosen and tossed in, not only to recreate the traditional yet personalized taste of the congee but to help my body heal. I imagine my mom waking up early before work to make cháo gà. From stewing the rice in the salty chicken broth to slicing the fresh vegetables for the garnish, my mom works hard to recreate this dish.

Cháo has not always been this intricate dish but rather food for the poor. Stale rice is boiled in water to create the thick consistency. I imagine my parents, starving as children during the Vietnam War, also being served cháo; yet theirs is different, it's stripped of its garnishes, flavorings and chicken and left only with the bland, tasteless rice base. I imagine my grandma, hovering over the most pathetic pot of cháo, rationing scoops of it into small bowls of her eight, starved children—feeling isolated and alone, waiting desperately for her husband to return from re-education camp.

I can't help but wonder what such meals bring my parents back to their youth. Does cháo remind them of their days during the War? The days where they were unsure of when their next meal was or if their fathers would ever be released from re-education camp? Does cháo elicit the same feelings I feel towards it? The feelings of love and empathy?

Although cháo was originally food for impoverished people, it has been redefined as a meal served during the winter and flu season. My mom serves cháo gà when we are sick, from when we were young to now when we are miles apart and in college. Cháo gà has become redefined for my mother as an opportunity to express her love for us. When she makes cháo gà she is seemingly happy. She hovers over the large pot of simmering flavors...stirring and stirring. I continue digging into the steaming porridge, my frail body ravenous for my mom's home cooking and embracing of her love.

✻✻✻

"Bao! Đi làm này chó mẹ."[3] My mom shouts from the kitchen. She shoves a bag of crisp, white, bean sprouts into my hands. Old newspapers cover the table. Piles of bean sprout roots cover the Vietnamese text of the paper. I hate this task. From as early as I remember, I was always the one who had to pick the roots from the bean sprouts. It was tedious and monotonous. What made it worse, was the insane amount of bean sprouts my family consumed. My family loves bean sprouts, typically one bag held a few pounds of bean sprouts. One by one, I had to pull the roots of the bean sprouts. I hated this task even more because the only reason we had to pick the roots off was because if we didn't, they looked "ugly". The larger my pile of "pretty" bean sprouts grew, the more aggressive I became with the bean sprouts. I started shredding the roots off and throwing the beansprout in the new pile, annoyed that I had to do this tedious task again.

My mom glares at me from the kitchen as I continue ripping the poor bean sprouts, "Trời ơi, Bao không muốn làm thì tôi làm!"[4]. This is her guilt tactic. She makes herself unnecessarily stressed, and then

3. Do this for me

4. If you don't want to do this then I'll just do it!

when you try to help her, she finds a small detail to criticize then takes over and does it herself. "I *can* do it and *am* doing it." I sass back as I continue tearing apart the bean sprouts.

My dad comes over from the arguing of our voice. He's calm and nice. His personality contrasts with my mom's driven and critical one. He takes the seat next to me, "How come you have to stress your mom like that?", he grabs some bean sprouts and picks off the sprouts. Through my dad's voice alone, I start to relax. Picking up the bean sprouts and following my dad's actions. "I'm just annoyed that she's criticizing something as small as one bean sprout." My dad chuckles as he helps me pick the roots, "You're the same way," he pricks the browned root of the sprout, "both of you! Always have to do it your way or her way. You can never be wrong can you?"

I look up back at my dad. He's aged. The small patch of hair is grey, and his wrinkles are beginning to form from premature stress and stress even now. Although his personality is calm, he hides his stress extremely well. He's even more stressed than my mom. If I ever thought I was the responsible child, I cannot compare myself to my dad. During the Vietnam War, my grandpa was a prisoner for nearly half of his childhood. As the eldest son, he had to mature quickly and take care of the rest of his six siblings. Even now, he continues to work day and night to help provide his children the opportunity to go to college.

While there are times in which I am easily upset by mom, my dad is a reminder of the reason behind my feelings. My mom can be critical, nagging and stubborn. All traits in which I share too, yet, the intentions behind her traits are out of love. Like my dad, she's had to assume responsibility at a young age when she was forced to work in order to support her family. Her traits stem from her traumatic childhood during the Vietnam War. She is critical, but only because she was forced to. When she was twelve, my mother worked at a bakery. Each pastry had to be perfect in order to sell well. She is nagging, but only as a way to ensure herself that her children have not had to experience the hunger and fear she endured. Lastly, she is stubborn, but only because of her tenacity.

My mom is rolling spring rolls for my birthday. Already there are dozens of spring rolls and I have to control myself from sampling one. Spring rolls, or *gỏi cuốn* are my favorite food. I love the satisfying yet refreshing taste of each ingredient that is all conveniently contained by the rice paper. Rice noodles, pork, eggs and various herbs are wrapped tightly by the thin clear rice paper. The long, green vegetables sprout from the end of the spring rolls. The vibrant, orange shrimp pops under the clear rice paper. The entire table is covered in plates, stacked with each component of the spring roll, ready to be wrapped.

"Ngay cả khi hôm nay là sinh nhật của Bao, thì Bao vẫn nên giúp đỡ."[5] I felt bad having my mom make such a tedious meal, so I happily start grabbing the ingredients and helping her roll the spring rolls. Besides, rolling spring rolls is a way for us to bond. I always crack jokes about how my lack of skill and various shapes and looks of spring rolls. This contrasts with her expertise and years of experience in cooking. Her spring rolls match her expectations: perfect and uniform.

Although at times my mother's personality and mine clash, over the years I've learned to notice her forms of affection. During high school, I struggled trying to understand my mom's language. I wasn't aware that love goes beyond words and that my mom's love was always represented through the meals she made each day.

It wasn't until college did I learn to really value the traits that my mom holds. I terribly misinterpreted her attempts to express her love to me. These attempts were often overshadowed by the clashing of our dominating personalities. Underneath our quiet and seemingly timid nature, we are fierce and passionate. We care *too* much, to the point where we aren't afraid to defend our values. Sometimes these values conflict between us. For years I thought that our petty arguments drove a wedge between us, where I couldn't even be around my mom without an argument ensuing soon after. Yet, after

5. Even if today is your birthday, you should still help if you want to eat.

leaving high school, I realized that our similarities are actually a blessing. I've learned to understand my mom more through myself and learned to decipher her ways to communicate with me.

Communication extends beyond words. My mom breaks our language barrier through food. As I continue college and am away from home, I take each dinner as an opportunity to learn more about my family and my culture. Dinner is a chance for families to take a break from their stress and enjoy a meal together, often sharing experiences and stories. When communication may not be clear, people can share their emotions through the food they eat.

*** 

It is a quiet Saturday evening, I look over my textbook. Words like *bánh patê sô* and *gỏi cuốn* stand from the long list of vocabulary. I'm finally back from college during winter break. Finals have passed, but I'm still reviewing my Vietnamese textbook. I want to study for my mom. The University of Michigan offers a class for people like me. People who also face a language barrier with their parents. Each day in lecture, we learn new terminology while reviewing some familiar ones. Although at times I am still embarrassed of my Vietnamese, I'm learning to become more confident.

"Bao! Đi giúp bố!"[6] My mother shouts over the simmering pot of *phở*. *Phở*, or beef noodle soup, has become an increasingly popular meal outside of the Vietnamese community. Phở Joints like, "P *hở* 99", "*Phở King*", and other variations of the same name are scattered across the United States. You can easily indicate the presence of a Vietnamese community based on the amount of Phở restaurants in that area.

There is no dish like *Phở* that represents and embodies Vietnamese culture. Vietnam's history spans for over thirty-five hundred years, yet *Phở* is a relatively new dish. The dish was birthed during the colonial era, a result from the intermingling of Vietnamese, Chinese,

6. Go help your dad!

and French culture. *Phở* is made from simmering the scraps and left over bones of cow carcass. Rice noodles and spices are imported from China, and thus *Phở* was created in attempts for poor street vendors to appeal to the tastes of Chinese and French merchants.

For my family and I, *phở* is defined as a meal of connection and nostalgia. My mom serves a pot of *phở* every time my family is home together. As we are all college students now, we are only connected once a year for Christmas. When I smell *phở*, I am instantly thrown back into my mom's kitchen and eating a meal with my family. Her pot of *phở* has become popular among family and friends. The strong flavor of the broth comes from simmering bones, oxtail, charred onion and ginger as well as steeping various rare spices; this process takes several days, but it is worth the effort.

"Dạ, tôi đi giúp bố xếp bàn."[7] I reply as I start grabbing all the necessities for the dinner table. At this table, we lay out soup spoons and wooden chopsticks. I grab a set of the ceramic rice bowls. Each bowl has a beautiful, hand-painted, blue floral design that was intricately crafted in Vietnam. The bowls contrast greatly with the cheap, artificially white foam plates they are placed atop on. My mom, after preparing the food all day, finally plates the meals. She sets plates of the fresh thai basil, pepper, limes and the "pretty" bean sprouts for the *phở*. It's been a few months since I've gone back home for a family party, but I'm ready for the good food and the sense of familiarity.

\*\*\*

The night continues. My house is overflowing with laughter and gossip, both a mix of English and Vietnamese. Young toddlers of the newer generation race around the house laughing and playing as their mothers follow attempting to feed their running mouths. On one side, the older men drink beer and share stories of their week often banging the dinner table in fits of laughter. On the other side are the younger

7. I'll go help dad set the table.

adults, sharing stories or memes from college and joking with one another. My mom is still busy in the kitchen, preparing the bowls of *phở* for everyone in our families. Yet she is different. There's a wide smile on her face as she gossips in rapid Vietnamese with my aunts. Her eyes are crinkled, and her head leans back when she laughs. Her cackle is distinct: loud and high-pitched.

This is the side of my mom that I am most proud of. When she is able to relax and have fun. There are times in which I feel as though I don't have a firm understanding of who my mom is, yet these moments I am confident that I know her. Despite not being able to communicate that deeply with my mom, I learn to understand her through her actions. These moments remind me that actions speak louder than words—moments when she interacts with her family and friends or when she prepares food for others. The best way to understand the actions of my mom, is to understand the significance of her family in her life. From supporting her family throughout her childhood to nourishing her kids today, her love to others is the main drive in her life.

My mom sets a steaming bowl of *phở* in front of me. The bed of white rice noodles lay beneath the deep red, thin, cuts of meats. The beef balls, tendon and tripe swim in the brown, clear, beef broth. The bowl is garnished with onion, cilantro and a pinch of pepper. I toss in a handful of crisp bean sprouts and fresh thai basil. I squeeze a slice of lime and drizzle the dark hoisin sauce and bright chili sauce across my bowl. Across the house, my relatives follow the same process each bowl personalized to their tastes. I grab my chopsticks, twirling noodles and scooping broth into my broth. My body is eager for this meal. I shove the *phở* into my salivating mouth. When people ask how *phở* tastes, I mention the feeling I get from each bowl. For me, the feeling I get from a bowl of *phở* is equivalent to receiving a warm hug from my mother as well as the familiarity I sense at each family dinner.

# EMILY PINKERTON

**Graduated, December 2019**
**Major:** English and Art History
**Reading:** Flash Fiction

Emily graduated in December, but still weaseled her way into doing Café Shapiro one last time. You may recognize her from the Sweetland Center for Writing, where she was indeed a tutor despite the fact she looks 16. Right now she is hoping to get one (1) acceptance into an MFA program.

*Nominated by: Michael Byers*

# ATO

In just a moment he'll ask the bartender to make it a double. She doesn't know he's done this; she's distracted, helping another couple take blurry pictures on the dance floor of the White Star in Detroit. She'll take her first sip of the drink after that, surprised that the vodka Sprite tastes more like just vodka, but drinking it anyway, since she'd promised herself only one drink tonight.

In ten minutes he'll ask if she wants another and she'll say no. Her empty stomach jolts with the introduction of alcohol, and she knows she'll be tipsy soon. When he asks again, she'll lead him to the dance floor. She's close to him, but not too close. When he pulls her hips toward his own, she'll need to remind him that she's here as a friend.

In twenty-three minutes he'll help her put on her winter jacket. She'll thank him for paying the three dollars for coat check, and they'll board the school bus together, giggling about the shirtless guy who wrapped his tie around his sweaty forehead and gyrated in front of his horrified date all night. When they pick a seat on the rented bus, he'll pull out a flask and offer her some Fireball. She'll decline. He'll take a couple long swigs instead.

In forty-one minutes, while the bus hurtles back to Ann Arbor, she'll rest her head against the back of the seat and feel her eyelids drooping. The bus will be mostly quiet now, at 1 AM, with the other frat boys and their dates either making out or trying not to puke from the bus's lurching movements.

In forty-seven minutes he'll nudge her arm and tilt his head to the left. The couple whose pictures she took earlier are blatantly hooking up a few rows ahead, a suspicious grinding motion indicating they might be doing more than just kissing. He'll wiggle his eyebrows at her and say they should follow suit. She'll laugh a little too hard.

In fifty minutes, as the bus exits the highway, he'll stroke her hair. She'll laugh again, not knowing if he's just being nice or if he's trying to hit on her.

In fifty-one minutes he'll try to kiss her. She'll pull away. He won't.

"What are you doing?" she'll ask.

"Come on," he'll beg.

She'll jerk her head back when he tries to kiss her again, more forcefully. He'll get mad that he took her to his frat's last date party of the semester, spent money on her, only for her to not have sex with him. She'll lean as far away as she can from him, trapped between the walls of the bus and his body, blocking her from leaving their row. That will anger him even more—he's not a creep. She agreed to come with him tonight. She should've known what she was signing up for.

He'll grab her tiny wrists in one hand so she can't shake him off, the grubby fingers of his free hand searching for the hem of her dress, trying to pull it up. Her eyes will be wide in shock, body stiff as she tries to comprehend if this is actually happening. When he reaches her underwear, she'll start fighting him, pushing her bound wrists against his chest for leverage, kicking her knees up.

In fifty-four minutes, he'll finally stop, when the bus parks outside of the frat house and the lights flick on.

Right now, he pulls out his wallet and walks over to the bar.

# Now the Dove and the Leopard Wrestle

In Oklahoma I met the storm chasers: ill-equipped young men, mostly drunk. They bragged to me in the cramped, smoky bar of the Franklin Hotel about the thrill, the adrenaline high. These kids who couldn't have been older than twenty-five chased tornadoes as a hobby in the spring months when the new, warm air currents collided with the cold, dry air like a pair of incensed bighorn rams. What morons, I thought. What absolute buffoons.

One of them, Bobby, or some hick name like it, had died the year before. Got sucked into the biggest one of the season. It occurred to me they seemed proud of this death; it reinforced their machismo, their testosterone-fueled gallantry. They were never able to recover one of Bobby's torn-off arms from the debris scattered across a three-mile radius. When they did finally find him, his face was so beaten up police had to identify the body through dental records. They leaned too close to me when they told me this, their drunk, waxy eyes widening with each gory detail.

They invited me to chase with them. It was May, after all, they said. Prime time in Tornado Alley. Being bored and unemployed and maybe a little bit high, I agreed. There was supposed to be a bad storm that weekend, with all the "fixins for a twister". Their words.

The boneheads pulled up to the hotel in an unmarked white van a couple days later, as promised, wild grins plastered to their faces. I tucked the last of my stash and a small metal spoon in my sock, and clambered into the backseat. Go Pros were strapped haphazardly to the kids' foreheads and chests, like they were Bear fucking Grylls filming his nature show. The interior of the van spoke to a history of rigorous chain-smoking. Fumes from the muddied beige upholstery wafted continuously up my nose, so much so that I could've sworn I got a nicotine buzz that first half hour. I rode that anemic high as we hurtled down crumbling roads and dirt paths on what I was sure was private property, and all the while the guy in the passenger seat dangled halfway out the open window, his binoculars informing the driver's course.

It wasn't very impressive when we found one. Didn't even touch down, actually. The atmosphere buzzed a deathly green, as it should, and golf ball-sized hail mangled the right mirror, which excited me and enraged the van's driver. The funnel, thick and grey and angry, stopped about thirty feet above the ground before it began its retreat back into the storm clouds.

I'd heard that tornadoes were supposed to sound like an oncoming train blasting its horn, but the one we watched whimpered as it lost momentum. The occasional loose plastic bag or lacerated twig slapped the van's windows pitifully. It seemed the tornado's dying force mirrored my own trajectory—an unimaginable fury rendered powerless by its own brief and fickle nature.

When I pulled the small, wrinkled baggie from my sock, the storm chasers didn't protest. This was part of the deal. Of course none of the idiots brought a spoon. Luckily, I planned ahead. After the first hit, I felt the ground slip out from under my feet and hang over my head, my body remaining in the van like a disembodied ghost. I imagined being lifted by the tornado that we should've seen, an immense, hulking beast. It didn't discard me. Instead, it swept me into its motion, and I circled the epicenter, gently, my fingertips reaching out to graze the lovely squall.

# SAM PINKUS

**Freshman**
**Major:** Sociology
**Reading:** Fiction Short Story

Sam was born and raised in sunny Los Angeles, California. From the age she could hold a pen, Sam has filled journals, written short stories, and ultimately plans on writing a Young Adult novel. In her free time, Sam enjoys going to concerts, trying new restaurants in Ann Arbor, and traveling the world.

*Nominated by: Nishanth Injam*

# I'm Sorry, Charlotte

It's a funny thing, really. We think we know everything, see the whole picture. Our judgment becomes so goddamn certain that at some point or another, our minds become closed off to any and all ideas that we just might be missing a piece of the story.

\* \* \*

Charlotte and I were six when Mother left. My twin and I held each other in our makeshift fort of protection, "the Igloo" we called it, drowning out the sound of Mother throwing things at Father. I heard my favorite set of plates hit the wall. We only had one set of glass, the rest were plastic. Charlotte winced as Lucky's fish tank crashed against the floor. I still miss that ugly goldfish.

In the Igloo, however, we were able to live a life that let Charlotte and I escape the horrors in front of us. We could be superheroes or famous people or soccer stars. It was the world we wished we had. A world outside of our tiny Virginia neighborhood. One day, around the time we were eight, once Mother was gone and Father was out drinking, instead of getting ourselves ready and to school, we stayed home. We spent the whole day creating an alternate universe with pillows and old toilet paper rolls and drawings. Charlotte was particularly good at crafts. I preferred to build. Into the evening, we constructed our colorful universe in the Igloo.

We called it Paradise. After all, anywhere but here was Paradise.

On one spring day when we were 12, Father came home drunk. Yes, this happened every day. Yes, Charlotte and I knew how to get him laying down on the couch, in an upright position.

Charlotte would cover him in a blanket and say a prayer. I would bring over the rusty trash can, a glass of cold water, and a molding piece of bread to our passed out father. He often forgot to go to the grocery store leaving us with rotting and smelly dinners. This night, however, was different. Charlotte and I were jolted awake extra nervously from our bunk bed. It felt like the whole entire small house was going to crash down as Father threw photograph after photograph onto the cold wooden floors. Once the walls and mantels were void of all life or proof of family, he moved to the furniture turning our sofa to shreds with his pocket knife, our floors hidden behind large shards of glass. When we gained the courage to try and stop him, he picked up one of the glass shards, eyes blazing. "Don't come near me you dumb shits," he said loudly through his bloodshot eyes. "Your whore of a mother should have taken you with her. For fuck's sake, I should have put you two out on the street for being such ungrateful assholes for everything I fucking do for you," this time yelling. Then, he did the one thing that I have had nightmares of since Mother left. I promised myself if he touched her, we would leave.

Before either Charlotte or I knew it, Father leaped at her. "You deserve this, you little bitch. You're a whore just like your mother, aren't you, little girl?" Unfortunately, Charlotte and I were both cursed with mother's genes. We were small. Charlotte smaller than I, but to put it simply, I was a 12-year-old boy without pubic hair in my near future.

I screamed, but nothing came out. I stood watching as my father violated my sister, taking her purity and innocence from her. She too was silent as blood spilled onto the glass-covered floor. The color had left both the cheeks of my twin and Father. I just watched, glued to the floor, unable to move or do anything. I screamed once again, this time nothing but a small wail escaping my white face and shrunken lips. It felt like it went on forever, days or months or years, the only sound filling the small, destroyed room, coming from Father's grunts and anger as he pounded into my broken sister. We were never the same.

*** 

"Kids, you are going to be late, get your tushies out of bed and downstairs; breakfast is on the table," I heard my wife yell to our 8 and 12-year-olds through her teeth brushing. I don't know how she did it really. She truly was my superhero. Before I could continue basking in my thoughts, she was coming to my side of the bed, placing a small kiss on my forehead, and drawing the curtain as she did each day for the last two months. I tried my best to give her my apologetic smile, the smile that told her I was so sorry for everything I had put her through as of late, a smile that told her I was trying to be everything she needed, a smile that wanted to scream "I love you and will do better." Nothing came out, it never did. A weak smile was the best I could muster up for my wife of 15 years who had nursed not only my beautiful children but my sorry ass for the last two months since I quit my job on Wall Street, making my bed and the hospital my permanent offices.

✳✳✳

There are three days in my 42 years of life that I remember perfectly. The day Charlotte was raped, the day I shared my vows with my beautiful bride, Joi, and the call telling me that Charlotte was sick with stage four cancer; she had four months, max, to live.

Maybe it was because we most literally shared the womb or because I had a pang of unwavering guilt coursing through my body since I was 12 years old. Maybe it was because she was all I had for so many years or because we eventually escaped a fate that was sure to kill us.

She was my north star, the strongest person I knew. The world was trying to take her from me and I couldn't protect her again. I tried to scream but nothing came out.

✳✳✳

Lugging myself out of bed as I did daily, I avoided the pale and brittle corpse I saw in the mirror. I ignored the questions I heard from the hallway of my children asking why they couldn't see daddy or why daddy was hiding. My wife's excuses began falling short and even so, they eventually stopped asking. I avoided the overgrown lawn as I entered my automobile. Mowing the grass had always been my job. I think leaving it grown was in some way, my wife's hope that I would return to normalcy and mow the goddamn lawn. We both knew I wouldn't any time soon.

As if on cue, the nurses dressed in blue greeted me at the front desk assuring me that Charlotte was stable, as they did each day. I nodded gratefully and handed Pattie, Charlotte's favorite nurse, her treasured glazed donut from the bakery down the road. "Don't tell the others," I would try to joke when I had it in me. Other times, I blankly handed her the bag. I did, however, always get the donut. It was in some strange way my attempt of living like Charlotte. She would want to make sure that others were taken care of in place of her. She never put herself first. It was just one of the many ways I would never compare to the beauty and grace that was my best friend, my savior.

✳✳✳

Before I entered room 465, I would take a breath and repeat the prayer Charlotte used to say to our father, back when she had faith in his goodness. "I love you like man loves woman. I need you like earth needs water. I look to you like wind does fire. I pray for you with everything I have. One more night, one more day, My world is not a life I can live without you in it." I then silently add, "you are everything he was not. You are everything she never could be. You are everything I want to be. I love you."

It never hurt to smile when I saw my sister like it did everything else. Even with cords coming out of her in every direction, she was perfect. She had always been my version of perfect. I kissed her right cheek and took my seat in the chair next to her. I would begin by making up stories from the work I had not been to in months. I would move on to information on the kids that I hoped was true; the sports they were playing, the awards they were winning, the top grades they were earning. She never answered, but I know she was listening. She always listened.

I would sit with her for hours, sometimes in silence, sometimes holding her hand, some times reading her favorite poems by Emily Dickinson and Edgar Allan Poe aloud. I know this is what she would have wanted. I could feel it.

"Theo, don't forget your cleats. You have a soccer game at 4:00 pm today. Ashley, grab your violin and put it in the car. Grandma is going to take you to practice after school," my wife told the kids as she applied powder and pink blush to her already rosy cheeks. She was so naturally beautiful. I wondered each and every day how she continued to put up with her husband who now lived in a world so far away from his family. She kissed my forehead and opened the blinds. Today, I found myself with a little extra energy. I squeezed her hand. I want to believe she knew that was my way of saying, "Thank you. I love you. I'm sorry."

Like clockwork, I handed Pattie her donut. Today, however, she did not make a snarky remark about why I was the reason she could never keep a diet or date a man longer than three weeks. There was something different in her eyes today. Something different in all of the nurses. Did they change uniforms or was the mood so obviously grey that their normally bright outfits looked just a bit more muted?

"Pattie, what is it?" I muttered as the color disappeared from my flesh. She told me Charlotte's health had rapidly declined the previous night. She believed she was only holding on until I arrived. I did not answer her.

I stood outside room 465 a few extra moments that day reciting my prayer. I knew this would be the second to last time I would say it.

She lasted just a few more hours. The nurses told me there was nothing they could do. I was silent. My mind raced with things I needed to say while my mouth remained sealed shut by imaginary super glue. I barely remember seeing my wife at the hospital. I didn't have the energy to move away from her as she tried to comfort me in her warm arms. Bless my sweet wife's soul, but she didn't understand that Charlotte was who I needed. Charlotte was the one to comfort me when we were 14 and hungry and stealing lemons from Ms. Dawn's tree down the road to make and sell bitter lemonade. We held each other in Ms. Dawn's dog house on the colder nights. She didn't know that Charlotte was the one to get us jobs at 16 working at McDonald's in the town over, 30 hours a week, in exchange for a bed in the backhouse of the owner's home. We shared that bed for 2 years like it was the Four Seasons in Beverly Hills. She didn't understand that

Charlotte stayed up for one year, unbeknown to me, sneaking to the main house's computer to find and apply for dozens and dozens of college scholarships to ensure we had a bright future somewhere far away from our desolate life in Virginia.

\*\*\*

"My sister was the greatest person I know. No, fuck that. My sister was the greatest person to ever walk this whole large ass universe. She brought joy to nothingness, strength to the deepest pain. She found happiness in darkness, she pushed on when one million cinder blocks did everything in their power to push her down.

We did a good job of hiding the truth for a long time. Charlotte always told me people would look at us funny if they knew our past. She was right. She was always right. And yet, all of you here deserve to know the truth about my sister. The person I grew with both physically and literally.

When Charlotte and I were young, our life seemed normal. That's a funny thought though. Is a toddler able to decipher normalcy? Charlotte probably could. She could do anything. And yet, what you couldn't see by looking at my beautiful sister was her past. She didn't want you to and in writing this eulogy I considered repeatedly whether to share this with you. It is time, I have come to understand, for you all to know who this woman was. She was so much more than a sweet lady who lost her life to fucking cancer.

At 6 years old our mother left. We didn't hear from her until our mid thirties when someone called and told us she had died. Charlotte and I ate dinner together silently that night. That was the only time we came close to recognizing her death. When we were 12, our father raped Charlotte. I didn't stop it. My sweet sister, I am so sorry. Our 14th birthday was the day we escaped that house. It was our birthday gift to one another. We lived off close to nothing for a while. Ms. Dawn's lemons and dog house kept us alive. We kept going to school. We knew our way out was education. Well, Charlotte knew that. She knew everything. We began working full time at 16. McDonald's kept us afloat. Left over chicken nuggets and Big Mac's made us feel full for the first time in two years. At 18, Charlotte and I both were given scholarships, that she had spent hours searching for, to Georgetown. It seemed like we had finally made it. I apologized to Charlotte before I went to sleep every night. I said I was sorry I didn't save her. So fucking sorry.

Nothing ever beat my sister down. Even when she got the diagnosis that her life was coming to an end, I could feel her smiling on the other end of the phone as she told me she had lived a beautiful life and she was thankful for her time on this earth. I don't know where this bravery came from. It sure as hell wasn't from me.

My sweet Charlotte, "I love you like man loves woman…You are everything I want to be.

I love you."

Rest easy sweet sister of mine. I am sorry."

✳ ✳ ✳

When I arrived home after the funeral, I looked at the lawn. Four months of being unkempt will make a lawn look pretty fucking ugly. It was going to stay that way. I continued bringing Pattie her donut every day.

# HOLLY PRICE

**Sophomore**
**Major:** Creative Writing and Literature
**Reading:** Fiction

Holly is a Creative Writing and Literature Major passionate about education and social policy. She loves to write fiction and non-fiction, but is an awful poet (not that it stops her). Some of her favorites are Maya Angelou, Kurt Vonnegut, William Faulkner, and Jesmyn Ward.

*Nominated by: Leslie Stanton*

# TRUST ME

gaslighting  (*present participle*)
manipulate (someone) by psychological means into questioning their own sanity.

It's not that I don't trust you, it's that I don't trust those other guys.

It's nice that you're looking out for me, but I can make decisions for myself. Not those other guys. I love you, but your fears are unwarranted. I'm going to the party. You can't stop me, and the minute you try and control me I'm out. I'm not going to be one of those girls who ignores their friends and completely changes their lives to make their boyfriend feel more secure or whatever bullshit.

You're going to wear that?

Should I not? What's wrong with my outfit? It's only a pair of jeans and a crop top, nothing crazy. There is nothing wrong with what I'm wearing.

No, I didn't mean it like that. You can absolutely wear whatever you want. I just think it's weird you want to dress up for a party, when you have no one to impress.

I wanted to feel pretty. I don't get dressed up for other people, I get dressed up to feel confident in myself.

I'm just wondering why are you wearing that when you have a boyfriend? I'm not saying you look like a slut or anything like that. I'm saying you look single.

Why would you say that? Why would you even bring it up if I didn't look like one? Why is the word that pops into your head slut when you look at me? No, I don't look slutty, I look like your girlfriend in a crop top.

I just want to know why you want to go out if you're not trying to get with anybody. That makes no sense.

I want to go out and have fun with my friends. Not everyone goes out to parties to get with someone or whatever.

Parties are literally only for hooking up. No one goes to parties to have a 'good time' with their friends. Guys go to fuck girls. I'm just looking out for you because I care about you.

I'm not a guy. I don't know how they think. But I can speak for women, and my friends and I don't go out to hook up with guys. *What if I get put in a bad situation? I really like this guy, I've fallen in love with him. I want it to work out.*

I'm never going to tell you not to go out. I never said that.

*He's not controlling me. He's not telling me not to go out. He's just telling me to be careful. Maybe I shouldn't go out. Maybe it'll be better for me and him if I stay home. I can have fun with my friends in other ways.*

I know it doesn't mean you're going to now. But with how you were in your past, I would just feel better if I came with you.

You can't always come with me. Me having fun with my friends is just like you having fun with yours.

I can't come?

No.

Why don't you want me to come?

I never said I didn't want you to come. I said you can't come.

So you expect me to just stay home while you're out at a party where a bunch of horny guys are, and not worry? If you're going to go out, you should at least text me updates so I know you're safe.

It shouldn't matter that there are tons of horny guys or whatever. It doesn't matter because I'm not going to do anything with them. I'm with you. I love you. I can absolutely text you updates if that would make you feel better.

I still don't understand why I can't go. How will I know you're not doing anything bad if I can't see you? How will I know if you go somewhere else if you don't tell me? You should also share your location, and snapchat me instead of text. So I know you're safe.

Not everyone is out there to sleep with random people! I'm not like that. Again, I'm with you – you're literally the only guy I think of. That's why I'm dating you. If I wanted to screw around with other people, I would be single! But I'm not! It shouldn't matter that guys are out there trying to get laid because they have been since the end of time. I'd appreciate it if you stopped acting as if I'm going to cheat on you.

I never said that I think you're going to cheat on me. However, most cheating in college occurs at parties.

So because I go to parties that means I'm going to cheat on you? You're right, you never said that. But you implied it.

You're not listening. I'm just saying that most cheating occurs at parties. And why wouldn't it? Let's take you and me, for example- only as an example, I swear. You dress up in those clothes and go to 'have fun' or whatever you do with your friends. You are surrounded by smarter, more attractive, richer, popular guys. You are literally surrounded by temptation. How can I not sit at home the entire time and worry?

Temptation? How am I not listening? And I'll change out of the crop top, if that will make you feel better, and wear less form fitting jeans. *I'm not even sure I'll have fun with my friends if I go out now, now all I'm going to be thinking about is you being anxious that something is going to happen to me because he's not there.* I know you're only looking out for me, but I'll be fine. I promise.

I'm not saying you're going to cheat on me, I'm saying that there will be temptation.

I know. But I'm not going to be tempted, because I'm not sure if I'm going to go now. I might just stay home, and watch Netflix, and talk to you. It'll be better for the both of us. I don't don't even really want to go anymore. I'm sure Nick will understand.

You're saying that Nick is at these parties?

Yes, my best friend Nick, remember? And why are you giving me a look?

I'm not giving you a look. It's just obvious that he wants you, or has wanted you in the past, that's all. Do you think he became friends with you because of your personality? No, it's because he thinks you're hot and if he had the chance he would fuck you, so he's keeping you around.

Why are you giving me a look, then? You have nothing to worry about. That's not why he became my friend, because I'm pretty sure he didn't have sexual thoughts at five-years-old. All that should matter is I'm not sexually or romantically attracted to him at all. He's just a friend, seriously. I know I hang out with him instead of you sometimes, but I can hang out with you more if it'll make you feel more secure. I just want you to be happy and not stress or worry.

I don't want you to be taken advantage of, that's all. I care about you. I care about you too, I love you.

I told you, my last relationship was shitty. She did horrible things. She would go to parties and flirt with guys and take her shirt off and snap her ex. I didn't trust her at all. I have trust issues, and I'm insecure about you with other guys as a result.

I wouldn't do that to you. I'll be better, I'll do better, I promise. I know trust is hard, but I'll prove I'm trustworthy. I'll stay home tonight, and I won't go to those parties anymore. I'll keep my phone on me at all times. I will text you immediately after receiving messages. I will be available to talk whenever you want me to. Here, you can even have my phone password (8209) so you can look in my phone. I'll prove I have nothing to hide. I'll stop hanging out with my best friend as much, until eventually it turns into me not hanging out with him at all and him dropping me for being a shitty friend. I may end up being a shitty friend, but I'll be the best, most loyal, most trustworthy girlfriend ever. You have nothing to worry about. Trust me.

# SANJANA RAMESH

**Senior**
**Major:** English
**Reading:** Fiction

Sanjana is a senior in the English department, and often a senior when it comes to stairs too. Having graduated from writing solely in cliches, Sanjana aims to defamiliarize the familiar, sneaking in the fantastical elements from books she loved as a child into her work. All work is strictly dedicated first and foremost to her cat, Nooni, partly because there is no one who's a harsher judge and partly because that judge can't really do much except meow her critique.

*Nominated by: Patricia O'Dowd*

# Haku

It was getting cold outside.

The skies were cast in mottled shades of bright white and slate gray with the barest hint of sun, shining. Fog had settled over the morning frost like a veil and the cold seeped into and under my skin like poison, spreading its icy tendrils within the crook of my elbow, the palm of my hand, turning my nails a deep purple.

The box was always open but I'd never had a reason to lay its guts bare before me: colored sweaters, and old dresses made of some floaty material I would never wear, and cardigans, and scarves, and old woolen shirts. But it was cold and I was cold and their time had come.

*

I met Haku in the fall of 2016. Or at least, I think it was 2016. It gets harder to remember with the barrage of pills clouding my mind and clouding my memories. Time works differently within the confines of my mind. The days seem endless and infinite, but memories anchor me to my sense of self like cornerstones. I can't remember if it's always been this way, but I tell myself that if I can't remember maybe it isn't worth remembering. In any event, the Tuscan air was crisp and new and the colors of the leaves were slowly blushing red, being touched with sunlight and turning golden. I'd fled across the world in search of a new home or a new life or a new beginning or maybe just a change of scenery.

I don't remember if I saw her when I moved in. I definitely don't remember if she was one of the twenty-three girls who had piled into my room on the first day. I'd like to think that I would have remembered if she had been there, but I do not pay deceit. I do remember what might have been the first time I saw her, though, and I remember thinking that she seemed so...feline.

I'd been walking out of the lobby right as she'd been walking in and when I'd turned because her shadow had fallen on me, I couldn't see her face. All I saw was the sun shining like a halo behind her tightly curled head and her long legs and the rings on her fingers and the trademark black Docs. She'd barely glanced at me before sweeping away in her distinctive gait, all shoulder-blades and long, ponderous strides. I'd left not soon after.

\*

"Oh my god, you dinosaur. You actually made a Facebook!"
"I did! Bitch, I miss you. How are you?"
"I miss you too. I've been good. How about you? How's London?"
"It's incredible; I wish you were here."
"Yeah."

\*

I'd like to say that we became firm friends almost instantly. That's a lie. We didn't really know each other for the better part of the whole year we "knew" each other.

We ran with the same crowd and we'd frequently congregate in her room because it was the nicest, and we'd have dinner together at a table under the high-vaulted ceilings of the dining hall that became *our* table. We went to the club on weekends and drank till there was no sane part of us left. We went to a diner, innovatively called The Diner, which had the only American food that tasted remotely American and she'd always order an Oreo milkshake. We went to operas. We went shopping. We went for fucking gelato, and even though there were only five people between us, Haku and I still hadn't said a single word to each other.

I knew her name. She knew mine. We didn't know each other. We were friends.

Three weeks after moving in, I ended up in the hospital for a week. I wish I'd been in for broken bones. Instead I was in for a broken mind. I'd left my phone at home, spending the week smoking cigarettes while writing on borrowed paper, under the watchful eye of a nurse who didn't understand the words she watched over. She was only interested in making sure I didn't spirit away the pen. I'd looked at the blue sky behind the bars on my windows, speaking broken Italian to a woman who didn't speak English, and sneaking tea in from the kitchen, and shutting the door of the toilet with my foot, and not taking a single shower because just because I was crazy didn't mean I didn't want privacy. My hair had never smelled worse.

When I got back, I found I had no friends left. It bothered me for a while and then it didn't. My ambivalence might have been rooted in a haze of weed and vodka shots and prescribed pills, but it felt real enough that it helped. Not talking to them meant not being around her. She was still in every one of my classes and when the others weren't looking, she'd hold my gaze and not say a single word. I always looked away first.

*

"SUN'S OUT LETS HANG!"
"*Dude, I'm sleeping.*"
"*Haku, I will only say this once...*"
"*Yes. I'm listening.*"
"*...get the fuck up.*"

*

The spring brought about some kind of new promise. It was a naïve thought at best, and I knew it, but the feeling persisted. The skies were a clear blue and the whole landscape had been transformed by the blooms that spread across the countryside like a beautiful disease. I reveled in the profound sadness and untold joy of enjoying it alone.

The fountain had been dry when I got here and had been that way for a while. I sat on its stone walls, warm from the afternoon sun, a cigarette between my lips and an empty heart. It was great here because it was frequented by few people, and those who did pass by were always just passerbys. I looked at the sky and wondered why my life was the way it was, why I had no friends and why that didn't bother me like it should and whether that meant that I had no feelings and how much evidence I had to support that. A week in the hospital had helped with the mental situation in some way, but it only served to lead to further doubts on the condition of my brokenness. Was I less so now? Was I more? Was it that going there was for the parts that could be fixed and being sent back was for the parts that couldn't?

"Hey. It's been a while."

I looked up. I nodded. I offered her a cigarette.

"Yeah, it has."

Haku sat beside me and we smoked my whole pack.

I can't remember how things turned out very well after that. I remember we started talking about writing and how we enjoyed each other's words and me saying how I thought she was a phenomenal writer and how she should write a book. I remember her saying she was. I remember, then, laughing at the ironic note in her voice when she told me that her editor had written to her this morning but she was ghosting him like she was ghosting her parents and her psychiatrist and *yeah, yeah, it's a bad habit but what can you do, you know?* I remember how the evening fell and even as the sun disappeared from the sky, I still found it in her eyes and I wondered what it was that I felt and how I had answered my own question as to whether I could feel at all.

*

"I'm going to go get some wine."

"Chill with the wine. I've got vodka."

"I mean if you don't mind..."

"Bitch, of course I don't fucking mind."

"Hey, it's been hammered into me-"

"I know Alice. Just get to Coletta already. I'm with Salinger."

"Great."

*

"Haku, babe, hand me the goddamn Pax,"

She looked at my outstretched hand and then broke into a Cheshire cat smile. Smoke seeped through the gaps in her teeth, through her nostrils as she shook her head and pressed it to her chapped lips again, inhaling deeply, before breaking into a coughing fit. I rolled my eyes, rolled my hand towards her as she pressed the little black bar into my palm.

"You're fucking ridiculous."

"You would know, Al."

We lapsed into silence; my gaze was firmly fixed on her ceiling as I thought about how wonderfully comfortable this couch was and how comfortingly far the smoke detector happened to be and how weird it was that it felt like I was in a movie I would watch and adore and how that made me feel and how this was really my life and how it was because of her. I heard Haku shuffling off the bed. I turned my gaze on her. She winked at me and pulled the bourbon out of her bottom shelf. I opened my mouth to tell her that that probably was a bad idea and then figured that, if it *was* a bad idea, I better partake in it.

She held my hair back for the first half of the end of the night and I spent the rest consoling her. Her eyes were wet but her cheeks stayed dry and she held herself as she swallowed her tears and sobbed noiselessly on the too-clean tiles.

*"I always fuck things up, Alice."*

*

*"You doing okay, Al?"*

*"I'm scared."*

*"Is anyone with you?"*

*"No."*

*"Are you drunk?"*

*"Yes."*

*"Do you need me to come get you?"*
*"No."*

✳

*Hey, you home?*

My phone lit up and I texted her back letting her know that I was and that I could let her up and did she need me? She said yes. Yes. Yes. I looked around at my room, at the heaps of clothes in different places and the wine bottles in the corner. I heard her yelling for me downstairs.

When I buzzed her in, she shouldered past me into the hallway noiselessly. I pointed her to my room and she shrugged and said she already knew where it was. That gave me pause.

"How?"

"Oh, I was one of the people who called Silvana to come take you to the hospital when you broke down. Do you not remember?" Haku looked at me, "Never mind. Stupid question."

I watched as she put her bag down with a practiced air and then sat at the edge of my bed. We looked at each other. I crossed the room and sat down across from her. We pulled out our laptops and worked in silence for but a half hour.

Then, she pushed her laptop towards me and got up to stretch her legs, strolling up to the mirror. *For English,* she'd titled it. I read about how she didn't feel like she belonged and how every time she was in Japan it didn't feel like home because even though she was Japanese, she wasn't Japanese enough and when she was back home she wasn't black enough. She wrote about how even when she had been with Kia she hadn't been enough for her and that even when she'd taken the blame for the needles and the blades, she hadn't been enough for herself. I watched her poke and prod at herself as I looked through her words and when she said that not feeling enough was an extension of not fully being one thing or another but a combination of both but also neither at the same time, I couldn't help but find my own reflection in that mirror beside her.

# JACOB REPUCCI

**Freshman**
**Major:** Undecided
**Reading:** Fiction

Jacob Repucci is a dragon slayer hailing from Maine. He's been writing ever since he could spell, mostly about spaceships, wizards, or occasionally wizards flying spaceships. While science is his primary focus of study, he plans on writing all manner of stories in his free time. He's often found doing homework, formulating hot takes about the film industry, or staring off into space.

*Nominated by: Carl Lavigne*

# Titans

Erik Lindbergh leaned against the railing of the pier, gazing out at the Caravel-Class Starcruiser stretched over the ocean in front of him. A light on is front blinked rapidly, once for every time a signal from the Rosetta Signal was received. His pilot's license hung, dangling from his fingers above the churning Atlantic beneath him.

"Still considering, son?"

Erik jumped and turned to find General Regashi standing behind him. The thin Japanese-American was clearly sweltering beneath the hot sun, his military garb, cap, and his pepper-colored mustache.

"You can take the hat off," said Erik. "No one's watching."

"I'm still on duty, Captain Lindbergh," said Regashi.

"I'm not a captain," said Erik. "Haven't accepted anything yet."

Regashi sighed and moved to stand next to Erik. The two stood, watching the rippling waves stretched out as far as the eye could see.

"I've talked to the board," he said. "They'll only accept the best pilots for Persephone."

Erik sighed. "You'll need to keep looking then."

"I've tried."

Erik tapped his pilot's license against the railing, thinking.

"Not everyone gets this opportunity," continued Regashi.

"Not everyone wants it, either," said Erik.

Regashi frowned before taking a breath.

"I've wanted this since I saw my first Titan. They flew overhead during a military parade, just after the war on Mercury. I remember thinking, 'I want to be up there.'" said Regashi. "Every pilot in the force remembers a day like that."

"Not sure I remember something like that," said Erik.

But of course he did.

"Are we there yet?" said Erik, echoing the cry of children on road trips everywhere.

"What did I tell you five minutes ago?" said his dad.

"We'd get there at 11:00," said Erik.

"And what does the clock say?" said his father, pointing at the car's holo-clock.

"10:50..." said Erik.

"We'll be there soon," said his mom. "Are you excited?"

"I guess," said Erik. "I just wish I stayed home so I could play VR with Isabella..."

"We talked about this," said his father, putting his hands on his head, letting the self-driving car do the work. "This is a very special trip. Isabella wishes she could trade places with you."

"Yeah, but she *wants* to be a Titan pilot!" said Erik. "I wanna make VR games..."

"Maybe you'll make a game about Titans," said his mom. "What about that?"

"I guess..." said Erik.

"Look, there it is!" said his dad as they rounded a bend, pointing to a large glass building with a tall tower jutting out of it. "The National Titan Museum! Doesn't it look cool?"

Erik humphed. He was too young to appreciate architecture.

When the car stopped, Erik slumped out after his parents. They stopped in front of a plaque. It read,

MAY ALL WHO OBSERVE THIS MONUMENT ENGINEER PEACE,
NOT WAR

-John Vaucanson, 2884,
At the dedication of the museum

"Engineering," said his mom. "Ever thought of that?"

Erik grunted, prompting his parents to lead him inside.

They were greeted by a receptionist, who offered them a brochure. His mother handed him one, which he clenched in his fist. After redeeming their tickets, Erik's mom went to use the bathroom. This was when his dad took him to the side.

"Erik," he said. "Your mom and I worked very hard to buy these tickets for you. This is a very big gift that we gave you, and it's meant to be enjoyed. Understood?"

Erik nodded.

"Please smile for mom, okay?"

Erik tilted the sides of his mouth up his father stood up, before letting his face relax again. When his mom came back, he put on the same mask as they lead him to the big double doors to the next room. The mask evaporated as they entered.

A giant banner that read "THE MODEL A" was draped over the hanger-sized room. The walls and center of the room were lined with myriads of different mechs. Erik lead his parents to the first mech he saw, a grey behemoth that was little more than a tank with squatting legs and claws for arms. The plaque beneath it read:

"THE MODEL A-109

The first Titan to be put to military use in the Titan Program. Emergency commissioned to deal with the Asteroid Belt Crisis of 2590. Equipped with anti-spacecraft guns and a limited-range rocket booster, it excelled in traversing the asteroid belt to deal with threats to the then Council of Space Fairing Humanity (CSFH)."

"What do you think, Erik?" said his mom.

"People drove this?" he said.

"They fought in it, too," said his dad.

Erik dragged them from that mech to the next, to the next. Some of them had machine-guns, heavy laser cannons, or larger jetpacks.

Soon, Erik saw every single one of them, read every plaque.

"Are there more?" he said.

His father laughed. "We haven't even made it to the Model B's!"

They went through another set of doors to find another room, this one with the banner "THE MODEL B" above it. These ones resembled humans more closely, with two long legs, a sensor-head, and two arms equipped with weapons on the end. Kneeling, it was about twenty feet tall. Erik could only imagine how tall it could be when standing. Erik breezed through these ones, inhaling two centuries of space navy history in the span of thirty minutes. You could have quizzed him on the Mercury uprisings, the space pirate outbreaks of the 2750s, and the exploration of Saturn's rings, and he would have passed with flying colors.

His face fell at the last Model B titan he saw.

"The plaque says this is the latest model," said Erik. "Does that mean we have to go home now?"

His dad chuckled. "There's one more Titan to see...Remember that tower you saw outside?"

They walked through the last set of doors into that same tower. Erik gasped. Above him stood a mech that must be at least 100 feet tall, bearing a narrow shield that ran the length of its body. Sharp stabilizers with rocket boosters nested beneath them folded down behind its back. A holographic sign in front of it read, "THE MODEL C."

Erik read the plaque.

"THE MODEL C:

A proposed model that has passed initial testing. With more speed, maneuverability, and armor than the Model B's, this unit is slated to be a part of the Persephone Mission to Pluto to investigate the Rosetta Signal in 2910."

The mechs he had seen before had captured his imagination well enough; but this model was finally the one that captured his heart.

"I want to fly that," he said.

# HOLLY SMITH

**Freshman**
**Major:** Undecided
**Reading:** Short Fiction

Holly is from Huntington Woods, a small city in the Detroit suburbs. She has no idea what to major in, but hopes to go into social work and work in the adoption and the foster care system. She feels super grateful to be attending the best university in the world and enjoys reading, running, and spending time with her family and church.

*Nominated by: Carl Lavigne*

# Ever Since Tuesday

Back on Monday, I had been sitting in Mrs. Mitchell's class, watching the clock. Even though I couldn't really read it, I knew that when the big hand touches the 12 and the little hand touches three, it's always time to go. That's what Jordan told me.

Mrs. Mitchell was talking about how we needed to put on our listening hats, but I couldn't find mine because I couldn't see it. I was just pretending I had it on so I wouldn't have to 'face the consequences.' She kept saying we never respect her, but I didn't really care because I just wanted to go home. So I stopped listening and looked out the window, waiting for the little hand to let me leave.

...

After school, I saw Jordan watching for me outside by the bike racks. As soon as he spotted me coming, he turned and started walking towards our house without even waiting for me. I had to run super fast to catch up to him and almost even got hit by a car in the parking lot (but I still caught him).

"Jordan! Guess what!" I had a lot to tell him and not a lot of breath after running so fast. "Today Mrs. Mitchell was so boring but for science she brought in rocks and we looked at them and I almost snuck one home but Ania Johnson told on me and so I had to sit in the hall but while I was in the hall I saw Ania through the window picking her nose and so I told her that and that made her cry but she deserved it since she got me in trouble and so I—"

"Yeah, yeah, whatever," Jordan was in middle school, so now he never listened to me.

I kept going. "I had—"

"Shut up, Greg."

"But I—" When we got to the street, I tried to grab his hand, but he wouldn't let me.

"You're stupid."

I huffed and waited until we crossed to try again. "Okay, but–"

"Greg, *stop.* " Something in Jordan's voice had changed, so I looked up to see what he was staring at.

We had made it to the front of our house. It looked like normal–weed-filled yard and anthills sticking out the cracks in the driveway and paint peeling from the shutters.

But right now, Jordan was frowning at the window.

Mom and Dad were both inside, and that was pretty weird. Usually, Dad isn't even at home before I go to bed and I never see him in the mornings, so actually it was *super* weird that he was there. But I forgot all that when I saw him and Mom.

He looked mad, like really, really, *really* mad. He was shouting, and I imagined steam coming from his ears like in the movies I sometimes watch on the weekends. He started throwing things at Mom, and she kept trying to get away, but our kitchen's not that big, and she couldn't get away, and he kept stomping after her.

Without realizing, I grabbed Jordan's hand. This time, he didn't pull away.

It hurt really bad to keep watching, so we just stared at the ants at our feet.

—— *Wednesday* ——

On Wednesday, Gramma let me stay home for the day. Since she'd gotten here, her face had stayed crinkled up in this worried-looking frown, and she was acting kinda weird to me. So I spent the morning outside, watching ants march around and around and it was so cool. They were all stuck inside the chalk outline of my dad that the police drew on the cement in front of my house when he died on Tuesday. I was standing inside the outline watching them because they were so stupid, they couldn't figure out how to get over the chalk. But I knew how to get out because I could just step over the line and be free. But *they* couldn't, so when they *did* escape, I would stomp on them really hard. But I didn't stomp on the red ants–only the black ones because Jordan told me the red ants would sting like a bumblebee, and that made me nervous.

"Greg, get away from there!"

Gramma was yelling from the porch again, and I jumped. I think the reason she moved in was because Mom was crying a lot. Probably because of how Dad had just died. Gramma really didn't like me playing near the chalk outline, but I think if she saw the marching ants she'd think it was cool, too, and come stomp with me.

So I was watching really hard as one of the ants escaped the chalk, but it was a red one and so I wasn't gonna stomp it but Gramma yelled again and I was startled and my foot landed on the red ant. Ever since Tuesday, when Gramma moved in after Dad died, loud noises made me jumpy. I knew the crushed red ant really wanted to sting me like a bumblebee, so I ran super fast up the driveway to the porch so it wouldn't get me.

When I got inside, I was gonna tell Gramma how she had made me step on the red ant and how that made me mad and how now we were all gonna get stung, but I saw Mom sitting up in her room which was weird because ever since yesterday, she'd been hiding under her covers.

This distracted me, and I lost what Mrs. Mitchell calls my 'train of thought.'

Anyways, I peeked inside her room, quiet like a mouse, and it smelled really bad. It was all dark because the windows were closed and her sheets were all twisted, kinda like the tornado I saw in a movie. Mom was in the middle and her eyes were black and red like the ants were. She was rocking back and forth like she used to do with me back when I was a baby. I tried to wave 'hi' because I hadn't seen her since yesterday which was when she saw me through the window, but when I did, she screamed, and I jumped.

So I tumbled out of her room because it scared me so bad, and I bumped straight into Gramma who knocked me over because she is a 'big boned woman.' I thought Gramma was gonna say sorry to me, but instead *she* yelled at me and shook her finger at me because I made Mom scream. I tried to tell her I actually didn't do anything, but she kept being mad so I ran to my hiding spot.

I hadn't been in the shed since yesterday, so when I pulled open the doors, it was still laying on the floor. It was still shiny and black, which was cool, like the black ants in the outline, but now it was cold and creepy and it made me kinda nervous, like stomping red ants.

—— *Thursday* ——

I went back to school late and all cranky the next day, which was Thursday. I hadn't slept a lot the night before, but Gramma was still making me go. She'd been using her 'business voice' on the phone all morning with some lady, and so now she was rushing me and pushing me down the front steps. She was saying I needed to 'get out of the house' and 'fill my brain with learnin' so I wouldn't end up dead on the driveway.' So I sighed really big and dragged my feet down the block toward school. When I turned around to make a face at Gramma through the window, I saw a car stop in front of our house. A lady with straight yellow hair and the biggest sunglasses I had ever seen stepped out. She stood on the curb and looked our house up and down, starting from the weeds in the driveway to the crooked shutters that Dad had never fixed. From where I was, I could see Gramma fidgeting on the porch. I stuck my tongue out at her, but she didn't notice so I just ran to school.

...

At school, Mrs. Mitchell told us to draw a picture of those rocks from Monday, but all I saw were ants. Ever since Tuesday, ants had been marching marching marching marching marching all over my mind and I couldn't get them out. I tried swatting scratching swatting scratching, but no use. They kept coming and I couldn't fight them off. It was too much and I had to scream, but if I did, Mrs. Mitchell would yell at me, so I ran out of class. I bolted out of there to escape the ants. They were all up in my ears, so I didn't hear when stupid Ania Johnson told on me, and I didn't hear when Mrs. Mitchell stuck her head in the hall and called after me. I just ran all the way home, and I didn't feel better until I was under my covers and had fallen asleep.

—— *Friday* ——

Gramma and Jordan were outside the little room Detective Scott and I were in. I could hear Gramma huffing and grumbling as she walked back and forth behind the closed door. Right before I had followed Detective Scott into the room, Gramma had yelled that I was 'just a child,' but she had sounded crazy. I knew I wasn't 'just a child' since I knew a bunch of stuff Detective Scott didn't.

"But what happened on *Tuesday*?" Detective Scott asked again. She looked concerned, almost like she was wearing one of Mrs. Mitchell's thinking hats.

I thought really hard back to Tuesday.

— Tuesday —

I had been planning on playing sick so I wouldn't have to go to school and see stupid Ania Johnson again, but I didn't even have to fake cough because Mom never ended up coming into my room to wake me up. I knew no one else was home since Jordan had already left. He always got up early on Tuesdays to walk to school with his 'girl but not girlfriend,' and I wasn't allowed to go with them.

I got out of bed, really quiet like a mouse, so Mom wouldn't wake up and make me go to school. I cracked open my door and peered into her room across the hall. I could see straight in because the door was still gone from that one time Mom locked Dad out and he came home all angry and sloppy and punched the door until his hands were bleeding and the door broke and fell off the hinges.

Sometimes I get sort of mad when I think about that.

She was still under the covers, so I figured I'd check the kitchen cabinet for any cereal. I was feeling pretty good about staying home all day. I stretched super wide and yawned as big as I could while I walked. My eyes were closed while I was yawning, and since I was stretching so wide, I hit a mug on the counter (but it was an accident!).

The sound of glass shattering rang throughout the room. My eyes shot open and there I was, staring face to chest with my dad.

I froze.

I tried to just play it off because there was already tons of cracked glass on the ground from yesterday when Dad threw a candle at Mom while they were fighting, but Dad wasn't buying it.

His eyes were dark and red, and his bottom lip was all puffy. He looked at me, and I could imagine steam coming out of his ears again. He started yelling really loud.

He called me names Mrs. Mitchell would've sent him to the hall for, and I began to feel really scared that he was yelling at me. But I switched from scared to mad pretty quick. My feelings were bubbling up inside me. Suddenly, I was so, so mad that I felt like I had red stinging fire ants climbing up my stomach. They were dying to crawl out of my mouth and sting Dad, but he kept yelling, so I swallowed them instead.

I squirmed; I couldn't stand Dad's screaming and steaming any longer. I bolted, escaping down the driveway to the shed. It's like a cave where a bear would live, and no one ever knows I'm there, so I look at and play with everything inside and pretend I'm a grown-up who doesn't get yelled at.

Inside were tools and trash and crunchy leaves and the lawnmower with spiderwebs on it. I started kicking all the leaves and tools because no one was there to tell me not to. But while I was kicking around, I saw something cool.

I spotted it first because it was shiny, and when I picked it up it was heavy and black.

Holding it made me feel like a superhero from those movies I sometimes watch on the weekends.

While I was inspecting it, I heard the screen door slam and knew Dad was coming, so I kicked it aside and ducked behind the lawnmower.

...

Once Dad was gone, and I'd given it a couple of hours just to make sure, I went back inside the house. I lugged it inside, too (just in case). I knew it would help me feel better. And then Mom would feel better and finally wake up. She'd be proud of me.

So I was just carrying it around the house for when Dad showed up again. I was spinning it around on the couch, pretending to be a soldier, when I heard him coming. I knew it was him because he was yelling from all the way down the street. The clock on the wall told me it was almost three o'clock.

I snuck outside and waited out on the porch. I kicked around at some bugs until I could see him coming. I knew what I had to do. If I did it, his yelling and steaming would end, and Mom could finally wake up.

He stomped down the street, and I had to do it.

He stomped up the driveway, and I had to do it.

He saw me, and the little hand touched three, and I did it.

There was a muffled shriek, and Mom's face was pressed against the window.

*Wake up, Mom. Did I make you proud?*

...

Late that night, after the police cars were gone, and the neighbors had stopped standing outside, and Jordan had fallen asleep, and I had stopped crying, Gramma moved in. She dumped all her stuff in the living room because it was the only room with the TV and she 'had to watch Alex on Jeopardy.' But that didn't matter too much to me. I wasn't gonna watch any movies that weekend, anyway.

*−− Friday −−*

"That's everything that happened?" Detective Scott stared me right in the eyes. Her hair was yellow, and her eyes were squinty and gray like a rainy day.

"Yeah, I think so." I swirled the apple juice in my paper cup. I didn't feel like looking at her cloudy eyes and scarecrow hair right now.

"Okay." She was writing everything slowly, and she sounded kind of weird. She didn't yell, though.

Detective Scott stood up slowly and started towards me, like I was one of those bombs in those movies that explode when someone touches it. I don't know why, but my lip started to quiver. I am *not* a crybaby, even if Jordan says it, but my eyes started to feel fiery hot, too. I fought back tears, and I bit my lip so hard to stop it from shaking that I knew it would be all black and puffy by tomorrow.

# KRISTY SRODAWA

**Sophomore**
**Major:** Cellular and Molecular Biology
**Reading:** Fiction

Kristy grew up in the relatively small town of Midland, Michigan. Life has always fascinated her, and so she is pursuing a degree in biology and is currently an undergraduate lab assistant. For fun, Kristy loves to do all things creative, including oil painting, cross-stitch, and now writing! She has always been a bookworm, binge-reading fantasy novels for as long as she can remember. Now, she writes fantasy in a modern setting, and she is very excited to share her work with you tonight.

*Nominated by: Carl Lavigne*

# Excerpt from "My Mind's Eye"

I painfully pushed up against the cold, packed earth, moving myself into a sitting position. My chin throbbed and I could feel the blood drip down my torn skin, stinging as it did so. My whole body ached, every joint protesting as I slowly moved my arms and neck, assessing the damage. My right arm was cut from scraping against the jagged edge of the cavern, bleeding enough to be concerned but not enough to be scared. The fall might have knocked me out, but I had no way of knowing. There wasn't anything in this cave that hinted at the passage of time.

I poured the contents of my backpack onto the floor, plants scattering everywhere and my insect jars rolling across the ground with the disconcerting sound of glass rubbing against rocks. I struggled to make out the differences in my collection with my night-vision, but by using my inner sight I could identify each by the magic they gave off. I had a sixth sense for energy within the natural world, as all druids did. I pulled out two herbs, one dark green and another more of a silver color. The first would do wonders for my miscellaneous cuts and scrapes, whereas the other always helped me with aches and pains.

I closed my eyes and focused on the magic within the plants. Carefully, I extracted all that I could and molded it into one entity, kneading it in my mind's eye to bring it all together. This is what would lead the spell. The majority of magic was intention and visualization, but the plants I had picked to use had a natural propensity for the type of thing I wanted to do. Next came a base energy, something to give it the right amount of power. I tapped into the magic I kept stored inside myself, looking for a nice, simple, stable energy. I couldn't find anything.

In the forest I didn't bother to recharge that much, since there was energy all around me to use. I normally grabbed things that seemed of particular interest, like whatever the hell lead me here, and then filled up on trees and the river on the way out. I hadn't intended on chasing a powerful being into the cave system under the mountain.

Anxiety rose inside me. A repetitive 'no' was the mantra welling up in my head, and my lips moved silently to match it. I lifted my hand to my head, clutching my hair in desperation and panic. I started breathing faster and tears began to form in my eyes as I focused on the fact that I was trapped here, and had no energy to get myself out. I was stuck. A druid with only some plant clippings and a few bugs. I messed up, and now I was trapped. There was no way for me to get out. I shouldn't have chased that thing, I shouldn't have been so reckless, I shouldn't have messed up! How could I have been so stupid?

Anger flashed up, guided by the anxiety, and I grabbed the nearest jar and flung it at the wall as hard as I could. It shattered, spraying glass everywhere with a satisfying crash and released some of the tension that had built up inside of me. But only some of it. I had to focus on finding a solution or else I would go mad.

Storing the meager magic I had pulled out into myself, I sent a cursory glance over my other plants. There wasn't enough there to do much of anything. I paced around the cave, my hand trailing across the jagged rock. It wasn't very large, maybe the size of a small bedroom, but with a slightly smaller ceiling. Not that it benefited me in the least. The hole I fell through was nowhere close to a wall that I could climb up. I jumped, trying to touch the ceiling, and missed it by at least a foot. I sighed, letting my arm swing as it fell, and then resumed tracing the cracks in the wall as I slowly walked, trying to think.

I was surrounded by rock and dirt; the same thing to a druid, really. Neither had easily accessible energy, and both took enormous power to shift. Even if my figurative energy tank was full I wouldn't be able to move the rock. I would need to be surrounded by nature for that.

It is, however, much easier to change the physical being of something with its own energy. Really, if I was able to access the energy inside the earth it wouldn't take much. The memory of my last attempt flashed through my mind. I could still remember the metallic taste, and the rumble of the ground below me as I sent the energy back where it came from.

Rock, as you might expect, has a very withdrawn energy. It takes a lot of effort to draw it into a useable form. I was able to get to that stage, but I was not expecting such raw, electrifying power. The magic was too strong, too wild for me to control, and it just kept pouring out of the tap I had created. I threw the energy I had gathered back into the ground, ultimately causing a small fissure where the magic had landed and a very large tremor.

I kept up my wandering, trying to think of anything I could do to get out of here. Calling for help wouldn't do much at all; I was far too deep into the cave system, and no one else really liked the forest that much, especially near the mountains.

After what I thought was a few hours, but really could have been any quantity of time, I had no ideas. I sighed for the umpteenth time since I fell into this cursed cave and leaned forward, kneeling on the ground and gathering all my things into my backpack. No point leaving them scattered around the floor when they weren't helping anything. I brought it with me to the furthest possible point from the hole, and sat down.

I couldn't die here, slowly starving to death. I *wouldn't* die here. I squashed the panic rising in my throat and took a deep breath. I had to do something, and I only really had one option. I closed my eyes and focused on my inner sight, trying to enter some sort of meditative state. Magic washed over me. The lichen was pulsating, bursting with energy for its small size. I could sense the different flavors and frequencies from all the clippings in my bag, weaker but very distinct, and as I focused I could feel the low, steady thrum of the energy captured within the earth. The earth that sustained the world as we knew it; the ultimate source of all magic. I knew the hum was backed by power stronger than I could ever imagine. I had only felt the tiniest sliver of what it had to offer, and it was too much for me. But at the same time, it was tantalizing. Excitement built within my stomach as I thought of accessing it again. Fear was there too, a healthy temper to my enthusiasm. This time, I wasn't going to let it overpower me.

What would happen if I failed? Images of another earthquake filled my mind, a tremor large enough to cause the ceiling above me to come crumbling down, the hard rock easily crushing my bones and tearing into my soft skin. The scene played in my mind, over and over, and I could feel my panic rising with my heartbeat. With my eyes closed I could just picture a boulder caving my head in, killing me almost instantly, but not quickly enough.

I clenched my hands instinctively, a grounding motion. I needed to stay focused. I needed to be in control. I clung to the thrum of energy, and unclenching my fists I placed them on the rock beside me. It was cold to the touch, as expected. I took deep breaths, in through the mouth and out through the nose. With every anxiety-inducing thought I just turned back to the energy around me, and the sturdy feeling of rock beneath my hand.

As time went on, my panicked thoughts calmed down. I could breathe fully, and my muscles were able to relax again. I began to feel the energy from the earth, not just with my druidic abilities but with my *hands*. Excitement bubbled up in my chest, and it increased the sensation rather than distracting from it. This is what I was missing the last time. I had forced the energy out and into the air when I should have been pulling it into myself, using my body as a gateway.

With one more deep breath, I opened myself up to the energy, allowing it to flow into my hands. It did so eagerly, quickly traveling up my arm and soon encasing my whole body in warmth. Besides the sheer enormity of the power it felt comforting, and strangely familiar. The longer I let the power rush in the faster it did so, pouring into me at an exponential rate. It quickly became intense and I panicked, lifting my hands from the ground. Sparks burst forth in my inner vision, but other than that the connection was cut.

The energy sat inside me, overflowing my body. My hairs stood on end and I could feel a physical itching to release it. The amount of energy I had let in with my brief connection was insane, a testament to how much is stored within the soil. I could feel the air buzz, and I couldn't tell if it was from the energy that was now within me, or that which was still begging to be let out of the rock.

I focused on where I could see the gap and cautiously sent magic out to it. I could see it in my mind's eye, a yellow tendril reaching out from my body. I imagined the rock splitting down the middle until it hit the wall, and then peeling to the side. Small shards of rock crumbled and fell as the rock moved, scattering once they hit the floor. My heart lurched with every crash, but I had to focus on controlling the magic, putting it exactly where I wanted it, and not letting it flood out like it yearned to. I kept going, moving the ledge until I was sure the gap by the wall was big enough to fit me, and then I severed the connection.

# KATHRYN SULLIVAN

**Sophomore**
**Major:** Biology, Health & Society and Program in the Environment
**Reading:** Nonfiction Narrative

Kathryn is a Sophomore from Saint Joseph, Michigan. She is studying Biology and Environment and views her minor in Creative Writing as an escape from her science classes. She is passionate about environmental issues and plans on continuing her understanding and devotion to them in graduate school and eventual career. In her free time she enjoys playing on the women's club soccer team, exploring the outdoors, and, of course, writing.

*Nominated by: Aozoro Brockman*

# Half-Gone Home

When I was a little girl, my mother packed a wagon to the brim with grapes, pretzels, sand shovels, and floaties. There was just barely enough room for my sister and me, who were perfectly capable of walking. I could tell my mother loved Lake Michigan because she did this day after day, all for me to sit under a giant umbrella and whine about how I wanted to be at the pool instead. I'd tell her that at the pool I wouldn't have to tiptoe to avoid the feeling of sand in between my toes. She'd laugh at me and call me "Granny" for wanting to stay out of the sun while all the other kids played. At the end of the day she packed up the same wagon and pulled us up a steep winding hill. When I imagine this now, it is a wistful memory mixed with the guilt of my own innocence.

Late in the spring of first grade, my parents surprised my sister and me with a puppy – most likely to shut us up from begging for one. We named our dog Blue and walked him down the same steep, winding hill to the spot where the land met the water. We watched the sky turn colors, each sunset a pastel explosion unlike any we'd seen before. My family continued this tradition of walking to watch the sunset every night after dinner, regardless of the time of year, and sunsets became the dessert I never grew weary of. They are so beautiful that it doesn't matter how many times you've seen them, they continue to rattle everything inside of you. I've seen the sun color the space between skyscrapers cantaloupe orange; I've watched it reflect a dozen shades of rose against a river so still it could've been glass, but at the bottom of this hill, I found the most wonder. It was during these colorful moments that I questioned which game of luck or chance I had won. Growing up on Lake Michigan was something out of a storybook.

On many starry summer nights my family made a fire next to the water. We layered sweatshirts on top of sunburns and let gooey marshmallows drip onto the next day's cherry-pit spitting arena. The neighbors gathered with stovetop popcorn to share, commenting on how the beach had been a few feet bigger the year before, a topic that deserved a lot more attention than small talk. My sister and I fell asleep between the neighbor kids and the bonfire, or pretended to, so our parents would carry us to bed.

As the years passed, I eventually stopped caring about getting sandy. I longed for summer days when I ran in and out of the cool water and parceled through rocks to find the pieces of frosted beach glass we would later add to the jars in our living room – one for each summer. Each jar showcased dozens of hues of olive green, amber, and cornflower blue; a pebbled mosaic that would soon be compared to the neighbors'. These jars measured how many moments of the summer we witnessed the waves break and the rocks part and the sunlight peek from behind a cloud, just so one piece of glass could glimmer. During the school year, I learned this beach glass was once just a piece of a broken bottle or a cracked plate. It took over 20 years of tumbling through powerful waves before the soft, sharp edges became hard, weathered, and rounded. My teacher didn't mention these same powerful waves were getting bigger every year, taking a little bit more land with each tide.

When I was a freshman, an older boy took me on my first date. We went to lunch and talked about whatever it was that mattered in high school. He drove me home and we walked to the shrunken beach, which was mostly just made up of rocks. He tried to teach me to skip them, but all I could think about was how there was no more sand to get in between my toes.

The next year, the water kept rising. My three-year-old wish was granted; everyone went to the pool. A few local stores closed down because tourists didn't want to visit the beachtown without the beach. I drove down my street and noticed for sale signs lining house after house, a last ditch effort to get anything for their home that would soon be swallowed by water.

I wondered where the beach had gone. Many of the people in my town assured themselves this disappearance was a cyclical and natural process – as if the sand could seamlessly wash itself back onshore. This would not happen; the earth was grieving over the way we had treated it. There was nothing natural about solely acting on human convenience and ignoring the ways the earth was degrading as a consequence.

In reality, the cycle went like this: more moisture in the atmosphere was causing extreme weather patterns such as late, snowy winters and early, rainy springs. An increase in precipitation caused lake levels to rise, which created more evaporation and more moisture in the air. Members in my community mocked climate change, claiming it was unrelated to the rising lake levels. Meanwhile, the burning of fossil fuels continued to be the primary control of moisture in the atmosphere. They were right, a cycle was occuring, but many didn't know we were the ones causing it. Even worse, many of those who knew acted as if they didn't. They rolled their eyes at the people telling them something had to change and remained determined to do anything but change. They held their breath, crossed their fingers, and waited to see what would happen to their beach the next summer. They would later be the ones to throw money at a few band aids. Retaining walls, a preventative measure to keep the soil and rocks and sand in place, were chosen as the solution while recycling bins remained empty and plates piled high with barbeque meat. The "I'm only one person, anyway" attitude infiltrated any hope of altering behavior and made me realize people gamble all the time on things much more important than money.

At my small, conservative, private school, my classmates denied that there was any proof of climate change as if it wasn't destroying their own backyard. They, like much of the country, turned science into politics. I knew this was an injustice I couldn't ignore. The only time our teachers acknowledged climate change was when it was presented as a topic for debate – me and one other classmate against the entirety of our class. My throat tightened as I tried my best to convince my friends to care, to explain how privileged we are to believe that climate change wasn't a real issue. I argued our privilege was wasted when we idealized this opinion as a valid one. I wondered what they thought happened to the sand dunes we once sled down on snow days and if we would still share a connection were this whole town to wash away. There's something terrifying about watching your home crumble beneath you and looking around to find everyone deeming you insane.

A few years have passed and I still take my dog to the place where the land meets the water, though that place is now much closer to home. The hill my mother dragged us up in the wagon is halfway eroded, and trees that once lined the bluff have long been swept away. When the waves show their anger, there are staircases from the bluff leading to nothing but water. On calm, lucky days they meet a narrow strip of rocks just wide enough for a footpath. I used to sit by the water admiring the vastness of the lake and the sky and how they collide; now I wonder how many more sunsets I will be able to watch before my family leaves our home, too. I worry those happy memories of beach glass and s'mores for dinner will be tainted with the feeling of desiring something once pure, now simply gone. This may have already begun, I've left so many rocks unskipped.

I bring this nostalgia to my university where I long for a half-gone home. I spend my time studying the environment as if filling my brain with more knowledge will do anything to change the damage already done. My classes are full of stories much more heart-wrenching than mine. Stories of climate refugees and fires and poverty, all caused by the collective inability to care. I never deeply considered why I valued the earth and the countless wonders it creates; instead, I questioned why others didn't. In the middle of this questioning, I realized it was Lake Michigan that silently begs me to.

We all have something we would never gamble on. Somewhere so beautiful you can't help but dream, someone so seemingly faultless you can't help but love. You will do everything you can to hold onto these places and people because losing them will break you in a way you cannot craft into words. These feelings are so intense, they can only be remembered by the thing that broke you itself. My breaking is felt deepest when picturing the beach that no longer exists. I can try to put it into words, but there is no accurate way to capture the feeling of my childhood washing away.

I never wanted to believe that nothing gold can stay. But it never feels more true as I stand on the edge of a cracked sidewalk, looking down at only water where there used to be sandcastles and watermelon picnics and the potential of sunny memories. Instead, all that remains is a quiet rush of emptiness that could've been avoided if we cared enough to polish our gold.

Works Referenced

DOE/Lawrence Livermore National Library. September 19, 2007. "Increase in atmospheric moisture tied to human activities." *ScienceDaily.* https://www.sciencedaily.com/releases/2007/09/070918090803.htm

Frost, Robert. "Nothing Gold Can Stay." *Poetry Foundation.* https://www.poetryfoundation.org/poems/148652/nothing-gold-can-stay-5c095cc5ab679

Sebree, Tyler. July 12, 2019. "Beaches are simply disappearing along Lake Michigan; Great Lakes break all-time June records." ABC57. https://www.abc57.com/news/beaches-are-simply-disappearing-along-lake-michigan-great-lakes-break-all-time-june-records

# NICOLE TOOLEY

**Freshman**
**Major:** English and Education
**Reading:** Poetry

Nicole is a freshman from Ann Arbor planning to major in English and education. She started writing creatively in high school and has enjoyed continuing this passion in college through her research in literary journals and publishing. When she is not writing, she loves to read memoirs, dance, practice yoga, and travel.

*Nominated by: John Buckley*

# Lessons on Numbers and Words

Everything we learned,
I learned twice over.

Finding every exception to
the transitive property

like if Ben likes Molly,
and Molly likes me,

then Ben must love me.
A teacher asked me to

turn my phone off
and could you believe

I didn't. I just needed to know
if 37 was a prime number,

but the vibrations in my hand,
with the force of freckle-sized earthquakes

were distracting. Notification
after notification for every day I would be

gone. Absent. When I asked Molly
what *bereavement* meant

she made up jargon and
threw in *melancholy*

a vocab word that would
have earned her five points

in the fifth grade only, ten years later,
neither of us can explain what it means

to be given some words
and deprived of others.

She googles *bereavement*
in geometry class and

tells me it comes from
an old English word with

roots that go back farther than
my recollection of yesterday's lessons.

She tells me it's a state, gerrymandered
by my own two hands, in which I'm robbed.

To bereave then is to take
what is not yours to take,

to tell what is not yours to tell.
I power my phone off.

Press the side button
as if it were a pressure point between

the shoulder and the neck.
Imagine the aluminum collapsing in

as I hand it to the teacher,
and remember ten years ago

in the lice-filled couches
laughing with our skinny books

and wide smiles, we latched to
these little lessons never taught on living.

# When it rains in

Chicago, it is probably raining here too,
so I sit in the unfinished attic all day,
watch the pink cotton candy planked by damp cedar,
all of it dissolving under one sky.

I'm not quite sure how to explain to you
where this glass shack starts and where it ends,
why we bought a house with busting seams
But you've got to trust me when I say

I've heard that distance is all relative,
but then again I've read myths
and thought they were memoirs.
You've got to trust me when I say

mother's bell bottom jeans are back in style.
I dug them out of a Home Depot box
out of the bones of an attic, unfolded them like origami.

The creases still streak my thighs: instructions
on how to return to before.
Instructions I will never get from
the patina of mother's cheeks, of leather,

of new beautiful things worn and weathered old.
Only the water is falling on my lap
heavier now, erasing and ironing
with the weight of winter rain.

# When DaVinci Drives my Car

I looked out the rear view mirror of my car yesterday,
and everything was slipping away.

When background is the backdrop to all the backwards ways of life,
contort the contorted.

Maybe we ought to remind ourselves
we were always in drive.
That's how my mama says you survive.

Perspective is the antidote to all my brain's lies.

The rear view mirror in my car tells me:
Objects may appear closer than they really are
like it knows all the tricks I play on myself.

And today I'm feeling heavy with the habitual
in all the best possible ways.

The sun bakes my temples.
Tells me I'm allowed to remember,
Tells me you need to be in reverse to go backwards.
Common sense cost more than two cents
It didn't save me from our backyard's fence.

Strangely enough, sitting in that car,
I remember Holden and the ducks
and how we'll adapt even when we feel trapped.

I remember reading "The Story of an Hour"
and thinking we had millions of those left.
Time traveled too.

But for now, I put the car in park.

Find the back lawn's grass
feel the weight of my own mass.

And I promise you I am
Lengthen, lengthen, lengthen
like we are girls made of laffy taffy.
I am

DaVinci's man on the floor.
Pull me north south east and west,
command this presence.
How nice it is to feel large and demanding.

Even when I lie on the ground with my Mona Lisa smile.
Even when I drive around for a few aimless miles.

I looked out the rearview mirror of my car yesterday
with a smile that stayed a little selfish and told me everything,
everything in this life moves forward.

# RYLEY VERDE

**Senior**
**Major:** International Studies and Creative Writing
**Reading:** Fiction Short Story

Ryley Verde is from Fennville, Michigan; she is a writer and a big fan of brevity.

*Nominated by: Laura Thomas*

# Sarah's Baby

They called me Sarah's baby, but my mother's name was Norma. Her eyes and voice were kind and soft, but softer still were the ironed wrinkles of her hands and the plumpness of a big belly, bouncing and affectionate. Into that fat, glorious stomach of hers, I would push my face and scream as loudly as I could manage. When I fell into the creek and muddied my pants, I yelled. When my last sister abandoned me for college, I yelled and hollered and sobbed. When Papa made me mad or the other way around, she rubbed my back gently, soothingly, hushing my tears with stories of dragonflies and crocus flowers.

When I whispered into her big belly all my secrets, you couldn't hear more than a muffle. Her stomach ate them all, gobbling each and every secret. When my Papa told her to lose some weight, I patted her fat stomach and frowned... *it won't be comfy if it shrinks*, and when I told her as much, she only drew me in closer to embrace her full-bellied laugh.

*My kind-eyed baby*, she'd called me. *My reason for being*. I'd repeat those words in my mind years later, but at the time, they had only brought me to the conclusion to stop sharing my secrets, just in case.

I wish now that I'm older, I could wipe some secrets from my mind. Secrets that are mine, others that are not. I was born to the wobbly woman in the cat-eyed glasses and the leaning, mustached gentleman. Norma and Gene, in their threadbare glory. Photographed here, in staged sepia, was their wedding, fifty years ago to the day. They both seem overwhelmed, love and joy oozing past the frame so that I could almost believe that their love had started good and pure.

My mama told me she had never smiled like that day I was born. Sarah's baby. She'd had me at fifty-seven years of age. But no one in my family lives past seventy, and Mama was no exception. I planted crocus flowers on her grave. Here, now, little spots of the purple peek through the winter. Frost clings to the words on her stone, words I have memorized but can no longer bear to read.

Years ago, I had carved below the fancy, scrawling script of a name and a message which have no relation to one another, two words:

*Cosmos Traveler.*

And in her heart, she was one. Never in real life. She'd never even left the state, only twice the city. My Papa didn't want her gone, wanted her near, and for the love of her children, of me, she smothered her urges to leave.

My mama was thinking about leaving since she was twenty-five, but her other four kids weren't yet grown, and she simply couldn't leave. She tried once. My oldest sister found her goodbye note before my mama could retrieve it. I think if she had never had me, she would have left him much sooner. I learned all of this much later.

Later still, at her funeral, I'd learned that she'd only made it a half-mile up the road, barely past McFarland Dairy before she had swung right back around for her babies. She had packed only her finest pair of silk gloves, cherished, two dresses, and a bit of money. I wondered if she'd known she wouldn't be leaving that day.

My Papa never found out. If he did, he would've killed her sooner. Eleanor, my middlest sister, told me not to believe their lies, the ones that clung to Papa's shadow. The ones tucked behind his broad-brimmed fedora. The ones that whispered it was his rage that was the blow that struck her dead.

Whether Papa did it or not, she was found on the edge of our property, near the old Pine Grove forest where we would bury her.

That day, the wheat had been full-grown, so much so that we only found her as we came across the crushed stalks. I spied only her ankle, resting at an unnatural angle, her flimsy slipper dripping off her toe.

I was frozen, staring at that strangely beautiful foot. So broken its positioning, I had no desire to turn away. Her feet were baby soft. I wondered then if they had ever walked on gravel. Surely, at some point they had. It was my brother's big frame that moved to block my view; he had to shout at me over and over to get past the thickness of my thoughts. The realization hit slowly: I was being asked to go, to hurry, to get someone because Mama was dead.

I raced first for my Papa, but my thoughts were far ahead of me. Had she lain there long? Was she dead? Then those thoughts were chased out by ones of uncomprehending shock. Had she had lain there all day, watching her last day curl to ash, keeping time by passing clouds? Maybe she dreamed of the day that Elvis had given her a scarf. I wondered if she'd ever seen the ocean. I wondered if she'd ever felt at peace.

Then I was there, in the house, screeching and hollering for my daddy who came flying down the stairs shotgun at the ready. He saw my face and dropped it. And we ran to her.

Papa had come, Papa had called the cops, the cops had come, the cops had taken her away and had handed her over to some doctors who threw a sheet over her corpse. Then these doctors had cut her open and had moved around her bits before declaring it foul play; the cops had questioned me, and Andrew, and Papa, and while the whole town buzzed of her murder. But for all the gossip, her funeral was quiet, extending into deafening silence. My world had ended, but every other bit continued. The globe kept rotating. Papa went to work; I went back to school. And year after year passed until the pain wove into the normal fabric of my being.

I don't know if my Papa killed her, but I knew he had likely killed another, years before. The whole town knew and believed, but they knew better of my father's temper. They could see it on us and my Mama, but in those days, that was a man's own business. They kept quiet about it until the husband of my father's lover was found dead, a bullet through his brain. The town traded whispers until the whole community knew that my father had bloody hands. One and one doesn't make four, and my Papa was too likely for the murder to acquit him. My parent's refusal to comment only confirmed his guilt. And so the rumors grew, some saying he was Italian Mafia, others claiming he was an escaped killer from up North. Fewer and fewer people doubted my father's guilt.

We all scoffed. As if any respectable mafia would never be a roofer, even as cover. To me, he was a jokester and a people's person. Afraid of rejection, afraid of judgment. Magnanimous as the day is long. I knew him honestly as a poor, gangly old Italian who liked riding motorcycles and pissing off the neighbors by pretending to sell his land to his best friend, a three-hundred pound man named Tiny.

Tiny and his family was the hallmark of our golden years. The Mamas cooked up a feast while the Daddys were out in the field, hooting and hollering about how happy they were going to be as neighbors. The rest of the neighborhood didn't like Tiny and his wife. They didn't like that he and my father were loud and rowdy, but mostly they were mad cause Tiny was large and undeniably black.

And their anger gave Papa glee. And when my Papa was joyful, the whole world sang. He made music from the neighbors hollering, Tiny and him laughing, the beat of the crickets playing us long into the evening.

My mama would perch on his lap and laugh along. Those were summer days when work was good and we were flush with money that never lasted into the winter months. My father was a hard-worker but a terrible saver. But he made sure there was a roof over our heads and food in our bellies, and he always came home every night.

My Mama, she loved the joy of a full, friendly household. She used to love roses the same. When my Papa scraped together two pennies for our home, he planted her a small rose bush outside. She brought friends over in those early days, some with children playing at their feet or with us, others visiting for sweet tea and lively front porch conversation. The afternoons would pass lazily, laundry drying in a gentle breeze, the buzzing of insects harmonizing with the distant sound of windchimes.

Despite the Carolinas' summer heat, my Mama kept those flowers perfectly pruned and watered, even after the roses started to go missing. She lovingly tended each bud, coaxing them to bloom. The bush was an explosion of pink and green, all glory. Mama never missed a day of its care, even as her hatred of roses grew, even when her friends visited to show off their beautiful, romantic bouquets that had been left on their porch step.

These were, of course, bouquets from my father, who was a fighter, but even more so, a lover. And when it came to fighting about lovers, he was the best. My mother's friends who once brought their children would begin to come alone, visiting more often. They usually began to bother with makeup around the third or fourth visit. And each one, my Papa would sleep with. So eventually, my mother stopped having friends, and he found his mistresses elsewhere.

Mama had never been with anyone else. She's buried here, alone, on the back plot of his land. I sometimes think of moving her, but my family wants her here and she's dead, so what would it really matter? A *Cosmos Traveler*. She wouldn't want to rest here for eternity. I'd like to think her soul now travels uninhibited, this grave only a plot of land for us still living.

I saw my father grieve only once, when he believed himself hidden in the privacy of this grave. The kneeling, weeping moment was quieted by the woods, broken only by a short, sharp wail so quick and fierce I am still not sure if it was him or a wild animal that had made it. If he murdered her, he loved her too. He believed himself a good husband; he thought because he always provided, always came home, that it was enough.

My Papa's own father had been a staying man, but he had stayed quiet, even as he watched his wife take a hammer to their son. He had stayed quiet as he watched that son grow and leave before being grown, sixteen and enlisted. Each five of us children wear my Papa's internal scars. But he loved us, and we loved him. My mama, too, loved him still.

In the end, he couldn't believe she left him. She hadn't left the state, not even the city. She'd moved across town, and they lived in distant peace for three years before her death. His own death had been long and slow and dignified through Hospice, the last few months of his life seemed to soothe him. There would be moments, spots of wandering doubt, wondering how life could have been different if he'd found these little blue pills—the ones that soothed the mania—earlier. Then his mind would wander again, too tired for unanswerable questions.

My mama, for her part, spent the last of her years sitting in her sunroom, bright and lovely, facing a wealth of wisteria. There, she would sit and listen to her grandbabies tell her of a universe outside the Carolinas, big beautiful words to imagine behind closed eyes.

It was her reason for being.

# SUHANA VIRDEE

**Junior**
**Major:** Psychology
**Minor:** Creative Writing
**Reading:** Poetry

Suhana Virdee is a transfer student at the University of Michigan. She is majoring in psychology and is planning to pursue a PhD in clinical psychology with a focus on adolescents. She is also minoring in creative writing and has always had a love of poetry. She loves rhymes, wordplay, and puns!

*Nominated by: Aozora Brockman*

# Trellis

There comes a time when saccharine winds
curl against the skin,
and the seeds that took root in my lungs
bloom from deep within.

It gets dizzying, the oppressive feeling
of having nearly no air –
I clawed at my chest, but could not reach
the seeds I knew were there.

I coughed up buds drenched in scarlet ichor
sicker, sicker, I grew still
but the buds were beautiful and had such sweet scent
so I often forgot I was ill.

The plants reached out to the sun, and I
stretched out to reach with them
until I felt it in my throat
twisting upward – a stem.

Petals fell from my mouth with the tears from your eyes –
the taste of bitter wax –
and flowers have bloomed behind my teeth
am I beautiful at last?

Air I had not tasted in ages
filled me up once more
thanks to the bloom, though lack of use
has made my lungs tender and sore.

Summer comes and the flowers die;
in vain, I clench my jaw
but the plants are ripped out regardless,
my throat – bloody and raw.

Yet in my lungs there are new seeds
Until they sprout, I will tend to their needs.

# As If I Were in Love

Now I shall write you a poem
as if I were in love
to make you think my soul
might be fragile as a dove.

And I shall take you dancing
on a low-lit, starry night,
make you shudder – quake – gasp –
feel like everything is alright.

I shall grip you tight
in the night and in the day
to make you truly doubt
that I should ever stray.

Yes, I shall write you a poem
as if I were in love
to make you think I am capable
of anything of the sort.

# She's Too Gorgeous

You want to put her on a pedestal
as long as she's undressed
and tell her that you love her
then forget what you confessed.
You'll spoon-feed her lies
from your chipped, gold-plated cup;
you don't see her choke on truth
when it comes back up.
You put a crown atop her head,
it's just for her, and yet
you freely give out silver rings
which she will never get.
She's devoted, and you know
there's never cause for worry,
so why do you touch her like she'll be gone
in the morning if you don't hurry?
You make sure she knows she's yours
but you have never been
someone to belong to one
and reject all others, then.
You want to be the only song upon her lips
but you caused her first scars,
so darling, do not be surprised
when her eyes become void of stars.

You want to hurt her so she'll never forget you –
Honey, she would never let you.

# Purple

If you are violet,
my whole world
is tinged in lavender –
just enough
to color it all
in an inescapable hue,
but not enough that you
even notice the missing pigment.

If I am navy blue
and you are violet
I will paint my world lavender
and fantasize of indigo.

# Ocean

The ocean in my throat, pushing,
spilling out the eyes –
washing away promises
(bitter bitter lies) –
roaring, churning, drowning waves
crash from deep inside
Swallow hard, push it down,
I know how you despise –
waves, rain, ocean flood,
a strangled compromise –
in my throat, the ocean, pushing
just behind the eyes.

# Enlightening

Regardless of the weather,
I might shiver or I might sweat –
the ozone could be jealous
of our own internal climate.

Heat, to me, is not as clear
as summer, but it is true
that I can truly feel the warmth
only when I am with you.

And you, my dear, will always be
the sunshine to my flower
but missing you is cold –
over me, you have such power.

Lover, oh, if I could show
the depths of how I care,
that blinding light might burn you
and I could never chance that scare.

Or, if I could tell you how
I am frozen when you are gone,
I worry crystals may form on you –
eyelashes and hair thereupon.

So, my love, I shall simply say
that missing you is cold
and being warm is knowing
I am yours, always, to hold.

# ANDREW WARRICK

**Junior**
**Major:** Creative Writing and History
**Reading:** Short Fiction

Andrew Warrick is a junior at the University of Michigan. When not doing homework, putting his nose in a book, or spoiling his two dogs, he is a film critic for *The Michigan Daily*. He is currently editing a novel titled *Electric Rage*.

*Nominated by: Laura Thomas*

# Toasted

There was something weird about the glass divider. The private dining room's three windows still worked normally, displaying campus's weathered, Gothic buildings ringed with oak trees. Even now, smeared with March's grey snow, they made a better view than the dilapidated dining hall on the other side of the clear front wall. Yet Sam couldn't take her eyes off it. This wasn't driven by boredom (though Macie and Maddie, the two other members of the Delta-Delta-Telta-Sisterhood-Stewardship-Committee, weren't very interesting). And it wasn't because Sam liked to people watch, either. Sam had never noticed it before, but the glass elongated the dining hall like a funhouse mirror. So students lined up for food, filled their sodas, and ate, chatting with friends or nose deep in homework or (more frequently) their smartphones, without knowing they were being stretched and pulled taut like vellum on a frame. It was mystifying. Come to think of it, Sam had seen something like this before, in high school: Lucy's mirror, on that horrible, final night. Then, though, the glass glowed purple like-

Across from Sam, Maddie tapped her Airpods case on the faux wood table. "Anyway, yesterday's Annual-Rush-Week-All-Night-Danceathon was a complete success."

"I agree," Macie said through a mouthful of gum.

Sam nodded. "Our pledges really put their hearts into it." The three of them knew (from experience) that yesterday's Annual-Rush-Week-All-Night-Danceathon was Hell on Earth. Pledges danced naked for nine hours and took two shots of Tito's every hour. If any of the girls fell down, they were scribbled on with Sharpie until they got up.

From out on the sidewalk, a man roared. Sam flinched. He was probably on his way to the basketball game. Their team was in the Final Four.

"So-" Maddie took a sip of her Tahitian Paradise smoothie which, after a prolonged and vicious argument with the dining manager, where Maddie had brought up the name and occupation of father several times, she had special permission to bring into the dining hall.

"Tonight is the Annual-Rush-Week-All-Night-Quizathon." She slid a paper across the table.

*Question 1: What are the three golden rules of DDT?* **Sisterhood, Community, and Scholarship**.

Bullshit. Nobody, not even the DDT-Sisterhood-Stewardship-Committee, cared about any of that. The place was a glorified, alcohol-filled shark tank. All anyone seemed to enjoy were the parties which, lately, Sam liked less and less. But what else would she do with her weekends?

"He's *never* going to message back," Maddie moaned, staring down at her phone.

"Tinder Mike, right?" Sam asked.

Maddie rolled her eyes. "Macie, tell her."

"Tinder *Marcus*," Macie said.

Sam nodded, feigning recognition with a flash of her teeth. "Right."

Maddie used Tinder constantly, but never went on more than one date. She'd see each boy once, then block him on every social media app. She valued her ghosting ability so highly that, at her funeral, Sam expected to watch Maddie rise through the coffin and into the air to haunt more frustrated frat boys plumbing Tinder for some easy ass.

Maddie slurped her smoothie while Macie chomped wetly on her gum, fingering the zipper on her 1500 Dollar Arctic Albatross fur jacket. In high school, before Lucy had that blankness in her eyes, Sam and Lucy had hated girls like this. Those girls with the Macbooks and Lululemon pants and Clinique palettes, who made fun of her and Lucy for their PCs and ripped leggings and acne. And now they were Sam's best friends.

From the direction of the stadium came a loud bang. Probably a car backfiring.

She used to be thoughtful, artistic, one of those theater kids. Would high school Sam like meeting *this* Sam, from DDT? Probably not. But Sam couldn't be alone. That meant thinking about Lucy. And burying herself in schoolwork wouldn't help, her business classes were boring as hell. She'd just daydream and see Lucy's cheeks pulsating blue in that glistening purple mirror. As for meeting new people, every girl in her classes was practically the same as these two. Plus, Greek life looked good on a resume. So Sam toughed it out with DDT and Macie and Maddie, letting their vacuous crap fill her eyes and ears and head day after day, month after month, year after year. Lately, though, it was almost unbearable. The business classes, the parties, and the lunch meetings cranked along in an endless belt, stretching Sam from all directions like a piece of putty until she quivered, ready to snap.

A girl outside screamed, her exaggerated joy sounding almost like terror. Chills oozed down Sam's hair like egg yolk.

"Sam, is something wrong?" Maddie asked.

Macie popped a fat pink gum bubble. "Did something happen with Matt? I heard a little something..."

"No," Sam said, just before her throat turned to alabaster. Something *had* happened, but that was neither here nor there. She wouldn't be seeing Matt again.

"Speaking of Lambda Thambda, you know what I heard?"

"What?"

"Apparently they give every girl who's slept with five of their guys a toaster."

"Why?"

"I don't know, but it's funny. Sluts get *Toasted!*"

"Sluts get *Toasted!*"

In the cafeteria, someone fell against the salad bar, knocking a bowl of lettuce to the floor. Was it Sam's imagination, or were Maddie and Macie sneaking looks at her? Were they calling *her* a slut? Did *everyone* in DDT think that? Sam couldn't be whispered about again, like after Lucy's death. As the rumors spread, Sam hadn't been able to set the record straight, not with the suited men telling her she had to calm down and forget what had fallen into Lucy's backyard, just before she stopped showing up at school. If DDT turned on her, Sam would be alone, with only the memory of Lucy's blood-stained carpet to keep her company. Sam wished she was home. It was close by and Mom missed her like hell. Why didn't she go? Lucy, that's why. The town was filled with her.

Someone in the dining hall cried out. Red sauce splattered against the divider, dripping its fingers down the glass. The Hell? There was a chorus of screams- their team probably just scored and the celebration had gotten out of hand. From Maddie's phone came an electric chime.

"He messaged!" Maddie called, opening her phone with a flick of a manicured finger. "He....He's not..." Her bottom lip stuck out while her eyebrows twitched, like they were glitching.

"What'd he say?" Macie asked. Maddie's face went red and purple bruises spiraled on her cheeks. No. Just-like-with-Lucy. It-was-happening-again. Sam stood and moved around the table, towards the divider. The glass clouded and shimmered with wet, purple glisten. She had seconds. "Maddie?" Macie asked. "Are you OK?" Maddie's cheeks, now swelled completely purple, dangled on her jaws like balloons filled with too much water. "Maddie?" Macie reached for Maddie's arm right as Maddie's head exploded with a loud *pop*, slathering Macie and her Arctic Albatross jacket in thick red muck. Sam spun around just as Macie screamed and *popped* away behind her. She opened the door to the cafeteria and froze. Headless bodies slumped over the tables, counters, and chairs and were strewn about the floor, covered in steaming puddles of gore. Sam took a deep breath. Like-the-suited- men-said-stay-calm-stay-calm-stay-calm. Sam crept forward, stepping between splayed legs and crooked arms, some still trembling. Blood stuck to her sneakers like syrup. Her left ankle brushed against something sharp and wet and she shuddered, biting back a scream. Stay-calm-you-have-to-stay-calm. In the lobby, where people were screaming and the *pops* were unceasing, like muffled gunshots, Sam started running. She sprinted into her hall, vaulting over her now headless RA, who twitched in a dark red puddle. At her door, Sam pulled out her keycard and stepped forward, onto something hard like bone. Shuddering, she looked down. Sam clenched the doorknob as her thoughts turned red and her cheeks swelled. Sitting against her door, with a sticky note reading "XOXOXOXOXO- *Lambda Thambda*," was a toaster.

Sam screamed as the world stretched taught and snapped with a sharp scarlet *pop*.

# KITTY WILCOX

**Senior**
**Major:** English and Creative Writing
**Reading:** Poetry

Kitty is a senior studying English and Creative Writing. They are currently at work on a collection of poems exploring the ways our body relates to nature in various stages of recovery. You can find them in Ann Arbor, drinking tea upstairs at Crazy Wisdom bookstore or walking the nature trails of Bird Hills.

*Nominated by: Christopher Matthews and James Cody Walker*

# Purple Skin

We drive electric cars now and
read books without pages,
but every day, someone, somewhere,
is still stomping on dozens of mulberries.
In our old neighborhood, they dominate the sidewalks;
The tree gives its fruit to any boot.
I always thought they were poisonous;
Delicious things are never easy.
When my girlfriend fed me one
I was ready to die
and it was good,
bramble-less and sweet.

# At The New House

An odd amount of slugs on a single limb,
a sickly ochre color but they seem so happy.
My clothes always fit better when I'm far
away from home. I imagine I shed my self
each time I move. Bits of my skin still lingering
on the childhood bed, a piece of my lip beside
the coffee pot. Looking at a slug, you'd never
know that they have thousands and thousands
of teeth, that the slime left on the dead birch is
a liquid crystal. I want to put my face close
to their face and tell them something, but it
might make them too heavy. If you scare
a slug, they make their own tail fall off.
I left mine in the backyard by the blue swing.

# Drying the Basil From the Windowsill

With the new addition of a basil plant, we've become much more
stable, my housemate and I.
This morning I found her using a cat tower as a ladder to hang leaves
above the window.

She looked so remarkably large up there, pinching tiny leaves at their
tiny stems, and whispering
something all the while. Something happy. You could tell by her
cheeks.

I don't really mind all the waking up these days and I know this to be
progress. It used to be
that herbs masked the scent of those who didn't bathe and the yellow
sour of spoiled meats.

It used to be that basil on your windowsill could get you burned by the
church. It used to be
that I saw my body as a plaything and didn't want it anymore. Here,
take this skin, it's for you.

Pluck it, pull it, cover yourself in it. Wherever you'd like. Basil was once
wrapped around the
dead in Egyptian embalming practices. For the Greeks, it was a symbol
of mourning,

then hatred. For the Cretes, a token of love. An occult book I found
said that basil
would wilt in the hands of any woman not a virgin. It's taken me years
to learn the truth:

that because someone once tossed my flesh down beside their
   dirty cum rag
does not mean my body deserved it.

I offer my hand to her, still warm from gas station cherry coffee.
   Her fingers furling around mine, she climbs down.

We nestle around the windowsill. The basil alive under our touch,
   each leaf aiming for the sun, and green in our small palms.

# MARIA WILLIAMS

**Freshman**
**Major:** Biology, Health and Society
**Reading:** Non-fiction

Maria is a biology, health, and society major on a pre-Physician Assisting track. She hopes to work as a women's health professional in an integrative setting. She loves to write in her free time and is thrilled to be a part of Café Shapiro!

*Nominated by: Leslie Stanton*

# Unshakable

Community. Equality, simplicity. Charity. A handmade quilt, a glass of water. A ball of yarn, a wooden church bench.

Isolation. Injustice, tragedy. Poverty. A filthy factory, a child laborer. A streak of filth, so many mouths to feed.

These were the two worlds that Ann Lee experienced in her lifetime. She was born into the second one in 1736, a poor blacksmith's daughter in Manchester, England.[1] She was also born a visionary. Around age six, Ann was baptized into the established Church of England at Manchester Collegiate Church.[2] This is one of the only records of her early childhood, as was common for someone of her economic status in 1742. Ann's father, John Lee, was married to her mother, a woman whose name was never recorded and has therefore been long forgotten.[3] Many women of the time faced a similar fate: the names of their husbands were recorded, even in places of deep poverty, and theirs were discarded in the streets with the rubbish eaten by wild animals. This is the root of what would inspire Ann's desire for and promotion of gender equality in the future. Her name, unlike her mother's, would be repeated. Her name would be remembered for centuries to come.

Due to her family's poverty, Ann went to work as soon as she was old enough to do so. At the age of thirteen she cut velvet, and later sheared hat fur and prepared cotton for the looms. She hated the boring, mind-numbing work and long hours. Around age 20, Ann became a cook in a public infirmary, where she witnessed sickness and death.[4] This time brought her face to face with the tragedies experienced by the people of Manchester.

1. Bokyo, Boris. "Ann Lee, a Woman of Great Faith."
2. "Ann Lee Biography, Life, Interesting Facts."
3. Tipton, Meredyth. "Mother Ann Lee."
4. Yolen Jane. *Simple Gifts.* 9.

In the midst of all this pain, she created a world in her mind out of thin air, and as the machines whirred around her and pollution streamed into the air, all she could hear was the internal conviction that she would bring to fruition her imagined world of peace and harmony. Not only that she would, but that she *had* to, because behind her mild expression and piercing blue eyes, she felt from deep within herself an intrinsic truth was lying in wait at the core of her identity. This knowledge, a certain blessed assurance, was that she, Ann Lee of filthy, overcrowded eighteenth-century Manchester, was anything but ordinary. She was a part of something divine. As a young child around six or seven years old, she would look in the mirror and wait for angel wings to sprout out of her shoulders and allow her to fly.[5] Ann was a short and stout girl with a mild but determined face, and staring into her own eyes, she waited in complete confidence for her divinity to transform her. While her feet remained rooted to the ground, Ann's visions and hope for the future soared.

Over time, the desperate images of Manchester wore on Ann's mind. It was a place of desolation, of soul-crushing work and desperate need. She often watched residents of her city stumbling out of the infamous gin mills at night. After long days working in the factories, they sought refuge in the bitter spirits that would lead them to seek company in other ways, which Ann found to be sinful and disturbing.[6] Here, she began to form her repulsion from sex and belief that lust was the root of all sin.

Ann spent years trembling with an ache for something beyond the slums of Manchester. When she was 22, she found refuge with Jane and James Wardley, a Quaker couple who made a habit of having very unusual worship ceremonies in the basement of their modest home in Manchester.[7]

These wildly odd gatherings would begin in silence. No one moved. Worshippers sat quietly, Quaker-style, as the ceremony began in

5. Yolen, Jane. *Simple Gifts*. 8-9.
6. "Mother Ann Lee Facts."
7. Yolen, Jane. 10-11.

complete stillness. After a few moments, someone let out a shout, a guttural shriek, and was joined by another person making a low humming sound. Several people rose and started to dance, shake, tremble. Soon the room was pandemonium, believers shouting and jumping and dancing and whirling around in circles, praising God in one of the most expressive and unorthodox ways the eighteenth century would ever see. The Quakers, who were known for their piety and self-control, were *shaking*.[8]

Ann found something very compelling about the Wardleys' methods of practicing their faith, and filled with the deep resolution that she herself was the second appearing of Christ, she continued to attend these gatherings regularly and gained followers in Manchester, the Wardleys included, as they became convinced that she was Christ's second appearing.[9] The shaking Quakers soon took on the name "Shakers." It was not long before the police caught wind of the seemingly absurd actions that happened repeatedly in the Wardley home, and promptly arrested Ann for disruption of the Sabbath. This happened multiple times as the gatherings became more frequent and caused concern to witnesses.[10]

Ann got married because she had to. Her father told her to marry a man named Abraham Standerin, who worked with him as a blacksmith, and she did. She was 25. The two were less than compatible.[11] While Abraham was a good man, Ann did not really have a choice in marrying him. There was not much opportunity or hope for an unmarried woman in Manchester in the year of her marriage, 1762, and Ann knew it. Abraham did not fully support nor understand Ann's views on celibacy, and evidently, they did not practice celibacy in their marriage. Ann became pregnant not long after their wedding. They lost the baby very soon after birth.

Quickly, Ann became pregnant again. And lost the baby.

8. Idib. 11.
9. Craik, James.
10. Mother Ann Lee Facts
11. Bokyo, Boris

And another.

And another.[12]

She was said to have been so desolate that her body would tremble from the ache within her soul.[13]

The deep pain and suffering that ensued only solidified her belief that sex and marriage were the root of a considerable amount of sin and pain. She would not share her bed with her husband during this nine year period of mourning.[14] This time surprisingly led her husband to join the Shakers himself.[15] Perhaps he too believed that the sexual act had brought pain to their family, and, like his wife, craved simplicity. Ann became determined to create the kingdom of Heaven on earth, and in order to do this, she was convicted that celibacy would be absolutely necessary. "The marriage of the flesh is a covenant with death," she said, "and an agreement with hell. If you want to marry, you may marry the Lord Jesus Christ."[16]

After being arrested in 1770 at the age of 36, Ann spent a particularly lengthy time in prison. She received no food or drink for two weeks, and her cell was so small that she could neither stand nor sit upright.[17] "It is not your bodies that are hungry, but your souls," she once said. "You must cry [out] to God for the bread of life."[18] This belief sustained her through this time of great tribulation, and her strongest religious epiphany came about during this particular sentence.

Alone and cold, Ann was in her cell trapped within both the physical walls and the confines of her own mind. Hungry, thirsty, and isolated, she looked to God for strength and guidance. Here, in this dirty, isolated jail cell, Ann heard God speak to her. She had visions of the

12. Yolen, Jane. 13.
13. Barker, Mildred.
14. Yolen, Jane. 14.
15. "Women in Religion: Leader of the Shakers."
16. Andrews, Edward Deming. *The People Called Shakers: a Search for the Perfect Society.*
17. Barker, Mildred.
18. Bishop, Rufus et. al.

original sin of Adam and Eve, which was their sexual relations.[19] Her opposition to sex solidified in addition to her conviction that in order to live righteously, celibacy was the only option. Above all, during her time in prison Ann became deeply sure that she was the second coming of Christ, the very spirit of God embodied this time by a woman. After gaining this insight, Ann knew that after prison she had a high calling to fulfill. Driven by this determination and fueled only by the small amounts of milk and wine that were given to her through a straw by one of her followers through the keyhole on her cell door, Ann persisted in faith and in living. As each second ticked by in that dreadful, lonely cell, she became more and more determined to hold tightly to her faith. According to Ann, Jesus Christ Himself spoke to her and became one with her in body and spirit.[20] Ann said to her followers, "You must not be discouraged, for Christ has everything you stand in need of. I feel the blood of Christ flowing through me to you, not in small quantities, but in fountains."[21] She knew that she was Christ's second coming, and soon she would finally be able to act on it. It was after her time in prison that Ann took on the name Mother Ann,[22] a name her followers would use to refer to her for centuries to come.

After Ann was released from prison, she discussed with her husband the possibility of their immigration to the United States. There she would have religious freedom to continue her Shaker ways and promote them, free from the watchful gaze of the Church of England, gaining still more followers to add to the small community that believed in her methods of worship and that she was Christ's second coming. Reluctantly, Abraham agreed, and they departed for the States.[23]

19. Bromley, David G. *Testimonies of the Life, Character, Revelations and Doctrines of Our Ever Blessed Mother Ann Lee, and the Elders With Her.*
20. Bromley, David G.
21. Bishop, Rufus et. al.
22. Rudy, Lisa Jo. "Biography of Ann Lee, Founder of the Shakers."
23. "Women in Religion: Leader of the Shakers."

The voyage to America was, like Mother Ann, anything but ordinary. It was three months before they reached New York, and during the trip aboard a ship called the *Mariah*, Mother Ann and eight of her followers worshipped freely in their Shaker fashion. The captain of the ship responded with disdain, threatening to throw them overboard if it continued. Ann told them to ignore him. Shortly after and while they continued to worship, it began to rain. It poured and thundered and crashed, and the boat sprang a leak. The passengers aboard the *Mariah* became fearful that it would sink, and turned to Mother Ann for guidance. She assured them not to worry, and that an angel had told her that they would reach America safely. The storm eventually passed, the ship continued on its way, and the stunned ship captain told the Shakers that they were free to worship as they pleased.[24]

With that, Ann's pilgrimage to the United States sojourned onward. The short, stern-faced, thirty-eight-year-old visionary led her little band of eight believers across the ocean with nothing but her blessed assurance and her eyebrows furrowed in determination.

Once the Shakers reached the United States, they found refuge in the home of residents of New York who allowed them to stay for a short time until they found jobs. They did this after Mother Ann approached them and informed them on no uncertain terms that she was, in her words, "commissioned of God to preach the everlasting Gospel to America . . . and an Angel commanded [her] to come to this house, and to make a home for [her] and [her] people."[25] She worked as a housemaid and soon learned that there was cheap land up for purchase about 100 miles north of New York City. She and her followers purchased a large plot of land and began building the very first Shaker colony near Albany.[26] It was at this time, in 1774, that Ann's husband Abraham left her, unable and unwilling to adhere to the new Shaker lifestyle. She never heard from him again.[27]

24. Boyko, Boris.
25. Boyko, Boris.
26. Boyko, Boris.
27. "Women in Religion: Leader of the Shakers."

The men, then referring to themselves as the "brethren," began clearing the land and building structures for them and the Shaker "sisters" to reside in.[28] Mother Ann was sure from the beginning to put an emphasis on working hard and finding joy in work, a very different concept than the one she complied with in Manchester. The work of the Shakers would not include the dark, filthy textile factories she knew long ago. Instead, they worked outside in the clean and quiet air, brothers harvesting crops and working the land, sisters cooking and cleaning, later going on to weave cloth, make poplar baskets, and sew clothes.[29]

The place was simple and sustained itself through members' selling high quality goods in town to provide what little income that the community needed to thrive. Removed from most of civilization, this place was perfect for the kind of counter-cultural living situation Mother Ann wanted for her Shakers. They named their communities the United Society of Believers in Christ's Second Coming.

A hallmark of the Shaker communities was that they offered complete equality of the sexes in a time when such a thing was almost non-existent.[30] Ann preached about "Father-Mother God," the Almighty having both male and female attributes instead of only male.[31] Ann believed that she herself represented the feminine parts of the Almighty incarnate, while Jesus, her counterpart, represented the masculine ones. The Shaker communities were run by a panel of elders, both male and female, who took charge of different duties but made community decisions together.[32] This was unheard of in the late 1780s. Because of this, once the Shaker communities began to blossom, they had a ratio of 1:3 male to female members.[33] The Shaker life offered women a choice apart from the usual cookie-cutter wife-

28. "Women in Religion: Leader of the Shakers."
29. Lowry, Lois. *Like the Willow Tree*.
30. "Women in Religion: Leader of the Shakers."
31. Lowry, Lois. *Like the Willow Tree*.
32. Bromley, David G.
33. Gershon, Livia. "The Shaker Formula for Gender Equality."

and-mother mold that was expected of them. Ann did not want any other woman to marry because she had to.

After a religious revival in other parts of the country, people came to visit the Shakers, and many converted, leaving them with the intention of starting their own Shaker colonies. Communities began their foundations in New Hampshire, Massachusetts, and Maine.[34] At the age of 45 in 1781, Mother Ann took "missionary tours" throughout New England in order to promote the creation of further Shaker colonies.[35] Eight more were formed as a result of this attempt to spread the Shaker lifestyle.[36] However, during these tours many Americans found Ann's teachings to be heresy and responded in brutal ways, subjecting Mother Ann and her followers to stonings, mob violence, and further imprisonment.[37] After her release, she lived only a short time.

Ann, the mother who had given birth to these colonies, died at the age of 48 in 1784.[38]

The Shaker colonies were in their infancy, with followers only just beginning to find truth in the simple wisdom of Mother Ann's famous adage, "hands to work and hearts to God." But her colonies would go on to outlive Mother Ann in ways that she never expected.

The communities that Mother Ann had planted seeds for continued growing after her death. Over the next century her teachings were recorded and passed on, Shaker songs were sung, worship ceremonies continued, and communities continued to crop up, even in her absence. In the mid-nineteenth century, Shaker colonies reached their peak with around 6,000 total practitioners of this religion that was once considered complete lunacy.[39] Members lived in peace with one another, celibate and hard-working, devoted entirely to prayer

34. Boyko, Boris.
35. Benowitz, June Melby. *Encyclopedia of American Women and Religion.*
36. Boyko, Boris.
37. "Women in Religion: Leader of the Shakers."
38. The Editors of Encyclopaedia Britannica. "Ann Lee: American Religious Leader."
39. Reif, Rita. "Shaker Design at Whitney Museum."

and bringing the Kingdom of God down to earth. The Shakers frequently took in orphans who had lost family members due to the Spanish influenza and other tragedies that struck the United States, ready and willing to bring them up in the Shaker way and instilling in them their teachings of hard and joyous work.[40] They learned these crafts through the ways the community sustained itself: by selling the fine-crafted soaps, silverware, furniture, clothing, poplar baskets, and candies in town made with perfect attention to detail by the Shakers. Once these children reached adulthood, they were given the choice of whether they wanted to fully become members of the Shaker community, and many chose to stay. Many others carried the strong skill-set they learned from the Shakers into more traditional jobs outside of the Shaker community. Shaker contributions to the outside world through their innovative inventions such as the washing machine, circular saw, and flat broom are often not accredited to them.[41]

While successful at their peak and efficient in their self-sufficiency, the inevitable decline in Shakers due to their commitment to celibacy took its toll on their population.

At its nineteenth-century peak, there were 18 functioning Shaker colonies.[42]

Today, there is one.

Two followers of Mother Ann Lee are living, Brother Arnold Hadd and Sister June Carpenter.[43]

These days, the Shakers don't shake. In fact, the communities put a stop to the wild dancing and whirling around during worship because once there were many very old Shakers who were unable to move in such a way, it was no longer something they could do all together.[44] The Shakers did not want inequality to exist in the community, so

40. Lowry, Lois. *Like the Willow Tree*.
41. "Sabbathday Lake Shaker Village."
42. Blakemore, Erin. "There Are Only Two Shakers Left in the World."
43. Blakemore, Erin.
44. Lowry, Lois.

they did away with the activity. However, throughout their entire existence, music has been a vital piece of community life. Singing is a daily ritual. One of the most famous Shaker songs, Simple Gifts, captures the essence of Shaker life.

> 'Tis the gift to be simple,
> 'Tis the gift to be free.
> 'Tis the gift to come down where we ought to be
> And when we find ourselves in the place just right
> 'Twill be in the valley of love and delight.[45]

The two living Shakers remain deeply devoted to the teachings of Mother Ann. Brother Arnold said in an interview in 2014 that "One of the great geniuses of Mother [was] that she lifted up physical labor to a place where it was spiritual. It's our duty to express God's love in daily life."[46] Quoting the late Brother Ted in the same interview, he added, "The Shakers are very practical people. We are to make life as little hellish for each other as possible."[47] Throughout the centuries of Shaker living, this has remained a noble goal.

At Sabbathday Lake, a Shaker colony, it is 5:00 in the morning. The deeply devout Shaker lifestyle is evident all around: every corner of the room is scrubbed to perfection, clean and simple, produced and maintained by a people committed to a favorite adage of Ann, "hands to work and hearts to God." As she liked to remind them, "There is no dirt in heaven."[48] The sun has not yet crept over the horizon, but the two remaining Shakers are soon to rise, eat a light breakfast, pray, and go to work. As said by the late Brother Ted, "There is no place in America where you can feel a sense of a life having been led so long and so faithfully as you do at Sabbathday Lake."[49] As the Shakers start to rise before the dawn creeps in, the only sound to be heard is

45. Lowry, Lois.
46. "Sabbathday Lake Shaker Village."
47. "Sabbathday Lake Shaker Village."
48. Bishop, Rufus et. al.
49. "Sabbathday Lake Shaker Village."

an old-fashioned grandfather clock ticking in the corner. Simplicity, hard work, prayer. There is little else. The stillness of Sabbathday Lake is in stark contrast to the chaos of the world around it. The aura surrounding this place has the same dedication and unshakable peace in the face of worldly chaos that resulted from Mother Ann Lee.

Community. Equality, simplicity. Charity. A handmade quilt, a glass of water. A ball of yarn, a wooden church bench. The world that Mother Ann endured so much hardship to create is here, and is one of the oldest sustained religious practices in America. Through more than a hundred years of growth and decline, triumph and tribulation, persecution and freedom, the Shakers, like the legacy of their Mother Ann, have persevered.

## Bibliography

Andrews, Edward Deming. *The People Called Shakers: a Search for the Perfect Society*. New York: Dover Publications, 1963.

"Ann Lee Biography, Life, Interesting Facts." Famous Birthdays By SunSigns.Org. SunSigns.org, 2017. https://www.sunsigns.org/famousbirthdays/d/profile/ann-lee/.

Barker, Mildred. *Our Mother in the New Creation*. New Gloucester, ME: The United Society of Shakers, 1963.

Benowitz, June Melby. *Encyclopedia of American Women and Religion*. Santa Barbara, CA: ABC-CLIO, 2017.

Bishop, Rufus, Seth Y. Wells, and J. P. MacLean. *Testimonies of the Life, Character, Revelations and Doctrines of Our Ever Blessed Mother Ann Lee, and the Elders with Her: through Whom the Word of Eternal Life Was Opened in This Day of Christs Second Appearing*. Hancock Pittsfield, MA: Printed by J. Tallcott & J. Deming, Junrs., 1816.

Blakemore, Erin. "There Are Only Two Shakers Left in the World." Smithsonian.com. Smithsonian Institution, January 6, 2017. https://www.smithsonianmag.com/smart-news/there-are-only-two-shakers-left-world-180961701/.

Boyko, Boris. "Ann Lee, a Woman of Great Faith." Ann Lee, A Woman of Great Faith, 2014. http://libertymagazine.org/article/ann-lee-a-woman-of-great-faith.

Bromley, David G. "The United Society of Believers in Christ's Second Appearing (the Shakers)." Sociology of Religion. Accessed December 11, 2019. http://www.people.vcu.edu/~dbromley/shakers.html.

Craik, James. *Old and New*. New York: D. Dana, 1860.

Gershon, Livia. "The Shaker Formula for Gender Equality." Jstor, February 1, 2018. https://daily.jstor.org/the-shaker-formula-for-gender-equality/.

Lowry, Lois. *Like the Willow Tree: the Diary of Lydia Amelia Pierce*. New York: Scholastic, 2011.

"Mother Ann Lee Facts." Your Dictionary. The Gale Group, 2010. https://biography.yourdictionary.com/mother-ann-lee.

"Sabbathday Lake Shaker Village." Sabbathday Lake Shaker Village, 2014. https://www.maineshakers.com/.

The Editors of Encyclopaedia Britannica. "Ann Lee: American Religious Leader." Encyclopædia Britannica. Encyclopædia Britannica, inc., July 28, 2016. https://www.britannica.com/topic/Shakers.

Tipton, Meredyth. "Mother Ann Lee." Mother Ann Lee. Accessed December 11, 2019. https://spider.georgetowncollege.edu/htallant/courses/his338/students/mtipton/annlee.htm

Reif, Rita. "'SHAKER DESIGN' AT WHITNEY MUSEUM." The New York Times. The New York Times, May 30, 1986. https://www.nytimes.com/1986/05/30/arts/shaker-design-at-whitney-museum.html.

Rudy, Lisa Jo. "Biography of Ann Lee, Founder of the Shakers." Learn Religions. https://www.learnreligions.com/ann-lee-4694324 (accessed December 11, 2019).

"Women in Religion: Leader of the Shakers." History of American Women. Accessed December 11, 2019. http://www.womenhistoryblog.com/2008/12/ann-lee.html.

Yolen, Jane. "Mother Ann and the Blessed Fire." In *Simple Gifts*, 8–9, 10-11. New York, NY: The Viking Press, 1976.

# DOMINIQUE WITTEN

**Senior**
**Major:** Creative Writing
**Reading:** Poetry

Dom was raised in Detroit, MI in a pink house her friend once described as the color of raw chicken. She remembers riding the DDOT bus home and never going pass the red house on her bike. She enjoys drag shows and using emphasis on the wrong syllables. Dom can be found at one of three places: working, going to school or passed out over a half-written poem on her futon. She writes about the fractals of worlds she experiences between the characters she meets. She writes about growing up with her biological mother and her adopted mother (who is biologically her aunt) and the effect not having a two-parent household had on her life. Because Dom struggles to remember things such as where she put her coat in the dead of winter; her poems serve as the snap shots she can't seem to shake: the lingering moments. In her struggle to create a time capsule, she writes poetry.

*Nominated by: Sarah Messer*

# The antagonist

in my story is a woman without mercy, she exists only as highlights of a nine year-old tethered to Langston Hughes's bruised *crystal stair* she stares at the moon mimicking every move of the man in the sky in hopes he studies her too at age two she was rose petal mid-winter winning smiles from strangers in shopping centers sparking honey hues like firecrackers held for the first time the first time I diagnosed her as monster I tripped over our four year distance the second time her hand reached for mine I snarled with heated nostrils and she became the monster.

# Two Dollars and a Nickel

She is always there,
laying in the same spot
under the once white bench
near the birch tree.

Her face stuck in the second before
a smile, holding frame like
a polaroid of the simple times
with big hair and big attitudes.

Her eyebrows searching for
the last thought washed away
in the memory of the person
she used to be good at calculus.

She says she was the tallest and
the tattle tale of the siblings.
Too much pride to give up a fight,
not enough fight to give up pride.

In eighth grade, the boys – and the men
noticed her big breasted and fed well
with the good fat. The boys and the men
imagined themselves above and inside her.

Underneath her she kept the essentials:
pipe and lighter locked away in
the big pocket of a men's XXL
dark brown trench coat for warmth.

Last December during our weekly shared
meal of gas station coffee and bow tie donuts
her eyes clamped to the cement and she paused
from the grease and sugar to say

*I put hyphens in all my babies' names.*
*Did you know that bed bugs could swim?*
*My Daddy invented the step stool on the UPS truck.*
*Do you think God remembers making my heart?*

In her world we eat pancakes in the shape
of rocket ships and she teaches me
the colors of the rainbow
paying special attention to green.

But she is always there,
draped in an aged sadness
contagious as the habit
she formed all those years ago.

Her children come here sometimes,
to give her crocheted socks and gloves.
On Wednesday we all came, toting
a box of chocolates and paper airplanes.

Me, I don't have the gift of forgiveness
to give her because I remember,
when we'd read stories before bed
and play with her red lipstick.

Now, she is another woman
who asks if a little cash can be spared.
So, I give her all my change,
before I say,

*Happy birthday.*

# Metacognition

i was 10 / making green beans with / salt / sugar and butter / cuz momma likes it that way / salt and sugar / both with enough power to kill on their own / but together they cancel each other out / momma loves food / i stopped her from cooking when i had to start cleaning the dishes / i don't want children / i don't think i'd do it right / i think they'd be just as fucked up as i am / unable to cry in private / for fear someone will break into my journal / everything is screwed up in my head / my mind goes from magenta sharpies / to photocopies / to not being able to tell my therapist thank you / i think i'd be a gentle flower if i believed in reincarnation / or a pygmy sloth / my dentist yelled at me / about flossing more cuz i got a dead tooth / and a deadbeat daddy / i've never met the man my birth mom says was a basketball player / or in jail for attempted murder / after someone made fun of his name being tracy / the headpiece of my headphones broke / i've learned how to be in public again / i still can't look a stranger in the eye / my cousin in the navy says / sometimes dolphins hump submarines / before they kiss the blades of propellers / every man i've kissed i've fucked / every man i fuck / is missing / the ability for me to love / them back

# Toxicology

When the man I was fucking
spilled his semen on my thigh
I took a sample and tasted
a salty history to prove that
some masculinity was a bitter
flavor similar to the way I
imagine water from stripped
lead pipes tastes: toxic.

# Until Death Do Us Part

Commemorating Junebug's southern twang and Jaquanda's hips

Under the gaze of the little dipper. Waiting until the street

Lights turn on to stop a game of pickup basketball with a blue crate.

Taming the bébé kids by beating them until their throats close.

Unsteady hands when a white police officer asks you to

Reach for your ID and still get shot reaching for your skin

Even though we were all born from Black Mother whose baby was stolen.

# Momma wants to know if I write letters to God:

I say *no*
>       and hear
Her exhale
>               let
>       out     sloppy over the phone.

Momma says she fulfilled her tithe when she raised me in church.
Momma says God has His eye on my heart.

I wonder
>               if he blinks
>               when I say
>                       *I don't know*

*if I believe.*

I fear Prophets
>               who twist
>               gospel for
>               profit.
I fear Saints
>               who make religion
>               a puppet exercise for
>               prejudice.

If God has His eye on my heart
>                       then he knows
It breaks
>               when parents say
>                       *I love you*
>               *but...*

"I love you

          but we <u>must</u>

          muzzle you for

                          company."

"I love you

          but please attempt

          some modesty in your

                *lifestyle*     *choice.* "

"I love you

          but I hate

          the        sin you

                  dress up in."

Momma wants to know if I pray:

I say

    *no*

       to her last

             attempt

                    at hope.

I don't pray Momma,

But Momma I am

          good,

I still learned to love

          *the Saint*

             & 

          *the Sinner.*

I gave my love to the girl who won't swallow carbs but plans to swallow her mom's pills.

I gave my love to the boy who isn't *man enough* to persist after refusals of his advances.

I gave my love to people who tiptoe in restrooms in case someone deems them predator.

321 | Momma wants to know if I write letters to God:

Momma do you know

                    I am good?

I think you worry we will find
        different
sides            of the horizon.

I think you worry we will rest
               with wrestled
               hearts.

I cannot sit with pretty posture in a pew painted in the blood of people
*we* deem sinners.
I cannot sit with hushed lips while people are murdered for a choice
they never made.
I cannot be afraid your love will dissipate if I choose to love someone
for all their parts.

Momma, I do not write letters or pray
                  but because your God taught me
                  love has no judgements
                  for you
                  I will
                  try.

# ADRIAN WONG

**Junior**
**Major:** Music Composition
**Reading:** Essay

Adrian is a Music Composition major who was born and raised in Hong Kong. He strives to create music that is engaging to perform and listen to, and aims to create an emotional connection with his audience through imagery, drama, and unapologetic conviction. Adrian's music takes inspiration from a wide array of subjects, ranging from the natural world, intersections of Chinese and Western culture, to the personal, day-to-day occurrences in life.

*Nominated by: David Ward*

# Bright's Question

Every Friday since sophomore year, I would rush from the library to my hour-long composition lesson with Bright Sheng, grappling with my manuscript paper and my freshly-printed scores while wrestling with my backpack as I clumsily knock on his office door. He would then look up from his desk, or from his piano if he was demonstrating something to his previous student, and slowly saunter over and let me in. He would always be dressed in the same black jeans and black leather sneakers with white soles, and either a particularly stylish mint/seafoam green wool sweater or a black sweater with a medium blond trim along the sleeves near the collar. Pretty trendy for a Chinese-American in his sixties.

"How are you?" would always be his first question, and I would more often than not stammer out an answer about how *overworked* and *tired* and *stressed out* I am, to which he would usually give no visible reaction and ask no further questions. Sometimes, he would comment on how much work I am doing and how it is a good thing to be busy. I guess that teaching at Michigan for more than twenty years essentially desensitizes you to all the anxiety and angst that young musicians get on an almost daily basis. That's not to say he does not care, though – on the days when my stress level noticeably exceeded my usual threshold or when I was so *overworked* and *tired* and *stressed out* that I actually got sick, he would genuinely try to help, like when I got the flu earlier this semester and was coughing all over his office. Bright offered me the fruits his wife bought for him ("These are very expensive, very good quality dates. Very soothing for your throat.") and the familiar-to-most-Chinese-people Chinese cough medicine that he keeps in his office ("Go on, don't sip it – gulp it down quick so I can give you another spoon."). This was one of my happiest moments in college. He was showing that he cared about me the way Asian elders showed they cared – not by stating it explicitly, but through little actions that unexpectedly make your day just a little bit better.

If someone had told me before my sophomore year that that would happen, I would not have believed them. Bright had garnered himself a reputation in the university that was difficult to pinpoint. A friend of mine showed me an alignment chart they made of the composition professors at Michigan, and Bright was a "neutral evil", and I can see why. Apparently in last year's auditions he didn't shake any of the auditionees' hands. He also would sometimes express rather controversial views about certain composers or composition practices in our seminar. One such example, which caused so much of a stir that one of the students published an op-ed in the *Michigan Daily* about it, was when he accused Pierre Boulez, a considerably influential composer and conductor in the 20th century, of ruining generations of composers, because Boulez rejected the study of all pre-20th-century music. Bright himself, despite working in a musical language that is obviously post-19th-century, is a fierce proponent of "studying the classics", and he is often quite vocal about it too – he often laments to me about how young composers only listen to living composers when doing pre-compositional research, while ignoring pieces by masters like Beethoven and Bach and Brahms who had "proven" hits that worked. "師古不泥古", he told me once, "learn from past but don't imitate the past". He was often quite headstrong about this and frequently brings it up in interviews, and I often wonder how one is able to have such strong views about music when it is such an abstract form of art. I admire Bright's self-assurance and confidence in what he believes in, even though some might misconstrue it with "evilness". These are traits that seem miles away for someone like me, who often feels quite *overworked* and *tired* and *stressed* about his own music and never knows whether it is any good or not.

Bright exudes confidence to such a degree that even my parents, who had only met him once, could feel his "aura", as they put it. He is not tall, perhaps hovering around the 5'6"-5'7" range, but his presence often commands a room. Perhaps it is the way he walks with his head titled slightly up and to the side on his very straight spine, his toes pointed outwards with every step. Or perhaps it is the way he sits. In our lessons, he would lean back on his black swivel chair at a (to the inexperienced swivel chair user) dangerously obtuse angle, sometimes resting his feet on the spindle of my inferior non-swivel chair as he pops almonds and walnuts and other trail-mix-like snacks into his mouth. Or perhaps it is the way he talks – he rarely uses filler words and phrases, and gets straight to the point. His emails are a great example of this. I once emailed him two paragraphs stating my concerns about a drastic change he suggested I should make in my music. I included the proposed roadmap of the piece and asked whether it was indeed what we discussed in our lesson, and presented a couple of questions about pacing and emotional impact the new configuration would bring up. He replied with "Your understanding is correct. Best, B". That, I thought, was a sign of a person who knew they were good at their work – not the (frankly) disappointing and somewhat frustrating one-line answer, but when they can sign-off their emails with a single letter.

I, on the other hand, have always signed-off my emails with my full name, and very occasionally (if I felt like being "casual" and "friendly" or when I was addressing a friend) just my first name. I have gotten myself into the habit of slouching, looking at the ground as I tread from one place to another (the freezing weather in Michigan is also partly to blame – growing up in sub-tropical Hong Kong, I am very much inclined to minimize the contact surface between me and the harsh snow). I do not own a swivel chair, and have been drilled by various teachers growing up to never lean back on a chair's back legs ("There was a very promising goalkeeper on the Liverpool F.C. youth team who broke his back that way and never walked again," said Mr. Bailey in second grade). I catch myself using "like" and "um" and "uh" and other filler words, and my sentence structure is rarely succinct, often stretching out to an extent that it becomes a five-to-six comma run-on sentence, often using multiple synonyms to get my point across, which, although sometimes is useful and beneficial to the reader to get a clearer idea of what I mean, can quickly become excessive and unnecessary, tiring out the reader as they try to decipher and understand what I was really saying.

This meandering quality of my speech and writing sometimes bleeds into my music too. There were two or three pieces in the past year-and-a-half where Bright suggested that I should cut rather substantial chunks out as they "don't really say anything – I'd much rather you get to this high point in a more straightforward manner". This was when Bright had the most fun in our lessons. He would jump up from his chair, grab his red colored-pencil and my music, plop down on the piano, and start playing the sections that he deemed to be structurally weaker. "You don't really need that," he would say, playing the piece while omitting the section in question, "you hear how the preceding and succeeding sections actually connect perfectly?" I would then (often) agree, and he would then gleefully grab the red pencil and draw a huge "X" on the offending bars of music.

The first time we did this was also when he cut out the most music, although he was not the person who instigated the change – I wrote eight-and-a-half minutes of music for a choir that could only perform a six-and-a-half-minute piece in a competition. We had to remove two minutes of music – easily two weeks of work! But Bright showed no mercy. He drew red "X" after red "X", occasionally ripping the paper with the amount of force he asserted on the pencil, making decisions that I would have taken days to decide in mere seconds. I remember myself laughing in disbelief after listening to the new version – it was so much more streamlined and effective and there were no "floating" passages that did not belong anywhere. However, during that lesson when I looked on, jaw agape, as Bright literally tore apart my music, I was reminded of one of my lessons with Professor Kristin Kuster, my composition professor freshman year.

Professor Kuster is basically the opposite of Bright (I genuinely do not know why I am using "Professor Kuster" to address Professor Kuster and "Bright" to address Professor Sheng in this essay. Professor Kuster actually told me to address her as "Kristy" in our first lesson and I would never address Professor Sheng as "Bright" in real life. I still call Professor Kuster "Professor Kuster" though – maybe it is my Asian upbringing, but calling a professor by their first name just seems wrong). She is tall (amplified by the fact that she often wore black high-heeled knee-length boots, which were often paired with black skinny jeans, a black button-down/blouse, and a black shawl, which blended her entire being into a long, looming shadow), blond, white, and usually pretty cheery and bubbly in our lessons. Basically, the opposite of myself. Not that we did not get along – quite the contrary, in fact. She is highly popular among the students – despite Bright being a "bigger name", Professor Kuster usually has twice the number of composers in her studio. "Never cross out your music!", she exclaimed as she pointed out one place where I did so in my manuscript, "there is never 'wrong' music, it's just music that's in the wrong place!" She then told me to always circle the offending section, and draw a little looped tail on the edge of the circle. "It's not bad, it just doesn't belong there!"

Whereas Bright helped me a lot with my music writing and laying down a good foundation of craft, Professor Kuster actually helped me a lot with coping with my confidence and self-esteem problems. I started composing relatively late compared to my cohort, and was amazed and terrified to hear about the accomplishments of some of them during my first week at Michigan – they were commissioned by a professional string quartet, they got their work performed by an orchestra, they put on an original musical, they went to Juilliard pre-college. Me, I have never even gotten a single piece of mine played by actual musicians. I only knew one other composer my age during high school, and he was not the most motivated person – he finished a bunch of his college application essays in class, two hours before the deadline. So, I did not have anyone my age with which I can compare myself before college, and as a result I had no idea where I stood. It did not help me psychologically when, out of the ten schools I had applied to in the U.S., Michigan was the only school that accepted me (it was, however, my first choice, which was such a stroke of luck that I still often express my disbelief to whoever I am talking to whenever the subject of auditions or college/grad school applications gets brought up).

Once, I was having a particularly rough week and did not bring anything to show Professor Kuster. She graciously offered to end our lesson early and told me to spend the free hour resting and recovering from the hectic schedule I was on. As I stared into my *exhausted* reflection in the glass table in her office, the culmination of *self-doubt* and *anxiety* and *stress* and *culture shock of living in a different country* and *missing my family* and the *horrible weather* and the *creative block* finally hit me. Before I can stop myself, I blurted out:

"Why am I here?"

"What do you mean?"

I told her about all the awesome things my peers were doing and how I was only accepted to Michigan and I listed all the awful things I felt about myself and my music. As I was explaining, I started to see a sliver of a grin starting to form on Professor Kuster's face.

"Every year freshmen ask me this question, and every year I'll tell them that I won't answer them."

Not expecting this response, I pressed on and asked her why.

"If I tell you why, then you'll just hold on to that aspect of your music and not develop anything else. Trust yourself that you are here because we think you deserve to be here."

It was genuinely quite reassuring to hear that my professor had faith in me, and I was soon able to dig myself out of that rut.

Yet, as anyone who works in a creative field knows, frustration never ever truly goes away. During my sophomore year, I found myself having another rough week, but for a slightly different reason: I was finding it hard to like the music I was producing. For the very first time, composing started to feel like a job, and while I've been warned multiple times by my family and friends and composers' interviews on YouTube that that might happen, I was truly in shock about how much I dreaded walking into a piano room and taking out my pencil and manuscript. I walked into Bright's office that week with less music than I would have hoped, and all we could talk about the music was covered in a mere fifteen minutes. After he finished, there were a good thirty seconds of awkward silence as he turned to his iMac to check his emails while I pondered about whether to end my lesson right there or tell him about the roadblock I have hit recently. I chose the latter, and knowing that Bright is not the type of person who would remember my music during my audition two years ago, I opted to address my insecurities through a different route.

"Are you always happy with the music you write?"

He stopped scrolling through his emails and swiveled his chair towards me.

"What do you mean?"

"It's just that I have been feeling not the best about my music lately, and I'm wondering whether you have had the same experience where you had written something that you are not happy with."

Bright started furrowing his brows and leaned back steeply on his chair, head titled to one side as he tried to formulate a response.

"I'll tell you what, let's go to my website and go through it work by work and we'll rate everything out of a 100."

He pulled up his website, and the familiar red and black color scheme, the photos of his latest opera, and his recent headshots (one was a close up of him seated in front of a Steinway in his black sweater, resting his chin on his baton-clad fist; the other a medium-wide shot of him leaning on one leg in a green field, laughing away from the camera in his black winter coat and black jeans) greeted me – I had perused it countless times during college application season and the summer leading up to studying with him. He clicked on his works-list and started rating every piece.

"That I'll give a 97. That a 95 – I wasn't too happy with the structure. Oh, this I have a lot of problems with and I'll probably revise it soon – I'll give it a 93..."

We soon went through all eighty-something pieces. He did not rate a single piece below 93. I pointed this out to him.

"Well, you have to be happy with what you put out! Just revise it until you feel good about it!"

Compared to what Professor Kuster said, this was obviously less of a quick pick-me-up. But I learned a valuable lesson that music is never finished – it just gets performed and there is always room for revision. Hearing him say that he would be revising a piece he wrote in the late-80s/early-90s put a lot of pressure off of trying to make my music *perfect* the first time around. However, even after these two conversations I had with Professor Kuster and Bright, the tiny voice that says "you're not good enough" in my ear appears every now and then. Sure, it is now a whisper rather than a shout, but the feeling of "not good enough" still lingers on, sometimes enveloping me like a giant greenhouse, trapping me in an inescapable cycle of doubt and fear.

Chinese New Year came around not long after that, and I, along with two other Hong Kong composition majors who were studying in Michigan, were invited to Bright's house for New Year's dinner. We arrived at his mansion, thanks to his wife picking us up from the music school. He sauntered out, head titled and toes pointed outward, of course, to greet us. His seven-year-old daughter was not far behind, hiding behind the door frame, wary of these three complete strangers entering her castle.

As we entered through the front door, I was quickly reminded of the reason I applied to the University of Michigan. On the mantlepiece next to one of his Steinway grand pianos ("There's another one in my library so I can write while Fayfay [his daughter] is practicing, and one in the basement if my wife needs to practice as well.") were pictures of Bright with various world-class musicians and politicians. There was one with the cellist Yo-yo Ma, for whom he has written several pieces; there was one with Leonard Bernstein, arguably the most influential American composer-conductor ever, with whom he studied and worked as an assistant for the last five years of Bernstein's life (Bright's full title at Michigan is actually "the Leonard Bernstein Distinguished University Professor of Composition"); there was one of him shaking hands with Aaron Copland, "the Dean of American composers"; and there was another one with him shaking hands with then-president Bill Clinton – Bright received a special commission to create a new work for the White House state dinner that year. The list of important and influential musicians (and people in general) on that mantlepiece was absolutely mind-boggling.

With great difficulty, I pulled myself away from the mantlepiece. As I turned around, I was met with a giant, colorful, and (for the lack of a better word) bright 8-feet banner, one of the press materials for his latest opera, *Dream of the Red Chamber*, which was premiered by the San Francisco Opera in 2016. That was not the only opera-related memorabilia in his house. There were also several pictures of the production of his 2003 opera *Madame Mao*, which was about the life of Mao Zedong's wife. Bright grew up during the infamous Cultural Revolution himself, and was sent to Qinghai and the age of 15, a province bordering Tibet. He worked as a pianist and percussionist for a music and dance troupe there for seven years, studying folk music, and, secretly, Western music. He became one of the first students to be admitted to the Shanghai Conservatory after the Cultural Revolution ended. Bright then moved to the United States to get his master's in Queen's College and his doctorate at Columbia in the 80s, where he was students with what we now call the "first-generation" of (highly successful) Chinese-American composers: Bright, Tan Dun (best known for writing the soundtrack to *Crouching Tiger, Hidden Dragon*), Zhou Long (who won a Pulitzer), and Chen Yi (who has received fellowships from the Guggenheim Foundation and the American Academy of Arts and Letters). He soon became an American citizen, winning numerous grants and awards which elevated him to the position he is in today.

Once, during a lesson, I asked Bright about him "making it" in the United States and whether he has advice related to forging a career as a composer. I was rambling on about my concerns of (possibly) being an immigrant composer and working against a traditionally white-dominant field that (frequently) equates diversity with tokenism, when Bright stopped me mid-sentence.

"It's good that you're thinking about all these things, but the first question you should figure out is what kind of composer you want to be."

"What do you mean?"

"Like what sort of music you want to write, what sort of things you want to do."

One could hear a pin drop as I concentrated to think of an adequate answer to this, admittedly, basic, but often overlooked question for a lot of young composers. I must have had a pretty quizzical look on my face because he then went on:

"It was actually Leonard Bernstein who asked me this question when I was studying with him, and I told him I wanted to compose and conduct orchestras – I wanted to be like him!" he said as he got up from his swivel chair and walked over to the little station stacked with boilers and cups next to the grand piano to pour himself some recently brewed tea.

After Bright said that, I knew my answer to his question

immediately. I want to write beautiful music for the best musicians in the world. I want my music to influence people. I want to use my music to open up conversations about controversial topics. I want a commission to write an opera. I want to prove that someone who is not white or of European descent is capable of making it in classical music. I want to have three grand pianos in my mansion, one for me in my study, one for my beautiful child, and one for my loving wife. "I WANT TO BE LIKE YOU!" I almost screamed at the top of my lungs – but I did not. Maybe it was because I did not truly believe in myself that I was able to achieve that lofty goal, or maybe it was because I did not want to seem like a fool grasping at straws in front of the person who knew the quality of my music best. What I know for sure was that I did not say it because I was embarrassed – whether because of myself or of my admiration of Bright, I still do not know up to this day.

This conversation happened a year ago, and I do not know whether I would have answered Bright's question honestly even now. Yes, compared to where I was last year I am now in a way better position in my career, thanks to the mercy of a couple of judges in several composition competitions, and the good friends I have made who trusted my music so much they performed it multiple times. But despite all these "achievements", I still feel unfulfilled. Do not get me wrong, I was definitely happy and excited when they announced that I had won the so-and-so prize or when audience members reacted favorably to my music, but that feeling was, always, so fleeting. I would soon be back in my natural self-doubting state after a couple of hours. "Did they really like my music?" "Was I awarded that just because they saw who my professor is on my CV?" It almost seemed like I *wanted* to feel miserable, and that I was afraid and suspicious of success.

And so, I would continue to scramble my way into Bright's office and be *stressed* and *overworked* and *tired* almost every week, and the frustration that accompanies the pure, unadulterated joy of putting down notes on a page would always be there. I've already accepted that the little voice that whispers incessantly "you're not good enough" and "you'll never achieve your dreams" would never go away. Yet, slowly but surely, I have started to see these things as old friends – old friends that keep me in check so that I never become arrogant or ungrateful about all the wonderful things that have happened to me so far. And meeting and studying with Bright is one of those wonderful things – so here's to more expensive fruits and cough medicine in the future.

# ERIKA WOO

**Junior**
**Major:** Economics
**Reading:** Poetry

Erika Woo is a junior studying Economics, with minors in Art & Design and Creative Writing. She loves poetry and slam poetry, Harry Baker, Walt Whitman and Steven Crane blow her mind! In her free time she dances to Christian rap, Japanese punk rock, and KPOP down the sidewalks of Ann Arbor or invents occupations that could incorporate all her areas of study.

*Nominated by: James Cody Walker*

# insecurity deposit

don't look into my eyes to see what they hide,
the insecurities inside, the tears I've cried
thinking I'm unlovable
thinking I'm incurable
because

my cheeks are too big
bone structure like a pig
my nose is too long
and my teeth are all wrong

my vocal cords are raw from shouting
my esophagus is acid from puking
and I don't have any guts,
my appendix is extraneous
but my stomach is bulging from emptiness

my words are messed up,
impure and hollow tin
my mouth is the root of all my sin
I need a rein on my tied tongue
I can't breathe: collapsible lungs

don't look at my back, it's abnormal
and my shoulders are hunched
posture broken from years of holding my head
confidence broken, dried up, dead

I have awkward elbows and scarred wrists
my nail beds have been abused and chewed
and my hands are allergic to a really long list
of people and their things
well, just about everything

with weak reflexes and knobby knees
I convulse every time I sneeze
my movements are robotic and slow
I lost my hand-eye coordination years ago

my ribs are hidden under folds of tender snares
and oversized clothes to hide a damaged colon
my thighs are burning from that first flight of stairs
my calves have fattened, my ankles have swollen

don't look at my feet, I don't want you to know where I've been
they aren't trail blazers, they are trial makers,
trudging through several feet of sludge and buckets of floods
it's no wonder my heart is too tired to pump the blood
that's blue, an unusual hue
I think I'm cold blooded and immune to heat
But you call me in, and I take a seat

You look into my plain brown eyes
and see behind the guise
you tell me I'm beautiful
and that fact is indisputable.

# What's wrong?

it bounces off the walls
"what is wrong with her?"
and I hurry along
head bent, eyes watering
letting the full weight of your whispers
hit my ear drums, sending waves of shock through my insides.
it rattles around in my brain a while
until it trickles down,
feeding my core like a slow acting poison
all the while echoing over, all over
resounding with a lie I've heard before
"something is wrong with me."

yeah, I see you,
from the corner of my eye
behind a closed hand
judging me and my lumpy baggage
you dance on my periphery
some perfect I know I will never achieve
and in that moment
I know I've missed the mark, missed the point
or snapped the pencil point
so that it makes no marks
jagged wood splintering scratching a red x through my heart

like cross my heart and hope to die
'cause anything "less than" is unworthy of life
abnormal is not okay but eccentric is just fine
I'll change my gait to walk like you
but you'll say I crossed a line
digging around in my brain while
trying to salvage my humanity

when you question my sanity
can you ask it how it's been?
ask whether the green is really greener on the other side
or if that's just a ploy to look down and ignore the brilliant blue
sky
ask if submission and quiet are synonyms
ask if it's still authoring my story under a pseudonym
can you let It know I'm doing just fine without it
that I've still got common sense with me
to hint that there's more to life
than seeking a temporary high
because striving for other's approval
leaves me dejected
labels me rejected
ejected from the hard drive
with an error message like
"error disc not compatible"
unable to read
cannot understand
that I don't fit in

the shoe doesn't fit
I'm not your Cinderella
not some project you can fix
and no "bibbity bobbity boo"
can change me into you
I'm too dark but too light for your narrative
too tall to be short, too short to be tall
they say I can't have it all
but are appalled when I don't have it all
together
gotta be better
gotta try harder
push more
chin up shut up
gut in chest out

get out
of my head
stop haunting my dreams
I know I'm not like you
and it makes me want to scream
and claw out of my awkward
weirdness that isn't just a phase
or burn down the labels that leave me ashamed

it's when I buy into your words
broke from spending all my time
investing in your lies
broken from letting them remold me
crunching my bones
twisting and pulling my skin
my eyes my lips
into an ideal
into a doll a clone
something unreal

it's when I believe that I'm not like you
because you told me so
when I try to change myself to fit your idea
of a pretty little girl
that is when I think
"what is wrong with me?"

# The perfect storm

The rain made it glorious
a delightful drum beat
to back the lovely melody
of the clouds rock and rolling
a thunderous wail and cry
leading the world into their dark vulnerable place
letting the sun take a break
from revealing the light
allowing the darkness to creep in
and the messenger winds carry anxious sounds in waves
whispering frantically into the souls of all in its path
causing the grasses and flowers to gather excitedly
bobbing their heads, hips moving in time
and the trees are swaying
to the boom boom beat
limbs raised heavenward

so the humidity thickens
as tension gains ground
the world praises its maker
getting ready for the drip
drip
drop.

and the rain made it glorious
adding a final encore
to the perfect storm

# I heard that a field of sunflowers burned today

I heard that it was out of jealousy.
that the culprit was jealous of their beauty.
their innate pretty countenance, rimmed in gold
a crown placed delicately on their head since birth

But I think it was out of jealousy
for their bold way of life
standing taller than the other flowers
bigger, more courageous
Their face an open book,
each seed nourished by their hard work
detailing the fruit of their faith
shamelessly following the sun,
wherever he turns
they follow, faithful subjects.
They stretch their necks
bend over backwards
all in an effort to bask in his pure light
to catch each and every ray
beaming from the beams they radiate joy.
Even when the sun sets,
they await patiently for its return
and at the end of their life,
heavy from bearing the burdens they carry,
they pass on to the next generation
knowing their time has come,
bowing to meet their King.
Anyone can look at a field of sunflowers
pointing to their life giver,
and know immediately where the sun is.

I burned a field of sunflowers today.
and I don't know where to look for the sunrise tomorrow.

# Double-Sided Tape

Side A

I wake up to a wet cloudy sky of fall,
casting eerie shadows around my gray walls
The sun doesn't shine, and I don't want it to
I toss around in bed for a solid three hours
mulling over what productive activity I should probably do
but that too, is too exhausting and its two o' clock
when I finally walk out of the bat cave
caving into the cuckoo clock swirling around and around in
my head carving out time, pockets of memories and blurry
reveries
I prepare lunch with my doubts
and eat with my fears, water the plants with my tears
Then look out the window only to close the curtains
There's no use wanting things I can't have

Like social skills
Confidence without a pill
Clear thoughts and a romantic life
A daily routine free from strife

I have the sudden urge to turn and run from it all
but finding no motivation to move my muscles
I collapse back into a pile of pillows and stare at the clock.

Tick tock
Tic tac toe
Three months in a row
I realize I've been in this slump

Suddenly anger bubbles up inside me and escapes my lips in a
cruel laugh, that quickly dies in a fit of coughing.

I haven't used my voice in weeks
I haven't seen another human in weeks
I slip in and out of sleep
Gaining weight to ease the blow
Of the floor beneath my toes
Every time I find it in me to crawl out of bed
And listen to the faint voice in my head
Telling me it's alright, it's all good
Telling me I did what I could

But the other voices whispering wisps of ideas and phrases,
incomplete thoughts and half phases.
Mummer the lies disguised in a flowing lullaby, in a sickly-sweet melody
Joining the fears in perfect harmony
I swallow hoping the push them down
Blink at the thought of another let down, sundown day
spent in a brilliant haze of gray, in between
a perfect reality and something not quite guaranteed

Stop. Eject, flip. Insert, close. Play.

Side B

I watch the sun wake up, turning my purple room brilliant
shades of reds, pinks and blues.
I jump out of bed, careful not to wake my friends living one
floor below who last night I met with at the elevator on the
second story, and proceeded to tell the story of my sister's
husband's best friend's cousin who had worked in the elevator
industry all his life, until the wife insisted that it was getting
late and shouldn't I be getting to sleep?
But I haven't slept, there's so much to do
Last night I organized all of my shoes
by material and then by occasion and then by color, so that
a rainbow covered the inside of my closet then I went to the
bank to deposit a check, but it was closed because it was two

am in the morning

So right now I have breakfast with anticipation and feed the cats with joy, having a discussion with them on the importance of vitamin C so you see it was then

I had the urge to go for a run, so I ran and ran and ran, and spontaneously joy bubbles up inside of me and escapes my lips in a bright laugh.

I make it to the stop and shop six miles down Valley street where I stop and shop for fruits and meats talking to everyone I meet and so it takes me six hours to make it back home where I stare out my window

and gaze at the 41st sunrise, which brings light to my purple walls like a flower in bloom

and sends streaks of brilliant hues dancing around my room.

# HAYLEY YU

**Junior**
**Major:** Psychology and Creative Writing
**Reading:** Fiction

Hayley is a junior who is majoring in Psychology and Creative Writing with a minor in Religion. She is from California and firmly believes that Michigan weather is not as bad as Californians (and some Michigan natives...) imagine it to be. She is honored to be nominated for the Café Shapiro Anthology and hopes to continue writing throughout her life.

*Nominated by: Laura Thomas*

# My Hope for You

It was in the autumn of 1987 that you showed up to my college apartment late at night on a rainy evening. It was two in the morning and you – your hair, your clothes, your face – were soaked. My first thought was to ask why you were at my crummy apartment, twenty minutes away from campus, of all places. I opened my mouth to say something, to ask the tentative question that had formed in my mind. But I looked at your eyes and it closed. I opened the door and you stepped in tentatively, like you had no right to enter. You smelled like fall, of decaying leaves and bitter rain. I remember thinking that you must have been outside for a long time for you to be perfumed like that.

I took your shoulders and led you gently to the sofa. You were skittish, like a wild horse afraid of a thunderstorm. I remember that you were all black – black miniskirt and a black tank top, black hair and black eyes, black lines under your eyes and black shadows obscuring your face. Everything about you was almost swallowed whole by the color.

*Stay here*, I said, and you nodded. Your arms wrapped around yourself and I wondered how someone like you, someone who always seemed to have a smile ready and plastered onto her face, could shake that badly. You seemed like a carefree girl, but I knew hard it was. You told me while you were drunk. Your head had been slumped on my shoulder and you slurred out stories like I was your priest. Like you were the one who had sinned against the family you had left in the hometown you hated.

But the stories you told me were about a brother who hated you, who did things no brother should do, and a mother who refused to believe you. It wasn't your fault, but you blamed yourself anyway.

I had my eyes too. I'd noticed how you hadn't been going to the classes we shared. I saw you at parties more and more frequently, acting wild and adventurous, the party girl who's up for anything. You played your role so well that I don't think the others ever noticed that deep rooted sadness in you. If that's what you were trying to accomplish, to disappear into a role you'd been casted in since your adoption, then brava... but where did it get you?

It landed you in bed during the day, unable to get up, trying to persuade your limbs to move, to *twitch*. It made you live to drown—I wonder now if you were able to survive only because you knew that night would come, and you would be free to drink, to dance, to have sex. Did you live to numb yourself? Did it really help? God, I wish that people would've realized what was going on with you. Maybe someone would have helped the girl who tried to make everyone happy but herself.

I left you in my living room to get a towel. You were bent over and huddled into the couch, like you were doing your damndest to collapse into yourself. It hurt to see you, someone who was larger than life, so small and defeated. No one should ever look how you did back then. It broke my heart – no, it *breaks* my heart to think of it now.

I walked into the bathroom to grab a towel. I remember how my eyes met my reflection and they were tired, but not unhappy. Your eyes scared me more than anything I'd ever seen, experienced, felt before. I'd always welcome you into my home, but they're the reason I didn't question why you were there. That dull black, so past terror that you couldn't feel it anymore... to this day, your eyes that night haunt me more than anything I've experienced—more than broken bones, broken hearts, broken dreams. Something that is broken can be fixed, healed. I spent years after seeing those eyes in every dark thing in the world. Like the night sky they were vast but empty and I, of all people, couldn't even begin to fill it. That overwhelming sensation of powerlessness makes my chest flutter even now. I feared that emptiness because I didn't know if I could pull you back from it.

I stared at my reflection for a moment more. There was panic, but I quickly schooled it to a neutral expression. I pulled off one of the towels from its hook and walked back out. You had not moved an inch, your hands clasped to your chest, your shoulders hunched forward like wings were about to sprout from your back, and for a moment I wondered if you were still breathing.

*Oh God*, I remember thinking. I close my eyes now and remember how my chest ached with the pressure of anvils squeezing my sides. *Did she do something when I didn't notice?*

Then I realized you were crying. It wasn't that you couldn't move, it was that you were paralyzed. Unable to move because of whatever demons screamed at you, you were trying so damn hard just to *breathe.* Your head was bent down, eyes shut. Now that I think about it, I think that I thought you looked beautiful. You were the first time I had ever seen despair so clearly displayed, and your pain was so hauntingly beautiful, the quiet loveliness of a graveyard on a sunny day. It was a horrible thought, I'll admit. But in that moment, silhouetted by the black shadows of the apartment and the sinister orange from the streetlight outside, you were the epicenter of a blazing warning flare that had finally gone off.

My heart hurt for you when I thought, *how can someone who cares so much about the people around her not care for herself?* I admired your selflessness. I *desired* it. And yet, I realized in a bitter paradox that generosity can be as deadly as selfishness. You taught me a lesson I think took you years to learn – we need to take care of ourselves just as much as others.

I sat down on the coffee table in front of you. Your hands were wrapped around your shoulders, like you were trying to keep something from spilling out. I gently draped the towel over your bowed head and began to dry the water out of your hair. Slowly, each strand, each lock. You had such long hair back then, thick and coarse as wire. You did not move, did not startle. You said nothing. It was the longest you'd ever gone without speaking, and it worried me.

I wanted to speak. I wanted to ask, *What's wrong? Are you okay? What happened? What can I do to help?*

The silence was unbearable. It was heavy; I wondered if I were to wave my hand in front of you would it feel slow, weighted, like how it feels to move underneath a riptide?

I wanted to speak so badly, but I said nothing. I peered at your face, your tears, and I knew you couldn't handle an inquisition. You were shattering from the inside out. There was nothing I could say or do to **make you talk**, no matter how much I begged or spoke.

So I closed my mouth. I wiped away a tear or two from your face. I lifted your chin, slowly, gently. I met your eyes with a steady gaze and an unspoken message.

*It will be okay*, I tried to say to you with my eyes alone. *I'm here for you, whatever you're going through. You're going to be okay.*

Your dead eyes stayed on mine for a moment, and then they drifted to the ground again. You had nodded vaguely, like you understood.

It felt like the tension had lessened somewhat. As a feeling of relief washed over me, I finally noticed the rain outside, the rain you had walked through to get here. It had lessened, now a gentle lullaby, *pip-pip, pap-pap.*

I went back to drying your hair, your face, your rain-soaked skin. I wondered if you'd been out long enough to get a cold. I hoped you would be okay. I didn't believe in God then, I still don't, but I prayed anyway. I don't even know what I prayed for.

Maybe that you would be okay. That you would be happy, if not tomorrow then... someday. That you would make it to someday.

You slept on my couch that night. I stayed up with you to make sure you wouldn't leave, that you wouldn't... do anything. I slept in the armchair next to you, the crappy one we got for twenty dollars at Goodwill, and fell asleep despite my vow to be up all night. I woke up with a start when I realized you were gone in the morning. You'd folded up the blanket I'd given you like the good Midwestern girl your mother raised you to be. I panicked, fearing the worst, when my eyes fell on the little note you'd left for me.

*Going home. Don't worry about me.*

- T

Your note, needless to say, concerned me. I went to the student administration office, I tracked down the girls who said they were your friends. I begged them all to tell me your home phone number. I managed to call you that night, but it was your mother who picked up the phone. When she asked who I was, I said, *a friend*. I don't think she believed me. I didn't tell her about the night before, I just asked if you were okay. She didn't understand why I would ask that, but she did tell me that you were home. Her brisk tone was too short to be motherly. I remember wishing, when she called you by your given name and not the one you had chosen, that you had just stayed.

Your mother hung up on me before I could ask for your address. I stood around awkwardly at the payphone for a few more minutes before I left. I tried calling for a few more days after, but every time your mother heard my voice, she hung up. I don't know why she didn't let me talk to you. Maybe she was afraid I would remind you of something bad, something that would upset you.

For me, that night feels like a dream even now. Had it really happened? Had the situation been as dangerous as I thought it was, or had I imagined the destructive glitter in your eyes, the pressure on your shoulders? In my desire to understand, I feared that I overestimated my role in your life.

Years later, you were in Chicago and I happened to see you carefully fold cashmere sweaters with loving hands in a Ralph Lauren's. I was so happy to finally see you again. Maybe I was relieved that there was a sparkle in your eye, that you seemed so full of life just like when I knew you in college. I remember fondly how we explored the entire city the next day, going to record stores and clubs. They smelled of old, wearing plastic and cigarette smoke from the vendor, but they had a lovely, grungy mystique about them. As we caught up with one another, I learned you were so happy because you had someone special in your life. A boyfriend. You said that he saved you and I smiled, but I wondered if you remembered what I had done. I wondered if it was wrong of me to hold onto that night if you had finally moved past it. I think I liked the idea of being important in your life. But that was selfish, right? You were happy. It didn't matter if it was him or if it was me. Your happiness was all that mattered in the end, not my own ego.

You married him in 1997, in a country club your mother frequented. You wore a beautiful blush pink dress that was lighter than the flush in your cheeks as you walked to your groom. Your hair was just as long and beautiful as it had been that night; you put it up in a beautiful bundle of braided hair. It was no longer the pitch black I had gently caressed dry in our youth; it was glossy in the cool afternoon light during the ceremony and rosy in the soft yellow during the reception.

As you stood next to your new husband, you gave us a smile that was so wide that we couldn't help but reflect it back to you. You looked so happy, so radiant, even if it was only for a moment. Was that the "someday" I had prayed for all those years ago? Were you finally happy then, T? Did I, of all people, help guide you towards that day? To happiness?

Your letter came in this afternoon. It reads:

*Dear G,*

*How are you? It's been a very long time since we last spoke.*

*I don't know how to say any of this, to be honest. It's been such a long time that I don't know if you remember.*

*You know the night I came to your place? I was a mess from walking around in the rain and sobbing. Do you remember how you let me in like it was nothing and dried my hair?*

*I want to thank you because you saved my life that night. I'd been walking around all night and I'd made up my mind that I was going to kill myself. I wasn't sure how – I had a few ideas, but no follow through.*

I paused my reading here as my thumb brushed over the few tear marks that blotted the ink. I saw how immaculately the rest of the letter was written and knew you left them there for me to see. I imagined you biting your lip as your chest heaved and tears rose in your eyes – maybe they were the tears that you couldn't shed that night. They slipped down your face and I wondered if you felt as relieved as I did. I continued to read:

*I don't even remember how I made it to your place that night. Maybe it was a coincidence, maybe it was fate. But when you let me into your apartment, when you dried off my hair with a gentleness that I didn't think I deserved... I think, at that moment, I knew that someone was there for me. That saved me. You saved my life that night, G.*

*You don't have to respond to this letter. I just wanted to say thank you, and that we should get together sometime.*

*Best, T*

When I got your letter, I took it outside. I don't know why; I live alone, after all. I think that I felt that the moment I read it would be somehow sacred. I unfurled the envelope slowly, like it was a treasure chest. The thick cardstock had hues of cream and beige and beautifully rounded edges and I was sure that you must have picked it carefully when I saw all those small little details. You had written your letter with precise cursive, not a single word crossed out. I wonder how long it must have taken you to find the words you wanted to say, never mind how long it took you to write them without a shaky hand.

I write my letter to you as I sit down underneath the olive tree in front of my home. The air smells like sunshine and freshly mowed grass. Fall is coming, but for now it is summer. It seems both so long ago and so recently that we were together that night. I think for years I wondered if that moment was all in my head. I'm glad that I know it was as important to you as it was to me. If nothing else comes of my life, I will always be proud of being there for you.

You remind me of the softening summer sunlight. We take the sun for granted – we see it every day and expect it to be there the next morning. We aren't always able to see it; a grey haze, thick or thin, will sometimes snare around it. But even when it is obstructed, it is still there. It just needs some time to show itself again, to come out from underneath the clouds that have hidden it.

A bird has begun to warble a soft song – no, it's taken off. It's flying high into the sky with its little brown wings. The trees sway around it; the bird's ascent into the sky has made even the long arms of the redwood trees move. The one bird is followed by one more, then three, then eight more. As they all follow the leader, the one who had the courage to go first, I think about how beautiful it is that a life can be saved by nothing more than drying one's hair.

CPSIA information can be obtained
at www.ICGtesting.com
Printed in the USA
BVHW041400010820
585202BV00007B/110